DEVOLUTION

DEVOLUTION

BOOK ONE OF
THE DEVOLUTION TRILOGY

JOHN CASEY

PHiR Publishing
San Antonio

PHiR Publishing
San Antonio, TX
phirpublishing.com

First edition: May 2021

ISBN: 978-1-7369081-0-5
Library of Congress Control Number: 2021905946

Printed in the United States of America

ALSO BY JOHN CASEY

EVOLUTION
Book two of The Devolution Trilogy

REVELATION
Book three of The Devolution Trilogy

RAW THΦUGHTS
A Mindful Fusion of Poetic and Photographic Art
(with photographer Scott Hussey)

MERIDIAN
A Raw Thoughts Book
(with photographer Scott Hussey)

THE BARN
A Mystery Novella
(co-authored by Doug Campbell)

For my family

"There are dark shadows on the earth, but its lights are stronger in the contrast."

— Charles Dickens

CHAPTER ONE

"Sir, looks like the meeting will take place. Still waiting on the banker." Lauren Rhodes regarded the Deputy Director for Operations, awaiting a response.

He didn't react. With one hand on the table, Phil Dittrich stared acutely at the middle of seven displays. At six-foot four he was an imposing figure with a personality to match. Everyone knew not to cross him. There was an unsubstantiated rumor that he'd personally fired multiple officers over the years and taken measures to ensure they were never heard from again.

A cardboard sign on the wall above read "The Pit." It was a joke—alluding to the room's bleak similarities with a since shutdown Agency black site prison and interrogation center northwest of Kabul, Afghanistan codenamed *The Salt Pit*. When they moved into these offices they'd filled the walls, ceilings and floors with soundproofing foam. A makeshift Faraday cage made the room unsightly. Wire mesh draped across each wall and across the ceiling prevented any remote EMI eavesdropping from anywhere outside the room. On the cardboard sign, someone used a Sharpie to scrawl *Arm* between the two words. It did nothing to detract from the tension in the ugly, smallish room, dimly lit by the spectral glow of the monitors.

"How much longer do we have the satellite?" asked Dittrich.

"Twelve minutes," responded one of the three CIA techs seated at the semicircular console.

"Talk about cutting it close. What about the backup?"

"It was denied, Sir. We didn't have priority to task it."

"Shit," said Dittrich. "And our man on the ground?"

Lauren broke in "Sir, Stone is five minutes out and we couldn't bug the house." With everything happening so quickly there was no opportunity. She walked to the center monitor and pointed to a ghostly white human form on the infrared satellite image. "There is one person already inside."

"OK team, let's do some good things." It was his quirky saying, an attempt at fostering unit cohesion. A teaming ritual. Everyone made fun of him about it behind his back. Lauren was sure he knew that, but he always said it anyway.

Dittrich stroked his short beard, pursing his lips. He seemed to ignore her. He was thinking that they shouldn't even be trying this with so little preparation. Weeks of planning were preferable, but on occasion, they were forced to act when the opportunity presented itself. They'd been able to crack a single encrypted message the day prior from Lefebvre to Aparicio, the banker, giving SCALPEL the location, date, and time, but nothing else. They didn't have time to investigate if the banker even left Panama. Dittrich hoped this is where he would deliver payment for what they surmised was one or more explosive devices intended to be used against American citizens in Europe. "This is all going to be a waste of time if we don't get the banker."

"Does the fact that we don't know the identity of the person in the house jeopardize the mission?" asked Lauren. "It could be the banker, couldn't it?"

Thomas Freeman, SCALPEL's field research expert and science technician, swiveled in his chair, tapping the screen with a pencil. "I've had satellite coverage for four hours now, and our suspect has been inside the entire time. The bottom line is, Aparicio wouldn't have had enough time to travel all the way from Panama and be inside the house before we had eyes on it. It is not him. You see this faint glow on the table? That's a laptop. Could be for a funds transfer. If they have Wi-Fi, I'll be tapped in as soon as Stone is in place."

"I'd like to know who he is as well," replied Dittrich matter-of-factly. "We might get the chance later, but for now, suspect X is part of this and that justifies taking him out. I wouldn't categorize it as collateral damage."

Lauren nodded.

The glowing figure inside the house wasn't moving, ostensibly seated and suspecting no complications. Certainly not what was about to go down in just a few minutes.

The tech at the end of the console piped in, pointing to a visible spectrum satellite display to the right of the infrared image. "OK, Ghost Seven is approaching—should be viewable at the bottom right."

"There he is," said Lauren as their operative walked stealthily onto the edge of the screen. He stayed near the wall of a large commercial building, working his way to the corner of the property and diagonally across from the house. He paused to survey the area, then moved deliberately across the street to the house where he stopped, lowered the backpack he'd been carrying and removed a small battery powered drill and two devices, flipping a switch on one of them, a small black box.

"I'm in," said Thomas.

Lauren had her head to one side inquisitively. "How sure are we this is going to work?"

"One hundred percent," said Dittrich. "The Puffer is relatively small but contains enough gas for a house twice as large. Doesn't even matter if all the doors inside are closed—it would just take a little longer. Within a few minutes of dispersion everyone and every thing in that house will be dead." Thomas was nodding his approval. "Even the rats."

Thomas was eager to explain. "We got it from the Intelligence Advanced Research Projects Activity program. IARPA. It was apparently handed over to them from their defense counterpart, DARPA. They didn't even tell us it was being developed, then one day they called and asked us if it was something we could use. The device contains a colorless, odorless toxin that when inhaled, combines with hemoglobin and prevents red blood cells from carrying oxygen. There are two unique characteristics. One is its incredible efficiency—the person is deprived of oxygen immediately and completely, and the effect is continued within the bloodstream, not just in the lungs. They pass out within five to ten seconds. Second, it is pervasive enough to kill within five minutes, and then the molecule breaks down into water, carbon dioxide, and a number of other natural compounds. It is untraceable after twenty minutes, with no residual indicators. An autopsy would indicate they'd drowned. It's perfect."

"Thanks Thomas, but save it for later," Dittrich snapped. "What's important is that it works. And that's a vehicle approaching. Should be Aparicio." He motioned to the top right corner on the screen to the right. "We need confirmation it's him. Lauren, once he's in there and we've determined the transaction is complete, give the go-ahead." She nodded. "How much time will this take?"

Thomas looked up from his laptop. "Sir, we're looking at three to five minutes if they get right to it. They might sit around and talk for a while first, who knows. Even if we don't crack the encryption, we'll have it all recorded, and I can work on it later."

"OK, good. Do we have comms?"

"Yes sir, we just received a text. He has eyes on the vehicle and a good view of the house. Audio is up if needed."

"Tell him to keep us apprised. We can't see much detail with these images, and I want to know exactly what's going on."

"Yes sir." The tech spoke quickly into his headset.

A surprisingly clear, hushed voice came over the speakers on the console. "Ghost Seven in position. Curtains are drawn on all windows, no visibility inside." He was moving away from the house now, settling in the shadows near the commercial building. "Puffer is in place. Window compromised. Vehicle approaching. Stand by for ID."

"What does he mean, compromised?" asked Lauren.

Dittrich pursed his lips. "He had to drill a small hole in a corner of the window to deploy the device. He'll fill it afterwards, but it could be noticed."

No one spoke. All eyes were on the automobile moving slowly toward the house. The seconds ticked by interminably as it rounded a corner and moved up the street. The area was well lit, though the adjoining properties showed no activity. The vehicle stopped just down the street from the house. Thirty seconds passed before he finally exited and began walking towards the house, moving past a dark colored SUV on the curb, probably belonging to the person inside.

"Ghost Seven, do you have a positive ID?" Asked Lauren, reaching for an orange-bordered file on the console.

"Negative," came the muted reply. "Fifty yards and closing. No evidence of a limp. And he's not carrying anything."

"Keep the chatter down," said Dittrich. "All we care about here is a positive ID. Time?"

"Five minutes twenty."

"If we lose the satellite we'll continue on audio," said Dittrich. "Is everyone clear?"

"Yes sir," they said, almost in unison.

"Target approaching twenty yards from the house" came Ghost Seven. "Slight build, short and definitely no limp. Younger. Does not appear to be our guy. Repeat, not our guy. Standing by."

"Goddamn it!" yelled Dittrich. He bowed his head, placing his hand on the back of his neck, rubbing." He lifted his head quickly. "Ghost Seven, did you get a good look at him?"

"Affirmative. He's entering the house now. I was able to get a good look just before he went in. Standing by."

Lauren cast a questioning look at Dittrich. He was staring at the screen. "Sir, should we go with plan B?"

Dittrich sighed, breaking away from the monitor. "Ghost Seven, disengage. Operation is a no-go. Repeat, no-go. Priority is now the vehicle. Put a GPS tracker on it. Retrieve the Puffer and exfil. And get the plate number on that SUV."

"Copy all—op is a no-go. Repeat, no-go."

Lauren shot him a disapproving look. "Sir—let's stay on the house. We need to try to ID both of them, and Seven can tail one of them when they leave. Let's get what we can out of this."

"Negative," said Dittrich firmly. "It's all about getting Aparicio, and Aparicio is not here. We don't have a plan for this. Thomas will get what he can electronically. Find out who owns the house. We'll talk after."

We can kill them, but we can't follow them, thought Lauren. *How incongruous.*

"Losing satellite in thirty seconds."

Lauren began thumbing through the Top-Secret file she'd been holding.

"Goddamn it" Dittrich said softly, slowly shaking his head. The image on the screen fluttered, then went to grey static. He turned to Lauren, lips pursed again. "This could shut us down. I spent more than one favor to pull this off. The whole show was riding on Lefebvre's man. He's not there and we're back to square one."

The speakers cracked. "Ghost Seven. Vehicle bugged. Moving back to the house."

"That could be," said Lauren, scanning the file, "but maybe the banker couldn't make it and Lefebvre sent someone else. If we're lucky, we'll ID this guy, find out who he's tied to, and we're back in business. Look here."

She held out the file and pointed to the middle of a page. "The banker has been seen more than once with an associate, who we thought could be a bodyguard. Maybe he's not. Perhaps he's an apprentice. A replacement."

"Ghost Seven. Puffer retrieved; window repaired. Moving out."

The second tech responded, "Copy."

"Ghost Seven out."

Dittrich looked at the file, shaking his head. "What are you getting at?"

"The banker's health has been in question. This kind of trip wouldn't be easy for him. Maybe he's retiring, and this is the new guy."

He looked at her squarely. "Lauren, I don't think you understand. We've been at this for seven months and have nothing solid to show for it. We've been operating on hunches and with little evidence. All we know is Lefebvre and Aparicio exchanged a few encrypted messages, and that Lefebvre never left Algeria. So, he's not in the house, and neither is Aparicio. What we have is a date and an address only loosely correlated to those communications. Why do you think we've gotten no collaboration from the DGSE, or the DGSI? As much as I'd like to think that by tomorrow morning we'd have IDd this guy, I'd still have nothing important enough to keep this party going. Add to that we have two unidentified targets in the house, and a shit surveillance plan. This is a total fuckup from start to finish. We've risked exposure unnecessarily." He paused to regain his composure. "I'll wait and see what you come up with, but unless it's both credible and immediately actionable, I expect the Director may recommend shutting us down. For two years now, SCALPEL hasn't produced the kind of results that justify the risk involved with keeping it operational. It's become too much of a political liability."

Lauren just stared at him for a moment, not knowing what to say. "I'll get what we need," she said resolutely, looking back to the file.

Dittrich nodded slightly, wondering if he'd made the right decision to put her on the team. She was the best he could find to lead this type of unit, but he was worried she might be too driven, and maybe a little too green. She'd only been an operative for four years when he tapped her for the position.

He turned, sighed, then recomposed himself and held out his hands, palms up at the group. Another weird mannerism that signified completion of whatever they were currently working on. Lauren always half expected him to clap twice afterwards, as if he were a blackjack dealer going off shift. "OK team. Let's meet next door to finish up. Tell Stone to head back to Paris. He can send us a report tomorrow. I want to go home and get some rest."

Lauren looked at the ceiling, then back at the file. Stone should dial in for the team's debrief. She stifled a sigh of her own, teeth gritted. She didn't like it when Dittrich came in to oversee their operations. He invariably ended up taking control. She didn't always agree with his decisions, and she couldn't do much about it. He was the Deputy Director for Operations, the CIA's top spy, responsible for all clandestine operations across the globe.

The monitors went blank as she looked around the room, then straight ahead. She was alone. What would she do if SCALPEL were shut down? Probably nothing as important. Nothing as challenging. She disagreed with Dittrich; sometimes it takes two years just to do the planning to take down a cell. And they were too small to focus on more than one op at a time. If SCALPEL were shut down, there was nothing in place to fill the void. "We've come too far to stop now," she said to no one in particular, her gaze coming into focus on the *Arm Pit* sign.

CHAPTER TWO

The next morning Lauren drove to work early. Their debrief the night before had been short. Dittrich called the Director beforehand. His tone had been negative. Almost demeaning. They were going to be shut down, she just knew it. She got off Route 66 at the Clarendon exit, navigating carefully through the early morning traffic and maneuvered into a small underground parking garage after flashing her ID at the gate guard. She marveled that such an operation could have been put into play in such a public area. "I suppose that's the point of it all," she murmured to herself. It was completely off the books. SCALPEL was a program tied to the Central Intelligence Agency's Counterterrorism Mission Center, a beyond-black program whose existence was privy to a small handful of people with a "need to know." Even the President, for reasons of plausible deniability, was in the dark about the details of its operations. The small suite of offices in Clarendon served as its headquarters. They maintained a safe house in Annapolis, Maryland and one in Berlin—both purchased through front companies and financed with money not even Congress was aware of. The house in Annapolis was theirs unconditionally. The Berlin site was shared with the CIA station there with the understanding that if SCALPEL needed it, anyone already there would have to vacate until they were through. They'd been trying to acquire a property in Paris for two years, but the French had always been good at keeping tabs on the CIA. The house had to be purchased, maintained, and used without the host government's knowledge. Paris Station already had two safe houses there, but SCALPEL could only use them for situations of lesser significance. They'd yet to use the house in Maryland. *Why would they?* She thought. Dittrich said they might need to rendition an enemy combatant to the U.S. at some point, and they would need a place no one, not even CIA proper, knew about. *Perhaps.*

Need to know. And she oversaw it all; when he wasn't trying to micromanage them, Dittrich was essentially just oversight. No one would ever guess the CIA's most secret counterterrorism program would be run out of a few rooms situated above a law office and a sandwich shop. At least she didn't have too far to go for a sandwich. *Or a lawyer*, she thought cynically.

She entered the elevator and inserted her keycard into the slot just to the side of the array of buttons. She rode to the second floor, pulling her keycard as the doors opened. She was intentionally early. If she had any chance of convincing Dittrich to give her more time, it rested on finding out who replaced the banker. She walked the thirteen steps it took to reach SCALPEL's door, with a mail slot to the side and a simple sign marked *Department of Homeland Security*. To the outside world, they were an administrative office that handled payroll transactions for Homeland. She slid her keycard through the reader. It beeped at her, and she entered her passcode into the terminal. The code was accepted, and she opened the door.

She dropped off her briefcase at her desk and proceeded straight to Thomas' relatively large office, which was strewn with electronics, weird gadgets, and boxes of manuals and files. There was no obvious attempt at keeping anything in any kind of order. He liked to say there was a *very* specific system, and that "the salient fact is," he knew exactly where everything was. More important, everything was placed in a manner that ensured its proximity to other items and files that were related to or necessary for that item's use. *Feng Shui*, he liked to say. Everything had its place. It looked like a geek's playground.

He was seated at his large, steel desk, several black cell phones lined up in front of him like overly large dominos. Batteries were lined up to the left of the phones, and a circuit board in what looked like mid-construction, with various potentiometers, resistors and wires protruding lay to the right. He looked up at her, his eyes rising without moving his head. "We know who he is." He cracked a smile.

"THAT is good news Thomas," she said seriously. "Tell me everything." She took a seat in front of his desk, leaning slightly forward, legs crossed.

"Well, first of all he's in none of our databases. No records at all. We checked with our contact at DGSI, and they said they had nothing on him, other than he was a French citizen, and some kind of computer science engineer who works in the wine industry. They did mention that the company, Château Group, is owned by his father and is being audited by the French IRS, but there's no chance of getting that data." He began shuffling though some papers on his desk. "The car was a rental. I hacked the rental agency server and got his name. After he left the house I tracked him on GPS to a beignet shop, and then to a house on Marseille's southeast side."

Lauren stared at him, waiting. "And?"

"Lefebvre's ex-wife's house."

Her jaw dropped. "Did the French Directorate ask why we were interested in him?"

"I told them it was part of our ongoing investigation of Hakeem Lefebvre."

"OK. Did you tell them he visited Lefebvre's ex-wife?" She hoped not. She didn't want the DGSI getting in the way. "Who is he, and where is he now?"

"No, I didn't tell them. I figured you wouldn't want me to. He stayed at her house for about ten minutes, then returned the car. Stone's already retrieved the GPS tracker. His name is François Martin. Thirty-three years old, born in Paris, lives in Metz. French Father, mother is from Syria. Château Group is the largest wine distributor in Europe. He's somewhat of a big shot—his father owns forty percent of the company."

She dipped her head, thinking. "What else. I need something that will give us more time. It needs to be big. Did you have any luck with the encryption?"

"They didn't use the laptop much during the meeting. I was able to crack the router, but they were using something else; perhaps a browser on a secure flash drive, like IronKey. If so it's impossible to decipher. And I couldn't get into the hard drive. Look, it's early still," he cautioned. "Let me dig a little deeper and see what I come up with. Dittrich won't be back from Langley until this afternoon."

"Alright. I'll see what I can do as well. Send me everything you have."

She walked back to her office, intent on studying her notes on Lefebvre, the banker, and the probable composition of the terrorist cell. As they go, this one appeared formative at best. SCALPEL was moving forward with little and inconclusive evidence. And until they had more, France wasn't going to play ball with the Agency. If they were able to get enough details about the money trail, those involved and what their plans were, SCALPEL could hand the information over to Agency proper and then over to DGSI. At that point France would have the ball and keep them informed on progress—a win. It was far better for the CIA to work collaboratively with a foreign government than to risk getting caught executing a black operation that violates international law and a nation's sovereignty. Of course, if they were caught the CIA would disavow anyone found to be involved. An unfortunate but necessary aspect of the job.

What they did know indicated a possible attack on U.S. citizens was being planned, and that the attack was likely to occur somewhere in West Europe. It was impossible to tell if it was an imminent threat. It could be weeks, months, or even years before they go active. When the evidence is scarce, it usually indicates the cell hasn't gotten very far with planning. The alternative was that they were exceptionally good at hiding their tracks—a troubling thought that compelled her to do whatever it takes to keep SCALPEL operational. No one else can do what they do. *No one.*

Lauren gathered everything she could on Hakeem Lefebvre. Born and raised in Algeria, he came from a family that controlled the mineral rights for large swaths of oil-rich land. He sent his son Sharif to a boarding school in Marseille when he was young. The mother, Hakeem's first wife, died in childbirth. Hakeem would visit Sharif in Marseille often in the first few years, and on occasion would bring him home to Algeria during breaks in school. Hakeem then became intimate with Sharif's teacher Salmah, whom he eventually married. She would accompany him and Sharif on the trips to Algeria. Salmah was a French citizen by birth and of Algerian descent. But after a while Hakeem stopped visiting. Salmah made a few trips alone to see him, but eventually the long-distance relationship soured, and they divorced. Sharif finished boarding school and contact with his father trailed off.

Probably because of embarrassment associated with his father's alleged terrorist activities.

For years Hakeem Lefebvre used his oil wealth to manipulate local politicians and industry, which also made him quite a few enemies. The politicians kept him out of trouble with the Algerian authorities, but eventually he came under the scrutiny of the governments of France and the United States, both of which had considerable industrial and economic interests in the area that were negatively affected by his activities. After a time, it became evident Lefebvre, with the help of his four brothers, was militarizing his large security force in what appeared to be preparation for an escalation to violence, perhaps to take control of foreign-owned assets. To make matters worse, evidence suggested Lefebvre was working with the al-Mulathamun Army to train his security team. This is about the time when Hakeem and Salmah were divorced. Salmah wanted to remain in France while Hakeem decided the protection of his interests and overseeing the training of his forces was too important to leave.

The al-Mulathamun Army (AMA) was an offshoot of the al-Mulathamun Brigade and designated as a Foreign Terrorist Organization under Section 219 of the Immigration and Nationality Act, and as a Specially Designated Global Terrorist entity by Executive Order 13224. The AMA had historic ties to al-Qa'ida. They were the real deal. Lefebvre was able to fly under the radar in part because he had the right politicians in his pocket and because Lefebvre hadn't done anything outwardly illegal to this point other than associating with the AMA, an organization the Algerian government did not recognize as a threat.

Upon formal recognition of Lefebvre and his AMA-aligned forces as a threat to U.S. interests and property, the CIA conducted a clandestine strike, sending two General Atomics MQ-9 Reaper drones from Sigonella Airbase in Sicily to take out Lefebvre's security team during a training exercise. Tony Stone was one of two SCALPEL operatives on the ground at the time to coordinate the attack. The other was Mike Collier, who is now Chief of Station in Berlin. Lauren always wondered how he'd landed that post, particularly after they were fairly sure his cover had been blown. They'd whisked him out of Algeria immediately. Then there was the political fallout that ensued. *Maybe he was just lucky to get reassigned out of SCALPEL before the shit hit the fan...*

It was a risky operation. The round-trip distance was right at the Reaper's flight range. Further, maximum range was unavoidably reduced. For the drones to remain undetected by radar or other aircraft, they were flown very low, about 15 feet above the Mediterranean and along a route that avoided seafaring vessels. The drones were fitted with external drop tanks to increase maximum flight distance. Nothing like this had ever been done before. As operations go, this one was *way* outside the box.

But it was successful. Each Reaper unloaded two AGM-114 Hellfire air to ground missiles and one 500-pound GBU-38 Joint Direct Attack Munition bomb. Lefebvre survived the strike; however, his four brothers were killed along with fifty-seven others, three of which were high-ranking AMA leaders. It more than made sense that Lefebvre has been plotting his revenge ever since, and the evidence was trickling in that he was planning something big. The one downside in the aftermath of the strike was an outraged Algerian government. Though they had no proof the U.S. was involved, there were reports of some fishermen along the coast who heard aircraft flying low over the water the morning of the attack.

Diplomatic relations between Algeria and the United States became strained in the aftermath. Algeria asked France for assistance to investigate the strike area. Though no formal accusations were made, relations with France took a hit as well. France did not take kindly to foreign nations violating the sovereignty of a country right in their back yard, particularly a country that France had controlled as recently as 1962. When all was said and done, neither Algeria nor France had any interest in providing help to the CIA in efforts to collect on Lefebvre, his associates, or the AMA—particularly on French soil.

Three hours later Thomas stopped abruptly in Lauren's doorway as she nosed through her small mountain of paperwork, a serious look on his face. "What?" she said expectantly.

"I think I have something we can use. Only, it's complicated."

"Well, we haven't been lucky with anything to this point, so I'll take complicated. Please tell me you found something on this Martin guy."

"Sort of—I did some digging and found he attended graduate school at the Sorbonne University in Paris from 2011 to 2012. Degree in computer science and automation. Guess who else earned a diploma from the Sorbonne in 2012?"

Lauren answered quickly "Lefebvre's son Sharif."

"*Yes.* Graduate degree in advanced political theory. But that's not even the interesting part. I pulled all the classes from 2011, 2012, and 2013. There were forty-one Americans who graduated during that period. Twelve who graduated in 2012. And one of those Americans has a graduate degree in advanced political theory."

"You have my attention." Lauren was fixated.

"His Name is Michael Dolan. He was there on a military scholarship; he was in the Air Force at the time. He's now a GS-14 on the Joint Staff and he's right here in Washington, working at the Pentagon." Then his eyes went wide. "Lauren, his apartment is just down the street in Rosslyn!"

"Well, what does that give us? What else?"

"There is more." Thomas paused for effect as Lauren fidgeted. "He barely graduated from the Sorbonne. Dolan was a top student for almost a year and a half, then his grades declined sharply in the spring of 2012. This guy was on the fast track in the Air Force—top of his peer group in everything military he'd been involved in before Paris. He graduated with honors from Boston College in 2004 with a degree in political science where he was a track and field star and something of a legend in taekwondo—a fourth degree black belt and national sparring champion. He was a top graduate in BC's ROTC program and entered the Air Force later that year as a second lieutenant. He's distinguished himself in every military training program he's attended, including pilot training. He was a Special Operations AC130 gunship pilot at Hurlburt Field in Florida and saw significant combat in Afghanistan. Then he went to the Sorbonne on a military scholarship. It was a special program, something very few pilots have the opportunity to do, particularly in special ops. They were grooming him. Three years after Paris he retired, with eleven years of service. Then he took the Pentagon job."

Lauren frowned impatiently. "What happened in Paris?"

"I'm getting to that. His training report from that period is still good but doesn't have the same shine as the rest of his record. He failed one class and barely passed another during his last semester. He was able to drop the failed class with enough credits to graduate."

Lauren could barely contain herself. "Thomas, get to the point please. Dittrich will be here in thirty minutes."

"OK, sorry. On a hunch, I hacked Dolan's private email. Fortunately, he's kept everything in his inbox all these years. Lauren, Sharif Lefebvre was a friend of his. And something bad happened in Paris that summer, something that affected Dolan deeply and strained his relationship with Sharif. There was a tragedy. Dolan's French girlfriend, a girl named Claire, died. She fell from a balcony at a hotel. Dolan was nearby when it happened but not present."

Lauren stopped fidgeting and tried to think. Frowning because she already knew the answer, she asked, "Did you get approval for the email account access?"

He shook his head slightly, first left, then right.

"OK. I'm sure you didn't leave any evidence. Dittrich will get it approved after the fact." She was sure of that. They didn't like to operate this way, but sometimes they were forced to comply with the law with a certain kind of poetic license. *For the greater good.* "Where does that leave us, and how do we use this information to keep the Agency from shutting us down?"

Thomas smiled slightly. "We send Michael Dolan back to Paris."

"What? How will that help in any conceivable way?" She was bordering on livid. "Goddamnit Thomas Freeman, you had me thinking we'd found something actionable. We can't send anyone to Paris, not at this point, and certainly not someone from the Department of Defense. Hell, he's got zero HUMINT experience. I mean, does he? No, of course not. *We don't exist.* We couldn't possibly bring him in. Even if we did, it would take months to prep him, and I don't even want to think about what paperwork that would involve. *What the fuck Thomas?"*

He didn't miss a beat. "No, he has no Human Intelligence experience. BUT, he does have a Top-Secret SCI clearance, and Special Operations isn't run-of-the-mill DoD. If we had to bring someone in from outside the agency, you could truthfully say we would want someone like Dolan."

Lauren shifted in her chair, doing her best not to interrupt.

Thomas continued. "So, what if we don't read him in? Not all the way, anyway. We brief him on the basics, give him some foundational instructions and training, and send him to Paris? I checked with the Pentagon—there is an intel sharing position at the DRM Headquarters in Paris. The person that's there now is supposed to leave in three months. We ask the Pentagon to replace him with Dolan. He's a perfect fit and he's fluent in French. He's not married, no children. He's a badass. We ask him to reestablish contact with Sharif, who works for Francopharma right there in Paris. Ironically, all we have to do is give him a phone and stay in contact. We can guide him through it."

"The spiPhone?" She laughed and shook her head. "Is that thing even field tested yet?"

"Sort of," Thomas said, somewhat sheepishly. "I gave one to Ghost Seven—Stone. We tried it out before the op yesterday, and he kept it live for me through the entire thing. Worked like a charm. The data was on monitor six, but no one was paying attention to it. We could finish testing it properly with Dolan."

"OK. I'll play along here. How does a degree in political theory translate to a job at a pharmaceutical giant? Is he a worker bee or management?"

"He's an executive. And I don't know, but I assume he's parlayed his father's wealth into opportunity. In any case, his grades were stellar at the Sorbonne."

"But I thought he was estranged from his father. Heck, he hasn't been in Algeria since he was twelve, and Hakeem hasn't visited France since 2006." Lauren paused while Thomas watched, trying to decide if he should answer, or if she was going to keep going. She kept going. "So, let me get this straight." She spoke slowly, wheels turning. "Let's say we can work the coordination to get him to Paris and into this French intelligence sharing position. Were he and Sharif close enough back then for that kind of contact to be useful to us? Is it even possible Sharif is involved somehow with his father's terrorist designs? I guess I am willing to consider this, particularly in light of evidence tying Martin to Sharif's mother. But the ex-wife is estranged as well. There is still so much we don't understand.

"We would need to have some guarantee of a return on this, and I don't see it yet. If we don't read him in fully, and we know we can't, we would have to read him into something. We can't just send him to Paris unexpectedly, give him a *spiPhone* and ask him to carry it with him everywhere in the hopes he ends up spending considerable time with Sharif. And even if he did, it is likely Sharif would tell him nothing, show him nothing at all that would help us. We would have to give him a credible story that is a realistic facsimile of the truth. We must tell him what Lefebvre is up to, and that we suspect Sharif. The truth would be the best reason for him to think he's helping the War on Terror somehow. We would have to create an operation that is a subset of SCALPEL, a subprogram. We'd need someone at Paris Station in on it. And we tell Dolan just enough to get him to go along with it without asking too many questions.

"We'd have to make it appealing in some other way I think. Not that a year or three in Paris isn't appealing, but he may have a reason or reasons for not wanting to go back—the death of his girlfriend, for one. And if his friendship with Sharif was strong, he may be conflicted about this whole thing."

Thomas interjected, "Maybe some kind of incentive pay?"

"Maybe. It sounds like he had everything going for him in his career, shit went south, and then he pressed the reset button. We need to consider that thrusting him into a new job in proximity to a negative past life situation combined with the stressors associated with clandestine work might break him. Again, he has no training for this. If that were to happen, we'd be in worse shape than if we hadn't sent him in the first place. Anyway, we can make sure the pay for the position is more than he's getting now without raising suspicions about where he's getting his money.

"It could be that a former special ops pilot might look forward to getting back into the fight, even if it's not from a cockpit. Let's forget the 'incentive pay' idea. It'd be problematic to explain. Our focus should be on how we include him. The plan. We'd have to read him in, covered and under a new program. Not necessarily so we can use him that way, but so we can disassociate him from SCALPEL while making him feel like he's part of something big. Back in the fight, but on a different front. It's not too far from the truth.

"He has no intelligence training at all, I assume?"

"Actually, he has quite a bit but it's all within the scope of his role as a special ops pilot. He was a consumer, not a collector. Not even an analyst. And no HUMINT at all."

"All the more reason to keep it simple. And in this scenario, I believe it could be an asset.

Lauren was tapping her desk with her middle finger. "We need to be able to incentivize Dolan to reengage with Sharif and to stay engaged. She paused, still tapping. "I have an idea, but I need to refine it.

"We'd need to give him time to settle in, to adjust. Maybe a French language refresher course in Paris, before he starts his job there? That would prevent us from having to remove the person that's filling the position currently until he's scheduled to do so. It also gives Dolan a better opportunity to link up with Sharif. More free time.

"God Thomas, if we weren't already doing some pretty outlandish things I'd say this was crazy, but we don't have anything else. And we have twenty minutes to prepare it for a pitch. Send me his military records, the emails that matter and anything else you have. I'll draw it up.

"Oh, and Thomas..." She stood up from her desk and looked at him squarely. "Everyone here believes so strongly in our mission. Even Dittrich, though he hides it well. Without SCALPEL, the CIA's visibility is seriously clouded in Europe and Africa. Especially Europe. Let's keep it going."

Thomas nodded.

They had failed to obtain any hard evidence that the Algerian Hakeem Lefebvre was financing a terror operation or that there was an imminent threat. They'd been unable to link the banker Eduardo Aparicio to Lefebvre at all in this plot, aside from sporadic and cryptic telecommunications between the two. This was not unusual, given most of Lefebvre's money was in Aparicio's bank in Panama. The U.S. government couldn't freeze Lefebvre's assets in the runup to the Reaper operation due to Panama's ironclad banking laws. Perhaps Lefebvre figured out a way to move his money without it being seen. All the while, SCALPEL's operational tactics were severely restricted for a host of reasons. These restrictions limited their ability to use traditional Agency assets. Heck, they had only one operative in Europe who was part of the core team. And they had no one who could get close to Lefebvre. Until now.

CHAPTER THREE

Michael Dolan woke to the slow, methodical build of *La Mer*, his favorite Nine Inch Nails composition. It wasn't a typical fan favorite. This was not a gritty, coarse industrial song. It was beautiful, orchestral. Composed by Trent Reznor as he contemplated suicide.

Dolan routinely allowed himself three minutes to become fully alert. The song was appropriate. It woke him gradually, calmly. It begins slowly and evolves note by note to a muted crescendo before easing back to a lightly melodic end. In a way, it mirrored his everyday life.

He stared up at the ceiling, focusing on nothing in particular. Then he began to gather his thoughts, prioritizing and building an agenda for the next seventeen hours. It was an easy thing for him. Very few people he'd known in life were able to memorize as well as he. For all intents and purposes, his memory was photographic.

First thing to do, exercise. He casually threw off the blanket and rose, turned on the light and slipped into his running gear. He grabbed his iPhone from his dresser, put a pot of premium dark roast coffee on to brew and left his spartan, one-bedroom apartment. The traffic in Rosslyn was just getting started. All those early-shift DC commuters. He zigzagged his way at a casual pace out of the urban community, traversed a footbridge over Route 66 and linked up with the Custis Trail heading west. He gradually increased his pace until he settled in at a seven-minute mile and began to concentrate, easing into his zone.

People tended to glance twice at him as he ran by. His rugged good looks, jet-black hair, and six-foot lean but muscular frame set him apart. He didn't notice them as he went over each of his meetings and tasks scheduled for the day, each process input and output, noting every prerequisite and unfinished requirement. It was his way of ensuring he would begin work in an itemized and efficient fashion. He finished his mental collation and held up his Garmin watch to make out the distance and time, squinting past tiny beads of sweat clinging to his eyelashes. Three point four miles. *Shit.* Too far. He slowed quickly and turned back, this time pushing to a six-minute pace. *That puts me four minutes behind schedule,* he calculated.

Dolan slowed to a walk within a quarter mile of his building. By the time he reached the doorway to his apartment his breathing and heart rate were back to normal. He went inside, dropped his house key, phone, and ear buds on the kitchen table and filled a tall glass with water from the refrigerator door dispenser. He drank it quickly and walked to his bedroom where he undressed and stepped into the shower. *La Mer* was still playing on his modest Klipsch stereo system on a continuous loop. As he dried off he was, as usual, whispering the barely perceptible French Creole lyrics from the end of the song under his breath. *An rien peut arrêter moi konin la.* Nothing can stop me now. His daily affirmation.

After a quick breakfast of two eggs, a small bowl of muesli and a glass of carrot juice he left his apartment and walked brusquely to the Metro station. He took the blue line toward Franconia. Two stops later he was at the Pentagon, exiting the dull concrete station with hundreds of others, a shifting mosaic of various military uniforms interspersed with business suits and similar dress. He had a nickname for them—*the Herd.* He despised the Herd. It was as if the Metro had some strange power over people, capable of temporarily transforming otherwise intelligent professionals into base, mindless automatons. He wasn't one of them. He refused to be. He'd never consider sprinting down an escalator to make it just before the train doors closed, especially if he were still in uniform. He'd never weave his way through the Herd desperately seeking a rare, unoccupied seat. He refused to spend his commute mere inches from six other people staring at his phone and scrolling through a vacuous, plastic life one 'friend' at a time, motionless and unaware of his surroundings. He wasn't one of them. He was different. He knew he was because he *was.* He was unique. Acutely aware. Capable of operating on a higher plane of consciousness that defied the impaired nature of the Herd. It was this ability in part that allowed him to overcome and wall off the dark, fragmented pieces of his soul. It was an enigmatic, almost circular logic that those compartmentalized pieces were also the catalysts for his relentless pursuit of perfection. It didn't much matter that he didn't yet understand how or why it worked for him. Only that it worked.

He found it interesting that the Herd would, after its quotidian demonstration of hive-mindlessness, end up passing through the tall, wooden front doors of the Pentagon and through security only to disperse immediately in myriad directions along the various floors, rings, and hallways only to end up in their appointed cubicle to begin formulating what they individually believed to be (right or not) some of the most important strategic decisions in the world.

Dolan's modest workspace was in the offices of the Joint Staff where he spent ten hours a day analyzing and formulating politico-military strategic plans and policies for U.S. forces in Europe. He walked into the nest of partitioned offices, looking straight ahead as usual to avoid eye contact with anyone who might pull him aside to discuss the latest office rumors, last night's Redskins game, or their cat. It wasn't always necessary as he was routinely one of the first to arrive.

Today he would give a key presentation to the general. He'd been over the details several times, but he wouldn't feel at ease until he knew it cold. He set his black Tumi knapsack on the floor at the foot of his desk and moved purposefully to the kitchenette to get some coffee brewing.

Back at his desk he booted his workstation and logged into his email. He needed to check if European Command in Stuttgart or U.S. Air Forces in Europe Headquarters at Ramstein Air Base sent him anything important. Europe started its workday six hours earlier. *Not too bad this morning,* he thought. Only twenty or so messages. He scanned the *From* column quickly, noticing nothing that might pertain to his briefing. Then one caught his eye, something from a Lauren Rhodes. The subject line simply read *Paris.*

He clicked the email open with an irritated anxiety, fading to curiosity as he read. It didn't make any sense—there wasn't enough information.

Mr. Dolan,

I have an interesting opportunity to discuss with you. I understand you've been stationed in France before, and at the Pentagon for almost four years now. There is a need for someone with your skills in Paris, a job with duties similar to those you are currently doing in J5. Please forgive the lack of detail. We would need to meet in person before I can fully explain. How about at the Pentagon courtyard at noon today? I'll be seated near corridor three.

Best, Lauren Rhodes

He frowned as he right-clicked her email address and reviewed the properties. There was no phone number, no office location, no useful metadata at all save an email address that indicated she worked for the Department of Homeland Security. He immediately experienced an uncomfortable mix of curiosity and dread. Paris. The mix of feelings threatened to become a flood of jagged, toxic emotion that would overcome him as dark images of guilt and loss broke through the carefully constructed barriers in his mind. But only for a moment. Long-repressed, painful memories some self-incriminating part of him desperately wanted to confront stepped to the fore of his consciousness, only to be pushed back in an instant. Quickly re-compartmentalized with innate precision. Only he couldn't hide everything, not completely. Which was a good thing. If he lost track of the things that bothered him most, they might come back stronger and he'd be unprepared. Dolan learned to interpret these memories as a positive thing. He could see in his subconscious where they were locked up and he knew what was in there. All of it continuously festering, roiling, gnawing. But contained. His anxiety ebbed however he couldn't shake it completely. *Understandable.* His two years in Paris had been resoundingly eclectic, an impossible collage of adventure, joy, cataclysm, and damage. How was he supposed to focus on his briefing at fourteen hundred hours when he had even a small part of this on his mind? And who was Rhodes? Again, he pushed it back.

The logical approach was to meet with her, to get and analyze the details. He could ask for his boss' opinion, and then reply with whatever was the best response. He emailed her back to accept the meeting, stating that he was looking forward to hearing what she had to say.

Dolan finished preparing for his briefing while various Joint Staff and other military officers and civilians moved in and out. He was distracted from his desktop occasionally to answer a question, or to say hello as someone passed by. He tried not to be impersonal. In truth he was well liked and respected in J5. He just had never had a desire to combine serious preparation with casual banter and interruption. When he was in a zone it was a good thing, physically and mentally. His zone was surgical and inertial. When he was in it the result was perfection and he could keep it going for a *long* time. His girlfriend Amy hated this about him. She just didn't understand that when he was working on important matters or doing something that required concentration she would have to wait until he was done. There was no way around it. It was how he kept his life aligned and productive. It was his paradigm for life management. The Germans had a proverb for this type of world view, a cultural cliché and one he liked to point out from time to time: *Ordnung muss sein.* There must be order. Dolan loved the Germans.

Stoic compartmentalization was something of which he was proud. It was a rare ability. It's what enabled him to lead and fly dangerous and difficult special operations missions in Afghanistan with extreme precision and success. Coupled with his high level of fitness and rigorous training routine, it's why he was able defeat almost any taekwondo black belt sparring opponent in short order. It was an ability that allowed him at any time to snuff out an entire spectrum of emotions that might otherwise cloud his mind and lead to an inappropriate or ineffective response.

He glanced at his watch and realized it was almost time to meet Lauren Rhodes. Anxiety crept forward again, which he extinguished curtly. There was no objective reason to worry. This had nothing to do with what happened six years ago. *Just meet with Rhodes and she'll explain everything.*

Down the hallway to the inner ring, Dolan descended the staircase and exited to the courtyard. He walked a path past the round lunch shack toward the corridor three exit, scanning the benches for a woman in civilian attire. *Would have helped had she told me what she was wearing. Or the color of her hair…*

That must be her. Dolan walked deliberately to a woman seated by herself and reading a book. She was modestly dressed in a navy skirt suit with long red hair, an Italian leather attaché under one arm. Mid-thirties, athletic and attractive. She looked up as he approached.

Lauren stood and smiled. "Mr. Dolan, Lauren Rhodes. Pleased to meet you."

"Nice to meet you as well." They shook hands. "Shall we discuss your email here?"

"Of course. This won't take long."

They sat down together on the bench. Lauren crossed her legs, setting the book between them. *Pride and Prejudice* by Jane Austin.

"Again, I apologize for the lack of details in my email. I'd love to be able to fill you in, depending on how this evolves and how receptive you are. This is an exciting opportunity."

"No worries, Miss Rhodes. However, I'd be lying if I said I wasn't curious. What is 'this,' exactly?"

Lauren smiled again. "I understand, and please, call me Lauren. Let me begin by telling you that if we decide to proceed beyond a vague description of what this entails, you will have to be read in. It's a covert program. I'll need you to decide if you want to participate in what I am offering before we leave this courtyard. You'll be required to sign a nondisclosure agreement." She reached into her attaché and pulled out a sheaf of papers. I have it with me. You will not receive a copy. If you decide not to participate our communication will cease and this meeting will have never taken place. Do you understand?"

Dolan's eyebrows furrowed. "Yes, but I have a few questions before we start. Can I see your identification? You work for DHS? I am concerned that I am being approached directly about something that in my experience would usually be brought to my supervisor first. And you can call me Michael."

Lauren nodded. "I was just getting there. But first, the nondisclosure. The fact that I am here in the Pentagon courtyard should be proof enough that my presence is related to official U.S. government business." She handed him a pen and one of the papers.

Dolan read the agreement. It was short, simple, and standard. Only there was no mention of DHS. The agreement was to not discuss the existence of, or any details relating directly or indirectly to EXCISE, with anyone other than those involved and read into the program. TOP SECRET SCI NOFORN was annotated in the header and footer.

Dolan looked around to see if anyone might be able to see the agreement or hear them speaking. There wasn't anyone within 20 feet. He signed it quickly and handed it back to her, a concerned look on his face. "It strikes me that we should probably be in a SCIF for this conversation. In fact, we should probably be in a SCIF for you to even hand me that document."

Lauren reached again into her attaché and unfolded her credentials wallet, letting it hang in front of him.

Central Intelligence Agency. An awkward sense of guilt suddenly coursed through him, as if he'd just been caught. *That's normal,* he thought. *You haven't done anything wrong.* So far, this was not what he expected. But some things were beginning to make sense.

"I cannot answer any more of your questions until I've briefed you in. That will happen at Langley. As you might imagine, my office has a Sensitive Compartmentalized Information Facility. Again, I need to know that you understand what I've explained so far."

Dolan was beginning to feel intrigued. "Yes, I understand. Please proceed."

"Good." She paused, looking straight ahead, as she gathered her thoughts. "I work for a part of the Agency that tackles national security challenges that require special care. Everything the Agency does is sensitive, but what we do, what we do with EXCISE is, let's just say it's *more* sensitive. We've been searching for someone who can work with us, someone with the right background and language skills who can grease the rails, so to speak. Someone who might have a history that enables access to certain individuals of interest without raising suspicion. We have concluded that you may be that person."

CHAPTER FOUR

The drive the next morning to Langley wasn't bad. Traffic was light, and the 10-mile trip took just 20 minutes. Dolan parked in the visitor's lot and proceeded to the original headquarters building. Lauren was waiting for him in the main lobby area where she gave him a visitor's badge and escorted him though security. As they walked past the north wall of the lobby, Dolan paused to look at Memorial Wall. He knew of it but had never seen it in person. 133 stars, each representing an officer who died in the line of duty. He gave his respects silently while Lauren waited, and they moved on.

"So, how was the drive?" she asked.

"Not bad. Not much traffic at all. How are things in the clandestine world?"

Lauren chuckled as they went up an escalator to the second floor. "Kidding aside, globalization is killing us. Technology has improved to the point that a dirt farmer in Uganda has the potential to disrupt global security and financial markets given the right education, resources, and a cause. At the same time, doing what we do without being seen is becoming increasingly difficult. And we are not where we want to be in terms of cyber security—it's a whole new front. The world is flat now and just about anyone can see past the horizon."

They walked down a long hallway and turned into a room with wood paneled walls. She shut the heavy door behind her, and they sat across from each other at a table large enough to seat eight. The room was small but decent sized as far as SCIFs go.

Lauren began. "I am the operations lead for a program called EXCISE. EXCISE is a black program. This means the U.S. government does not acknowledge its existence and will disavow anyone associated with the program should they be caught overseas doing anything illegal."

Dolan interceded. "I am aware of what a black program is. I've been involved with a few myself."

"Good, that makes things easier. Our mission is to identify foreigners in Europe and Africa, and to a lesser extent, elsewhere, who may pose a serious threat to U.S. citizens and national security. This information is then relayed to other programs within the CIA, other Homeland agencies and to our foreign partners in bilateral and multilateral efforts to prevent or mitigate and remove terrorist activity. We act unilaterally in some cases, but it is our last option by default. In this case, at least for now, unilaterally is where we find ourselves.

"You were identified as someone who has French language and cultural expertise, familiarity with Paris and the surrounding area, and a past relationship with one of our suspects. We have reason to believe this suspect and other individuals intend to commit acts of terror against Western targets in Europe, and we need your help. We believe your special operations background and other talents will simplify the preparation for this proposed operation."

Dolan's mind was racing. *Who could this 'past relationship' possibly refer to? Someone from Paris?* "No offense Lauren, but this sounds like the beginning of a Jason Bourne rip-off. I have no HUMINT background. How would you use me as a legitimate intelligence resource? I would need substantial training. And I have a job already. What am I supposed to tell J5, and more important, *who is this suspect?*" In less than a second, he went through his entire mental catalog of friends and classmates from the Sorbonne and Paris. None of them jumped out at him as a possible threat.

Lauren smiled slightly. "This is not Jason Bourne, not even close. Your role would entail primarily overt information collection, conducted during unscripted interaction with the suspect. It should be relatively easy. It is my understanding you were close to Sharif Lefebvre." She paused to take in his reaction.

Dolan bristled. Sharif. *Sharif?* For a time, they'd been almost inseparable. They double dated with Claire and Anne, who were also best friends. They all partied together, studied together, traveled across France and Europe, shared each other's secrets and dreams. It was probably the best seven months of his life. He was aware at the time that there were problems between Sharif and his father in Algeria, or at least that they hadn't seen each other or talked in a while. He never met Sharif's mom in Marseille but knew that they were close. Sharif was smart and well adjusted. A good French citizen, by all accounts. And they'd been good friends. But after Claire's death, that changed. Dolan was a complete wreck. He'd grown close to Claire and was fretting about how to keep the relationship going after he left. Marriage wasn't on the table, not yet anyway. He thought he was beginning to love her. He wasn't sure—he'd never been in love before. It was a new thing.

Then the accident. Dolan withdrew and had only sporadic contact with Sharif in his final semester at the Sorbonne. Once he graduated, he left Paris and the friendship was essentially over. They'd exchanged a few emails after Paris, but that was it. The falling out was a necessary part of his compartmentalization process. His realignment. *Ordnung muss sein.* But there was also something else. Something he'd repressed along with Claire's death, and now it came rushing to the fore. Sharif was there when she fell. Anne was already gone, and not in a good mood, by his recollection—it was just Sharif and Claire in the hotel room. Dolan left to buy a bottle of champagne. Claire was intoxicated that night, they all were. But he'd always felt it was such an unlikely explanation—she fell over the balcony railing. The tragedy created a fissure in their friendship, something he couldn't reconcile. Anne broke off the relationship with Sharif immediately afterward.

Lauren continued. "The intel sharing position is a cover. It's believable because it's established. We don't have to create something for you. While an ideal candidate would be a career intelligence officer, we feel we can sell you for the position because of the special ops background and your work with the J5. You don't need to worry about saying anything to your boss. We will handle all of that and your supervisor will be instructed not to ask you about it.

"You have robust insight into strategic U.S.-French bilateral intelligence and military interests. The role in Paris is more about growing and refining relationships in these areas than understanding and navigating the complexities of the international intelligence community. The guy currently occupying the position is rotating out in three months.

"It's actually a win for us that you have no intelligence background. This means you are off the DGSI's radar. The DGSI is basically the French FBI and their domestic counterintelligence organization. No one would suspect you'd be involved with something like EXCISE. They'd have eyes on a career intel officer from day one.

"And you may not even need to start the job. We plan to put you in a French refresher course. The school is called Lingua Europa, located at La Défense. If we get what we need in the first three months, we can just create a reason why you were deselected for the job, DoD would select a new candidate and you'd be back in DC at J5 with none the wiser. Or it could take two years. Either way, we'll make sure your job at the Pentagon is waiting for you when you return. You'll also have the option of staying in the job in Paris if you prefer.

"You would have periodic contact with an Agency operative who may or may not ask you to do certain things. He'll make sure you are apprised of important developments. Any information you collect, you will give to him. He is also there to help in any way he can, to make your job easier. But I'll be frank—this will not be easy. Especially if we are still operational after your language course is finished. After that you'll be doing a real, full-time job and will still need to execute your part in EXCISE.

"You should not be asked do anything illegal or dangerous." Dolan's head was swimming by now. "As you are not a trained operative, you will not be asked to employ tradecraft per se, except for simple observation and collection. We will brief you on how to communicate, collect, document, and deliver. Your contact's name is Tony. You will see him when you arrive in Paris, and you should never meet with him unless it is set up in advance. I will give you a phone to make these things easier, and for us to remain in contact. You will be able to call or text Tony, and those communications will be encrypted. I will explain later how to do it. Other than that, it is a normal cell phone, and you will be able to use it in Europe and we will reimburse you for the bill. Your paycheck will start the day you leave J5. To anyone poking around, it will look legitimate, like you are being paid by DoD. It should, since you will be. It's a good cover. Your pay will get a bump, as it is a GS-15 position and includes things like a housing stipend and a few other perks.

"There are many more details we will have to go over, but at this point I need reconfirmation of your willingness to participate. If you decide to back out now, for whatever reason, we will still need a debriefing that covers all your time spent with Sharif. And you have my promise that the Agency is committed fully to preserving your health, welfare, and safety. We will never intentionally put you in a dangerous position." Lauren suddenly felt uneasy, as if she had just lied.

"Finally, we are aware of Claire's death and how that may have impacted you. Heading back there now in what can only be described as difficult and stressful conditions, we'd understand if this is too much." Lauren held her breath for a second. "But given how you pulled yourself together afterwards, the occupational success you've had recently, and the amount of time that has passed since that tragedy, we are confident in your ability to succeed."

Dolan paused to contemplate the ramifications of what he was being offered. She never mentioned his breakdown and school trouble. Maybe she just doesn't know? It wasn't likely. He spent the last six plus years repairing his career. *His life.* After Paris he was set to return to a command position at Hurlburt Field. The ensuing investigation cleared him of any wrongdoing of course, but he was broken. He'd nearly failed out and that was not lost on his superiors. He began drinking more after that, to the point that he could barely function. He'd always been a hard drinker, but he also always knew when to stop. Those six months were different. At the time there was nothing else he could do to arrest the pain. It's the one time in his life that compartmentalization didn't work. Drinking was a suitable replacement. But as is the case with all forms of overindulgence, there was a law of diminishing returns. Eventually, it made things worse.

He quit a week before graduation. He was surprised by how hard it was, and how horrible he felt during those few days. It was the one time in his life when he'd considered he might be better off dead. After all, at the time he felt as if he were dying already. It was that bad. But he managed it and was able to walk the stage somewhat presentable and feeling better. Physically at least. He hadn't had a drink since.

Upon his return to Hurlburt he had two long conversations, one with his Wing Commander and another with his Group Commander. Each of them was focused on understanding more about his acute decline and how Claire's death might still be affecting him. Was he fit for command? He'd decided he wasn't. Or maybe his Commanders made that decision. It didn't matter, he didn't want it anymore. It wasn't that he'd given up or had no interest in leadership. He still wanted to improve, to lead and win, and to do his best. But he knew he wasn't going to be able to do the kind of job he expected of himself. He needed to heal, to set his mind straight. Better to let one of his deserving peers take the squadron.

He got back to flying as a line pilot, took on some rather menial additional duties and then he pretty much coasted. He was healing. But as he did, he withdrew further into himself. He was rarely participating in unit extracurricular activities. His job performance never wavered; he was still the best at what he did. He just decided not to compete for any increased responsibility. He would deploy twice more to Afghanistan during that time. His mind and outlook were as healthy as they were going to get and there were still too many reminders, triggers that periodically and without warning allowed the memory of Claire to affect him. He could handle it, but he felt he shouldn't have to. Ultimately, he submitted his resignation. He wanted out—a clean break and a new life. It was the only way to put all of it behind him.

Dolan knew if he agreed to this and returned to Paris there was a chance it might undo some of what he'd spent so much effort repairing. Usurp his compartmented mental paradigm. It might seem as if he were going back in time and opening Pandora's box. But he was also excited by the idea. His love of Paris still lingered. And his fondness of European culture—the languages, the food, the architecture, and history. Allowing himself to weigh options, he revisited his subconscious, that dark place. To lobby some detached part of himself for mercy, for a compromise that would suddenly give him the power to do this and still be successful in walling off any potential damage. He looked deep and saw it, a dark cube sitting alone in a corner, far beyond many others that were far less menacing. The translucent box pulsed with images of Claire in mid-fall. There were demons buried in Paris, demons that had scarred his soul. But they weren't *his* demons. He had to put up with them, but they didn't *own* him. He didn't create them, either. Due to events beyond his control, they were brought into existence and began to excoriate his soul, flay him layer by layer until there was nothing left. After all this time he wasn't quite sure why or how it all happened. A terrible, unfortunate case of cause and effect, an error chain, whatever. What transpired wasn't his fault. And it was buried. Imprisoned. *It can only come out if I give permission.*

At that moment, an agreement was reached. A capitulation. It didn't matter where he went next, that box would go with him, shuttered and impenetrable, pushed deeper and deeper into his subconscious as each year passed. It couldn't affect him now. He would be able to do this. Uncharacteristically, he pushed aside the long list of reasons he should say no. It was a challenge, to be sure. But to date, there was no challenge worth taking on that he hadn't conquered. His mind was set. *Nothing can stop me now.*

"OK. I'll do it. I can do it. What's the next step?"

Lauren subdued a sigh of relief. "Great, thank you Michael. This is good news, and I look forward to working with you. Let's get the Sharif debrief out of the way first. Right now, if that's OK with you. While we do that, I can have all the necessary paperwork printed out for you. There is quite a bit of it. Everything will be done on paper, by the way. No emails, no scans. I'll need to meet with you tomorrow at nine a.m. in our office in Clarendon to complete the inbrief and give you your phone. Fill out and bring all the paperwork with you to that meeting. You'll also have a polygraph tomorrow. If you can't pass it, we will read you out of the program and our association will terminate. You leave for Paris in two weeks."

CHAPTER FIVE

The Sharif debrief took four hours. She was tired and wished she could go home to a hot shower and a glass of wine, but first she needed to meet with Dittrich to brief him on the outcomes of her meeting with Dolan and to clear up some loose ends with Thomas before she met with Dolan again in the morning. Of course, Dittrich might just tell them they're being shut down, in which case none of it would matter…

She now felt she knew much more about their suspect, but it was based on who he was years ago. Too much time had elapsed since then. There was nothing Dolan told her about Sharif that shed any light on why he might be helping his father plan a terrorist attack. Dolan felt the same way. There were two things that kept coming to mind that kept her undeterred about Sharif's involvement, however. First, he seemed to be spending a lot more money than his position with Francopharma would enable, and second, the association between Martin and Salmah. Hakeem may have moved his money from Panama to France, and Sharif might in fact be the financier at this point, something they would have to investigate. Or Salmah Lefebvre could be the financier.

Beyond Martin's visit to Salmah's house the other day, there was no evidence that either Sharif or Dolan knew Martin while at the Sorbonne. But the three of them were in fact attending during the same period. She would have to ask Thomas to find as much as he could on Martin from that time, and about his life in Metz, his family, and his job with Château Group. So much to do.

Dittrich walked in, looked first at Thomas then at Lauren. He tapped a thin file in front of him on the briefing room table. "I need to make a few points crystal clear. We are EXCISE. We're it. No one else is briefed in. Those other two techs who come in during ops surveillance, they won't be read in. Stone is read in partially, as is the Director. Dolan believes he's read in, but of course, he isn't. No one above me is going to know about it and that's my call. I am authorized to launch temporary programs that are required to fulfill the larger SCALPEL mission. The irony of all this is that we are doing it this way so we only violate a handful, vice twenty-something international and domestic laws to continue a larger mission that breaks more than that on a weekly basis.

"I recommended continuation of SCALPEL to the Director based in part on the possibility that Dolan's interaction with Lefebvre's son might yield enough information to break this cell open. Since this new guy Martin was at the meeting in Marseille and because of his apparent ties to Sharif's mother we now have basis for assuming the cell has been activated. There are positive ramifications for the long-term continuation of SCALPEL's mission if EXCISE succeeds. I believe the risk is worth the reward in this case, and it could bring closure to a case that has remained open for many years now. That said, the risks are many and some of them we don't yet fully understand.

"My greatest concern is Dolan himself. He could bring down the entire operation in spectacular fashion, single-handedly. On the face of it he's a hard-charging special ops perfectionist who may do quite well in the role you've created for him. On the other hand, he's a potential head case, unexploded ordnance." His eyes went back to Lauren. "I need you to hold his hand. You will make it easy for him." Dittrich paused, eyebrows raised as he waited for a response from Lauren.

"Understood. I will take care of it personally." She was almost overcome with relief at the news of the continuation of SCALPEL.

"Oh, and Stone's part in this must be perfect. He must stay invisible while doing it, and he's someone else you'll have to manage. He's good, but he's eager. He's not necessarily the type of officer I'd want on this detail, but he's all we've got." He paused, then added with emphasis, "All things considered, EXCISE has *fail* written all over it. If it does, SCALPEL is finished and just as we've been given a second chance to continue.

"Thomas, you are going to be busy. Despite Stone's direct involvement and geographic proximity, you are Dolan's real lifeline. Behind the scenes. Communication is going to be critical. If he talks to Sharif, the team needs to know immediately. If he talks to Martin, we need to know. Immediately. And if he does anything suspect, if he breaks protocol or for some reason goes off the reservation, we need to know. Immediately." Both Lauren and Thomas nodded in agreement.

"OK. Bring me up to speed."

Lauren lined up the edges of the sheaf of papers in front of her, an index finger sliding down each side as she began to speak. "Well, we came up with cryptonyms, in the event we have to communicate in the clear, and for our documentation. Dolan's code name is 'Jonah.'

Lefebvre's son Sharif's is 'Shax' and Martin is 'Stolos.' I sent Stone my report on my first meeting with Dolan and the basics from our meeting yesterday. We went over every part of our plan as well. Thomas has an iPhone prepped. I'll give it to Dolan when he gets here tomorrow. Thomas?"

"The nice thing about Monitor is that it is just an iPhone. There is no added hardware, no unique network settings, no self-destruct mechanism. There is no way to distinguish it from the real thing." Thomas smiled as he held up the phone.

Dittrich looked at the black device. "So, we're not calling it the *spiPhone*. That's a relief. Why Monitor? Baby monitor?"

Thomas laughed. "No, although that would seem appropriate in this case. I named it after the monitor lizard, or Komodo dragon, though the double entendre was intended. The Monitor app is hidden. It does not show up on the screen. It exists in its own partition in the flash memory on the phone, and IOS can't see it, even if the operating system is upgraded. The only way to tell that something is there is if you are able to determine the total storage in use on the phone does not add up. To do that you'd have to be looking for it. You'd have to suspect there was something on the phone that wasn't supposed to be there."

Dittrich was intrigued. "How did you get the app on the phone? What if the phone is wiped?"

Thomas dipped his head to the side, holding his arms out. *"Please…"* There was very little code out there he couldn't bend to his will.

Dittrich was undeterred. "What if he loses it? What if someone else gets his or her hands on it? How quickly could they figure out the phone is a collection device? And is there any way to wipe it remotely?"

"We're in a bit of trouble if he loses control of it. Someone who knows what they're doing and has the right equipment on hand, such as a foreign intelligence service, could crack it. And there would be no way to ensure the future utility of Monitor at that point. We'd be unable to use it again. Dolan has been briefed that if he loses it, he is to contact Lauren immediately. Then I'll wipe it remotely."

"And how is that done exactly?" Dittrich seemed unsure.

"The iTunes account is ours. I mean, Dolan will think it's his, but we have access. All I have to do is log into the account and erase it.

"Monitor basically creates an encrypted peer-to-peer connection with a server I have in my office. Stone has a version of it on his phone as well, though his offers much less utility. Monitor allows us to control the microphone on the remote device and record whatever sound is nearby. Dolan can't tell that we're listening in. It also provides me with all GPS and accelerometer data. If he makes a phone call, or uses Skype, or sends a text we'll hear and see both sides of the conversation along with the coordinates of his exact location.

"There is about a five-minute delay, however. The feed is encrypted on the phone, then sent via VPN and bounced off thirty-one servers in nine countries. Each bounce changes the IP address. Then it's decrypted here in Clarendon. Anyway, by the time we are listening in the GPS location and audio are about five minutes old. Stone's app has less of a delay, because it only bounces off seven servers and the data feed is just location coordinates, requiring much less time to encrypt and decrypt.

"If he's taking a video or photos, we can see what the camera sees. We can also view photos and videos he's stored on the phone. But we can't control the camera live the same way we do with the microphone. There is just no way to do it without the user noticing."

Lauren cut in. "We've told Dolan he can use the phone however he likes—to call home to his parents for instance, and for daily use. As far as he's concerned the main reason he's to carry it with him everywhere, to keep it charged and to never lose it is because it's his lifeline to you and me."

"So, there is no possible way for him to know we're listening in?" Dittrich queried.

"No," said Thomas emphatically. "I've spent hundreds of hours bench testing just that. And oh, by the way, we will have access to his email. We even have access to other metadata produced by apps used on the phone. Any of it could prove useful."

Lauren shifted uneasily in her chair. It was one thing to break international law in the name of antiterrorism, but another entirely to use an American citizen and war veteran to further the aims of an illegal (but essential) government operation. And because he would be unaware of their eavesdropping, they'd be crossing a line they've never crossed before. Thomas pointed out that this was less of a concern because it would be happening outside the United States. They all knew it was still very illegal, however. The conflict she felt was kept in check solely by the thought that the needs of the many outweighed the need of the one. The greater good was the sole reason for SCALPEL's existence. Despite that, she promised herself she would do everything in her power to prevent Dolan from being harmed. It was essential she not lose sight of that.

"Lauren, are you listening?" Dittrich looked at her critically.

"Yes sir. Sorry. I was off on a mental tangent. Please continue."

Dittrich resumed. "The app Stone has on his phone. How is it limited?"

"As I said, Stone will only have access to location data," replied Thomas. "That's it. If Dolan's phone is on and has service, or is connected to Wi-Fi, he'll be able to track him twenty-four seven. He just won't be able to see or hear anything. We'll have to back brief him on important details we capture at our end. There's no way to give Stone the same data feed that we'll have here. Way too risky. It's an issue with encryption and decryption that we don't have a workaround for yet."

"OK. So, we know Dolan had an incident in Paris that affected him acutely. His French girlfriend, Claire Lafontaine, died tragically in a fall—an accident. He was allegedly nearby but did not see it happen. He was inebriated at the time, and his grades faltered in his last semester. I need you to fill in the blanks for me."

"Yes. There was an investigation by the French police, and a limited review of the case by the State Department, mainly to make sure Dolan's rights weren't infringed upon. The DoD conducted an inquiry that amounted to a review of State's findings. He was quickly cleared of any wrongdoing and there was no evidence anyone else was at fault, though Sharif was in the room at the time. He admitted that. She fell six stories from the balcony of their room at the Grand Rêve Hotel on the Champs Elysées. It's an old building and apparently the railing was quite low, about a foot lower than today's typical safety standards require. Subsequently, the hotel replaced the balcony railings for every room. So, Dolan left the room for a bottle of Champagne, which he couldn't get from the hotel due to the late hour. When he returned, she had already fallen. Her toxicology report indicated a blood alcohol content of 0.28. Dolan was required by the DoD to complete a short series of counseling sessions via the embassy to ensure he was OK. Then he completed his degree at the Sorbonne, where he was on scholarship from the Air Force Institute of Technology.

"Before the incident, his record was spotless, and superior in every way. Afterwards, he kind of withdrew. His grades went down, but he still got his diploma. He returned to Hurlburt Airbase in Florida and three years later he retired. He then took on a job as a General Schedule 14, which is like a civilian Lieutenant Colonel, with the Joint Staff at the Pentagon and his career seemingly back on track.

"Emails between Dolan and Sharif indicate there was a break in their friendship shortly after Claire died. Dolan receded from everyone who was close with him, even his parents back in Boston. Given how much time he and Sharif spent together though, one would think they would lean on each other to get through such a tough spot. It could be he thought that because Sharif was with Claire when she fell, he should have been able to save her or prevent it but didn't. Sharif acknowledged he was there that night, but said he was in the bathroom when it happened. There was nothing in the investigation by authorities that suggested there was any foul play.

"Which leads me to my final point. Though their friendship was effectively over, they have had sporadic contact via email over the few years that followed. It looks as if Dolan was trying to put the incident behind him and to make up for what he considered to be a negatively motivated discontinuation of their relationship. In fact, they were in touch just five months ago, when Dolan wished Sharif a happy birthday. The bottom line is, the timing is good. I believe Dolan will be able to reconnect with Sharif when he gets to Paris and convince him he is trying to mend or perhaps rebuild that friendship. And we'll have a front-row seat."

Dittrich frowned in thought, something he did a lot. "Are there any other red flags? It sounds as if Dolan has his shit together. But going from a straight-A graduate student in a renowned foreign university to nearly flunking out doesn't jive. I can understand a dip, but if this guy is who we think he is, he bounces back quickly. He resets priorities, reloads, and gets on with life. How long were he and Claire dating? Were they engaged?"

"They were together for seven months. They were not engaged. After reviewing his emails, it is evident they were serious. They were introduced by Sharif's girlfriend at the time, also French. Her name is Anne Bernard, and she was Lafontaine's best friend. Curiously, there is no evidence in Dolan's emails with Sharif of any communication between Sharif and Bernard since the accident. And there is the added factor that Dolan's career was tainted by a slightly less than stellar performance report. It could be that the combination of that with the death of his girlfriend was enough to have a profound effect on him for an extended period. And as we know from his Pentagon record, he did bounce back. He has a superior record with the J5. It just took him a while."

Thomas sat next to Lauren, eyes flitting back and forth between her and Dittrich, wondering when they could get back to breaking down the utility and capabilities of the spiPhone.

Dittrich appeared satisfied, at least for the time being. "All right team, I think we've covered most of what I needed to know. I'll need you," he pointed at Lauren "to send me your full report on Dolan and a synopsis of your discussions with him from yesterday," he then looked to Thomas "and I'll need a daily report on anything meaningful from your lizard phone."

Thomas chuckled. "Yes sir."

Lauren nodded as she pushed back from the table, again lining up the files in front of her before picking them up. "Sir, I'll be meeting with Dolan tomorrow at nine, and a few more times to go over protocols, and quite a bit of training. And to answer any questions he might have. Though I should get what I need from our surveillance, I do plan to contact him directly from time to time. Handholding."

Dittrich held up at the doorway. "Sure. Just don't overdo it. Stone should be able to help with that considerably. By the way, I shouldn't have to say that we don't tell him about Marseille. You can brief him on Martin, just not how we came to know he was involved. Oh, and read him in on the drone attack. He needs the back story to put some context around Lefebvre's motivations. And without a doubt, the second you might be worried he's wigging out or can't handle it, do whatever it takes to prevent Dolan from fucking this whole thing up." He left the room.

CHAPTER SIX

Tony Stone finished his espresso and gazed out across Place de La Concorde. Another fine April morning in Paris. He adored France. He loved the language, the culture, and the people. And the food of course. He harbored an extreme dislike for anyone who couldn't appreciate the French, or at least those who didn't make an effort. That thought lingered as he watched an American family stop on the sidewalk in front of the café. The plump wife flipped through pages of her travel brochure, head down and thumbing frantically, trying to figure out where they were or what there was to look at in the area. The husband, a fidgeting kid in each hand, sported a Members Only jacket and stared off in the distance. *These people are lost*, Stone thought. Not lost in Paris—just lost. They traveled to a different continent with no preparation, no education or understanding of the history or culture. What's the point? They'd be better off staying home watching television. Instead, they end up here with no context at all for what they are experiencing. Their motivations for visiting France were superficial. See the Eiffel Tower and the Mona Lisa. Have some French wine with cheese. Eat some foie gras and a croque monsieur. Then they'll go back to Omaha or Reno or wherever they flew in from with hundreds of digital photos and an assortment of vacuous, boring stories. They will return just as ignorant as they were before they left.

Paris had intrigue. It was a world away from his work in Algeria, which he had simply endured. And he was now in a place worthy of his abilities. There was an old-world spy subculture here that had somehow stayed intact along the Seine, long after Vienna and Berlin shed their clandestine allure with the fall of the wall and the end of the Cold War. Unlike Germany and other, lesser regional powers, the French maintained an elegant but effective geopolitical influence with all the attendant diplomatic, military, and clandestine activities. This was quite evident to him during his work in Algeria and it remained so throughout much of North and West Africa.

Algiers was interesting at times, and the one big operation he'd worked on there had, inexorably, followed him here. It was a personal coup, and he was extremely happy with the eventuality. Of course, he'd rather there were no bad actors at all who were intent on attacking the U.S., but then he'd be out of a job. It was unfortunate that a small minority would hijack and distort a religion in the name of revolution and radical change, and to do so repeatedly in such bloody, shocking fashion. It has happened throughout history and with many religions of course; this was nothing new. But the entire first world, nearly all of the second, and much of the third had matured past this.

It was the outliers they still needed to deal with, and it would continue into the foreseeable future. In this case Stone foresaw an array of complications with being a babysitter to a non-Agency asset, a bridge 'agent' who had absolutely no idea what he was getting into. But Stone was taking this as a challenge. His marching orders were clear— follow when necessary, respond and assist appropriately if Dolan contacted him, keep him out of trouble, and report. *Pretty broad*, he mused. Dolan was a puppet, and he was holding the strings. Or at least a few of them.

He waved to the waitress for the bill and wet his forefinger, pressing it against the flaky remains of his croissant and then to his tongue. He checked his watch, 7:30 a.m. His 8:00 meeting with Lauren Rhodes should provide him with the last necessary details for his plan. Though he bristled a bit at the idea of dependency on Dolan and being required to keep him in the dark about some aspects of EXCISE, he knew his own capabilities. He performed exceedingly well. It was the reason he was recruited for SCALPEL and then granted Paris Station. The way he saw it, Dolan could be the perfect project for Stone. To mold and create. Produce a thing of beauty. With his direction, Dolan would lead them to the information they needed to unravel the AMA cell and take them out. The plan of course was to get enough information for the Agency to be able to pass everything on to the French and let them take over. But the current bilateral situation made that plan difficult. By his estimation, they would have to go to extreme lengths to make it work. It was more likely that he would have to take them down personally. And he had no problem with that.

He paid his tab, leaving a nice tip for the young French waitress.

"Merci," she said with a smile.

"Je vous en prie." He winked at her and strode away from the small café in his blue Savile Row suit, skirting the outer security wall of the U.S. Embassy and around to the front gate. Once inside he walked with purpose to the second-floor briefing room, swiped his embassy badge, keyed in his code, and entered. He thought with satisfaction that he was alone in the room for a reason—no one else in Paris was briefed on EXCISE. Only he and the Station Chief were even briefed on SCALPEL. Stone booted up the classified video teleconference system, typed in the appropriate IP address and made the call.

Lauren appeared on the screen, sophisticated and beautiful as always. "Hello Tony. How are things in Paris?"

"Couldn't be better Lauren. You're looking well for two in the morning. Good to see you again."

"Thank you. As you know we're on a tight schedule and we have some important details to go over before Dolan gets there. To begin with, we have him set up in a nice hotel near your residence on rue Galilée. The Hôtel Flambeau. He'll stay there until the State Department is able to get him into an apartment. He'll be in room 313. He arrives at Orly on Thursday at four in the afternoon on flight 2112, Air France from DC. You will meet with him on Friday morning at nine O'clock. Do you have everything set up for him?"

Stone smiled curtly. "Yes. DoD owns the intel sharing position. As far as the defense attaché is concerned, he's just another DoD civilian in Paris, and although he's directly responsible for Dolan's well-being and administrative issues he'll be almost completely hands-off. Besides the housing office, neither the DATT nor anyone else at the embassy will ever need to meet him. I should have enough time tonight to fully review the *twenty*-page report you sent me yesterday. I've scanned it but still need to digest it. I must tell you; I'm impressed with how thorough you three have been given the time allotted."

Lauren dismissed the compliment. "Listen, I know I don't need to tell you, but I will anyway. You are being directed to blend into the scenery. When you leave the embassy to meet him, when you go to and from home, in fact anywhere you go from today until this is done you are to be as unremarkable as possible. It's your full-time job, essentially. You're the self-described definitive Francophile so it should be easy for you. I need you to lose the fancy blue suit and to look average. Don't wear a tie. You can't ever be seen with Dolan. You can never be associated with him by anyone else, ever. And you'll have to be doing everything right under the nose of your own station. Yes, the Chief of Station is briefed on SCALPEL, but not on EXCISE. It would be a good idea to get caught up on what Paris Station is doing as far as counterintel goes so you aren't caught in the crossfire. Do you understand?"

"Lauren, you are correct, you don't need to tell me." He was a bit put off by her directive tone. He could blend whenever and however he wanted. He knew she was right, but she should have more faith in him given his track record. "I am concerned about latency of real-time intel though. I'll have eyes on him when I need to, but you have the ears. My app only allows me to track his position, and nothing else. Shouldn't I have all the data? Is Thomas there?"

"No, he's prepping the phone for Dolan and doing some last-minute tests. We can't pipe the signal to you. We simply have no way to do it securely at this point. Thomas will be providing Dittrich regular reports about his activity, you'll be courtesy copied on Intelink. This is as good a plan as we must get you data that is as real-time as possible. We'll call you on your cell if we can pass information in the clear."

Stone nodded knowingly. This was all standard. "OK Lauren. What about the rest of our guys. Any updates on Lefebvre, Sharif, Martin, or Lefebvre's ex-wife? What about the banker and the unknown target in Marseille?"

"A lot of that is in the report. Here's what isn't. Late last year Lefebvre moved fifty million euros from his bank in Panama to an account at a bank in Zurich. We believe that Sharif or maybe his mother have access. We don't know how they did it without our knowledge, but it appears Aparicio probably used an elaborate scheme with hundreds of transfers though multiple banks to get it there undetected. It also clears up why there was no transfer made at the meeting near Marseille. We think they finalized a deal there, but still don't know if any funds have been used or transferred out. The account is basically invisible to us. One could also assume that Lefebvre is simply sharing his money with family and knowing that those funds could end up being frozen, he's taken special precautions.

"And we have information on Martin. He recently left Metz and hasn't been seen for a few days. We don't know where he went, he could just be on vacation."

Stone felt the hair on the back of his neck stand up. A small dose of adrenaline shot through his body, and he felt as if he had just fallen behind the power curve. "Well, this is all good information and I'm glad we are finally getting somewhere. At the risk of sounding negative, however, Dolan is useless unless he rekindles and maintains his friendship with Sharif. And if he doesn't do that carefully, if he stumbles, Sharif could become suspicious immediately and the whole plan will be shot. We need to do this carefully, to do it right. I have some ideas."

Lauren held her breath. On one hand Stone was a potential risk. He was a self-absorbed perfectionist with a penchant for going it alone. And it wasn't that he was oblivious to his character defects. In fact, he was well aware. He just didn't care. He relished his carefully crafted narcissism. He fed on the reactions his personality evoked from others. Yet he planned the strike on Lefebvre's team in Algeria exceptionally well, in part because he possessed a knack for creating productive relationships with the right people. He could pinpoint what people were best at and get the most out of them. His attention to detail was second to none. Stone was already involved at the deepest level and understood the intricacies of SCALPEL. He almost single-handedly uncovered Lefebvre's involvement with the AMA. And though they had yet to do so, the AMA had the capability of striking fear in North Africa and the West. For Stone at least, EXCISE was aptly named. They needed to execute thoughtfully and precisely, to remove the cell without so much as a hint of their involvement. Or to collect enough evidence to be able to hand everything off and pursue a bilateral solution with DGSI. In any other scenario the damage would be immediate and far-reaching.

Stone was young but proven, and his uncanny perception and ability to manipulate people in volatile situations yielded surprisingly positive results. His resume was well above average for an operative his age, but the summation of his persona, on and off paper, added up to a wild card. This is why Dittrich was worried about using him.

"Let's not get ahead of ourselves, Stone," Lauren countered. "Put your ideas together in a memo and send it to me. We'll evaluate here and let you know how to proceed, OK?"

Stone smiled at her through the glassy screen. "Of course. You'll have it by the time you finish breakfast."

"Great. Thank you, and I'll give you a call later to set up our next VTC."

"Hey, how did his polygraph go? I guess he passed, or our discussion would have been much different. Any flags?"

"Well, yes, he passed. We gave him Full Scope. No problem with the CI exam, but he had some trouble with lifestyle. We saw evidence of deception when we asked about involvement in a serious crime. Turns out he carries a lot of guilt about what happened to Claire. He also showed an inconclusive result when asked about use of illegal drugs. Again, it seems his perception about how much he was drinking in the aftermath of her death was skewing the score. After we removed Claire's death from the scope of the questioning and reemphasized the illegal part of the drugs question, he passed."

"OK, thanks. Good to know. Stone out," he said, still smiling.

The screen went blank. Lauren sank slowly back into her armchair and let out a measured sigh. She liked Stone, generally speaking, but disliked his candor and his approach. She would need to be careful with him.

Stone sat unmoving in the quiet, sterile room. He was thinking, carefully arranging these latest developments into their proper order, within their proper context. Assessing possibilities and crafting a way ahead. How much of his plan he would reveal to Lauren remained to be seen. He decided he would save a few curveballs in case he got behind in the count. He left the secure room and the embassy, stopping in his office first for twenty minutes to send out a few emails and the memo to Lauren.

Walking slowly along the north side of the Champs Elysées, he reminisced about his time in Algeria. Much different than Paris. More dangerous, for sure. He and Mike had almost been killed, but they'd successfully completed the mission. Well, almost—they hadn't gotten Lefebvre. And so here we are. *Time to go to work*, he thought with a grin.

CHAPTER SEVEN

Michael Dolan looked around his apartment. He packed five boxes, two suitcases, his Tumi knapsack and a duffle bag. They were stacked neatly near the front door. Everything else would go into storage. Once State was able to find him an apartment, they'd provide him with loaner furnishings. Other than a modest collection of books and various types of athletic and Taekwondo gear, he didn't own much. He'd always tried not to accumulate too much 'stuff.' He didn't want to be weighed down.

His mind then wandered to his girlfriend Amy. He'd been trying to figure out how best to break up with her for a month. Now that he was leaving DC it would be easy. As he thought about it, he realized there were several things about this radical change that were positive. He was relatively comfortable with his proposed role in EXCISE. Lauren did a good job answering his questions and briefing him on how things would play out. The training they'd given him had been straightforward and useful. How to use the iPhone to make secure calls and texts. How to recognize when he was being surveilled or counter surveilled. To execute dead drops and brush passes, common interrogation techniques. How to manage stressful situations, like being caught in the act of collecting information.

And they knew about Paris. As far as Lauren was concerned it was an unfortunate accident and it hadn't factored into their decision to use him. He felt relieved and somewhat empowered by that. Not because the CIA didn't attribute fault in that sequence of events to him personally, but that they had said nothing about his struggle in the aftermath. As if it were understandable. *I had nothing to do with Claire's death. It wasn't my fault.*

He quickly laced up his shoes and went for one last run on the Custis Trail. This time he went easy, taking in his surroundings as he ran, seemingly for the first time. The constant pressure of his Pentagon job was gone. He had nothing to collate mentally save a short list of accounts to close and people to say goodbye to. Amy would be difficult, but not overly so. She'd be hurt. She wouldn't understand why he was leaving so quickly. Why he was only telling her at the last minute. He realized he should also call his parents back in Boston.

As he ran, he went through his last day at work. His afternoon briefing to the General yesterday had been cancelled. His supervisor Colonel Sykes called Dolan into his office that afternoon, wanting to know why he was being pulled from the staff, why he wasn't notified earlier, and why Dolan would consider such a career move in the first place. It was a dead-end. General Thompson told the Colonel what he knew, which wasn't much. The cover story was that he was requested by name to fill a critical position in an intelligence-sharing unit at DRM Headquarters for Five Eyes plus France, based in Paris. Dolan helped Lauren craft some of the details of the story. That he couldn't talk about it made it easy. The unit's mission was to share intelligence between the Five Eyes Plus France countries. His experience with Special Operations and his mastery of the French language put him at the top of a very short list. That was all close to the truth. In a nutshell, it was believable, and it would work.

Lauren instructed him to remain silent about many of the aspects of his move. She also told him to be careful about advertising the refresher course. If anyone asked, the course was essential. He'd need to be able to communicate as a native, and he hadn't spoken French with anyone for years save sporadic contact with old friends from his time at the Sorbonne. To some it could look strange that he needed the course considering his fluency and having lived in France for two years. Added to that, it was a $35,000 expense charged to the taxpayer.

He was looking forward to seeing Paris again, speaking the language and reabsorbing the culture. However, it worried him he would be in and around the places, and at times with people who reminded him of Claire and of what happened to her. That night was a blur, right up until the point he'd walked into the hotel room, the crushed red velvet window drapes on either side of the open balcony door shifting silently with the wind. He remembers pushing past a distraught Sharif to the partially open sliding glass door and noticing her pink sequined clutch purse on the balcony floor. Leaning over the black wrought iron railing. And he saw her, sprawled unmoving facedown with arms and legs bent awkwardly on the street below, her sky-blue dress splotched with dark red, almost black in the yellowish incandescent lighting. Blood pooling around her head like a sick halo as sirens wailed and lights flashed.

Emergency response personnel were yelling at him from below in French, something about staying where he was, waiving their hands. He remembered thinking to himself how he'd returned through the rear entrance to the hotel. It was the quickest route back from the corner store. If he'd come through the front, he'd have walked right into the commotion now surrounding Claire's lifeless body. He just stood there, staring down and unable to move, his head spinning until the police entered through the open door. In the moments that followed he'd experienced a surreal, hollow disembodiment, a black nothingness. He'd felt *inhuman*. As if his thin shadow of a soul, all he'd ever had, just slipped away into the night.

Dolan shook his head to clear the images. Somewhere about a mile back he stopped enjoying his surroundings and allowed himself a slice of pain. This was oftentimes the only way he could feel any emotion at all. It was a sad, sardonic self-prescription that reminded him he was still human. Only he couldn't handle it this time—it came on too fast, too vividly, and it took on a life of its own with an innate prescience. As if it foresaw something he couldn't. He didn't know what it would do to him if he just let it all out. The imminent proximity of his controlled, stable life to that climactic event could be a powerful, negative catalyst. He had to focus. He felt he'd never be able to confront it and control its effects simultaneously. With a determined thought he put it back, throbbing, into its cage. He turned around and jogged brusquely back to his now bleak apartment for a shower in preparation for his difficult breakfast with Amy and final meeting with Lauren.

CHAPTER EIGHT

"What's wrong?" she asked under her breath as Michael approached. She was seated at their usual table in the Old Ebbitt Grill on 15th Street, their favorite restaurant.

She was visibly worried. He had been unusually curt with her on the phone. It wasn't on purpose. He simply had been unable to find the right words, to explain why they should meet. It was strange. It should have been as easy as any other time they'd met there for a meal. He came right out and told her.

"I'm leaving for Paris. Tomorrow." He pulled a chair out across from Amy and sat down, regarding her as she slowly shook her head with a confused look.

"What? Why? For how long?"

"Amy, I've been reassigned to a three-year tour there and it's happening now." He put his elbows on the table, his fingers interlocked. As Amy struggled to process what he just said, he studied her. She was beautiful. She was intelligent, driven and a good person. Everything that attracted him to her in the first place. But now he felt little for her. Just a sort of sincere, mild affection. As if she were already his ex and they'd moved well beyond any post-breakup awkwardness.

She looked at him intently. "Mike, it doesn't make any sense. They wouldn't just send someone to Paris for three years at the drop of a hat." Now she looked away, through the window, continuing. "And why wouldn't you have told me earlier. Even just a day earlier, if it were possible. If you genuinely cared about me." She looked at him again, tears welling. Her fair complexion was reddening, her lower lip quivered slightly. "Just tell me why."

He disliked having to do this but knew it was the right thing. He cocked his head slightly, leaned forward, and did his best to appear empathetic. Just enough to seem genuine. "Amy, I do care about you. Greatly. And you're right—the government doesn't usually do it this way. But this isn't a normal assignment. I can't say much more than that. There was a need for someone like me to go to France and to do something important. There was another guy lined up for the job, but something went sideways, and he could no longer fill the position. They asked me and I said yes. I understand this is difficult for you to take. I really do." He leaned closer to her. "But it's happening. There is nothing either you or I can do to change it. All we can do at this point is decide about what to do with our relationship."

"What to do?" She was becoming more distraught. "There is no manual for this situation. There is only one thing to be done, and you're doing it. You are leaving me." She wiped the corner of each eye with her napkin as a waiter approached and stopped short, recognizing an uncomfortable situation. He turned and strode away, melting into the noisy background. "I suppose I should thank you. I've suspected for a while now, you've changed. How you think about me. You're hard to reach, Mike. And now you'll be as far away physically as you've been emotionally." She dropped the napkin on the table, no longer trying to stem the tears now streaking her face. She looked at him for one last moment, got up and walked out.

He didn't even look to see her go. He felt bad she was hurt. In a twisted way, that made him feel better for a moment—at least he felt *something*. And now he was relieved that she was out of his life. A weight removed. *I should probably feel guilty about that.* But he didn't. *Not to worry.* The utility of any feelings for Amy was already exhausted, and it was easy to stash small, insignificant memories. Minor problems. They'd only been dating for two months. He quickly compartmented anything that would linger, anything that was threatening. There—*gone.*

CHAPTER NINE

Lauren was standing near a fountain wearing a greyish plaid wool skirt and a white ruffled silk blouse. *She looks different*, thought Dolan. Her red hair was pulled back into a ponytail. Not as pretty, more professional. *She's probably worried about how prepared I am.* "Good afternoon, Lauren," he said with a nod.

"Good afternoon." She shook his hand quickly and they both sat down. The location was quite different this time, a small park in Crystal City just south of the Pentagon. He noted the background noise of water splashing in the fountain, no doubt to cover their conversation. Though it probably couldn't get more public than this, the abundant greenery largely screened their position from commuters as they walked to and from the Virginia Railway Express station.

"Your ticket is inside." She handed him a large, navy-blue canvas bag with handles. It looked like something he might take to the beach. "There is also a folder with information pertaining to your hotel in Paris. It'll be a few weeks before State is able to find you a proper apartment. Contact information for the language school, information about the U.S. Embassy, and a separate file with quite a bit on your job, they are all in there. And your passport with a three-year visa." She reached into her purse. "Here is your iPhone, and the encryption card." The micro-SD card was inserted into a dongle, the other end to be plugged into the lightning port of his phone. A piece of scotch tape kept the card secure. Thomas had shown him how to use it. "Use it as you would if it were your own. Remember to take it with you everywhere you go. Again, it's your lifeline. I cannot emphasize that enough. Always keep the card safely hidden. Please tell me you understand. It's important, OK?"

He took the phone and white dongle, looked at them briefly, and placed them inside the blue bag. "I understand, and you have nothing to worry about," he assured her.

"OK." She crossed her hands on her lap and looked at him with a thoughtful gaze. "Michael, I have to say I am surprised how easily you've agreed to do this. I'll be honest, I'm curious about what's going on in your head right now. I know you have no immediate family besides your parents and it's relatively easy for you to just pick up and move but I expected you to be hesitant. I mean, in the spectrum of opportunity that's available to you, this is extreme. It's radical and there are many unknowns. Yes, we've done what we can to make it easier for you, but I would have expected you to ask more questions. I'd like to know what you feel about all of this personally before you go.

"You haven't said much at all about Sharif. I would be overwhelmed to find out a good friend of mine might be involved with something like this." He was hard to read and carried himself with a casual stoicism that was rare. As if he could be professional, genuine, and situationally aware without ever giving a hint about his own opinions, feelings, or concerns. It was impressive. Or it could be sociopathic. She hoped that wasn't the case.

Dolan thought about it for a moment. "It makes sense to me that you're concerned. However, I don't think there's anything to be worried about. As you pointed out I have nothing keeping me here. And though you may perceive that I am underwhelmed by the whole situation, I can assure you that's because I've thought this through to what I would describe as an extreme degree. I've weighed the positives and negatives" *a lie?* "and I've considered the impact of all of it on my life in general. I've been quite objective about it. In the end, I determined it's an opportunity that will benefit me more in the long run than it may appear. More important than that, this gives me the opportunity to serve my country in a different way. A direct way. I've missed being the tip of the spear, and frankly I'm tired of strategic planning and relationship building. Those things are important, and I do them well, but I'm not passionate about them. I'm fully on board."

She continued to study him, scrutinizing his demeanor and trying to divine something valuable to add to his words. She was unable, but he'd satisfied her concerns for the time being. "Alright. I'm happy with your answer. I'm going to leave you with this." She chose her words carefully. "We've obtained new information. Where two days ago we were ahead of the ball, I would say at this point we are behind." Dolan shifted slightly on the bench. "On the face of it, that means nothing to you. Your charge remains the same. Go to Paris, go to school, work with us and eventually, do your job at DRM. However, it is likely we will need you to accelerate your timeline for meeting with Sharif." He looked at her inquisitively. "I'm not being clear. What I mean to say is, listen to Stone and follow his lead. He will coach you and tell you what to do. We just don't have as much time as we thought, and you should work on rekindling that friendship with Sharif soon after you get there. That's it."

His eyes darted around the immediate area scanning for some interloper he knew probably wasn't there. He wanted to ask her *why* the timeline was accelerated, what had happened. "Well, that's about as vague as you can get," he said. "I'll be honest with you, Lauren. I may not know the entire backstory or all the details about what is currently happening and there may be good reasons for this, so I'm not going to linger on the topic. As I said, I'm on board, and I know what you want me to do. However, I expect that as our working relationship evolves and matures you and Stone will begin to fill me in on those details to help me understand better what the scope of my role is, and so I can put the desired outcomes of my work with you in the proper context. In my view this is essential if you are expecting results sooner than later."

Lauren was both caught off guard and pleasantly surprised. *At least he's showing me something now*, she pondered. "We will tell you what you need to know, Michael. As I said, just be flexible and follow all the protocols. If you do that, we'll be fine."

She smiled at him, and he was unsure whether it was sincere. Genuine or not, there was a finality to it, as if the discussion were over. He could reengage on the topic later. "Understood. Should I ever expect a call from you, or will I hear mainly from Stone?"

Lauren looked at him squarely. "I will only call you to pass important information when Stone cannot. I may also check in from time to time to see how you are doing, though there is no timetable for that. And again, you shouldn't call me unless it's absolutely necessary, and only using the encryption card."

"I understand. I have one last question."

"Shoot."

"I know it doesn't change anything. We are already in motion but why go through all this trouble? The risk involved seems excessive. France is a strong ally. Why don't you engage with your counterparts there and let them do the legwork? You'll have to forgive my ignorance, but I'm not up to speed with any international laws that may apply here. Why wouldn't you just work with the French government? They could surveil Sharif and Martin or anyone else, bug their houses and share the intel with you."

She paused before answering. She wondered why he didn't bring this up during their meetings. She could have reassured him then, but she missed it. *What else did I miss?* "Michael, it's a good question. But you don't have to worry about those things, let us do that. Suffice to say that we are working closely with the government of France on this. There is history, there are extenuating circumstances—the drone strike in Algeria is a primary factor—that require us to do some things outside the norm. Unilaterally. Though the French are strong allies their global and domestic priorities frequently do not align with those of the United States. In these cases, we reserve the right to do what's best for our country and our citizens. The fact is, other countries don't always do what we ask of them. And even when they do, they don't always do it the way we need them to.

"As I've said before, you will never be asked to do anything that we believe is beyond your level of ability to do successfully and safely. And the entire time we will be taking measures to protect you." She leaned forward a bit, looking him directly in the eyes and whispered, "You must understand this one important thing. Though you are technically not an employee of the CIA, you are an invaluable member of this team. EXCISE will succeed or fail depending largely on how well you do your job. I want you to do well in your language refresher course, and to do well in the intel job. But all of that is secondary. What you do for us comes first. Always. Promise me."

This was what he needed—an intriguing challenge that would yield real, positive results. He hoped the team would ease him in quickly, and that he would come to understand and enjoy the full impact of his participation. Something had been missing from his life, and this was going to fill the void. Something that would require complex problem solving and analysis, adrenaline, and if he was lucky, some serious hand to hand combat. "I promise," he said with a guarded smile.

CHAPTER TEN

The flight from Washington Reagan was interminably long. He spent a couple of hours reacquainting himself with a somewhat worn advanced French grammar book and the rest of the time mentally outlining a realistic plan to get in contact with Sharif. He was still wrestling with the likelihood that Sharif was a violent radical extremist. It was difficult to believe. Sharif was never a practicing Muslim let alone a fundamentalist. He never even mentioned visiting a mosque in Paris, let alone attending khutbah. He was full of life. Too full sometimes. Highly intelligent and driven, he'd expressed and pursued personal goals that did not align with revolutionary Islamism. Everything he'd accomplished in life would be undone. Dolan just couldn't envision Sharif changing in such a primal way. Something significant must have happened to catalyze such a complete transfiguration.

Dolan wanted to write it all out with a timeline, milestones, risks, and important facts. But he couldn't of course. And with his photographic memory it didn't matter. Lauren had given him some simple instructions for using code, however he wasn't to do it unless needed to get a written message to Stone. Unless it's done well, a coded message looks like a coded message and in the wrong hands could blow his cover and the operation. Though he understood why, it was concerning they didn't trust him with some of the more mundane clandestine efforts. They ran him though some quick training on these and other things, but he wasn't supposed to do any of it unless explicitly told to, or in the event of an emergency. It made him wonder how useful he was going to be to EXCISE. Hopefully, they'll trust him to do more as he proves himself. As the operation matures and he becomes more comfortable in the role. *Or, maybe they haven't told me everything…* Maybe he was being used as bait. He wasn't used to thinking this way—it was too haphazard, too chaotic. It bothered him that the rigid dependability of his scheduled life was in flux. It would have to be redesigned, rebuilt. That would take considerable time.

By the time he landed Dolan had sketched a rough draft of a plan in his mind for approaching Sharif. He got his bags, walked out of Orly, and flagged a cab. The Middle Eastern driver loaded his luggage into the trunk as he got into the back seat and settled in for the ride north. The morning traffic was just starting to pick up. He tried to continue refining his thoughts from the flight and found himself transfixed, gazing at the outskirts of Paris as they moved slowly by his window in a misty rain. It seemed weirdly unfamiliar, as if he were trying to remember the details of a movie he'd watched ten years ago. It just didn't seem like he'd spent two years of his life here. Of course, some things have changed since back then. But he wondered if he'd accidentally locked away random elements of his past life, parts of harmless memories and experiences along with the dark, dangerous ones. If this was the case, it wasn't good. Intentionally, and acknowledging the irony, he put that thought away as well.

He asked the driver to take a detour northeast on Avenue du Général Leclerc, toward Île da la Cité. He wanted to see Notre Dame Cathedral, what the damage looked like firsthand. The fire happened just two weeks earlier and took nine days to fully extinguish. The cause was believed to have been an accident as the result of ongoing restoration work. Luckily, many of the church's historic artifacts including a crown of thorns believed to have been that of Jesus Christ had been removed as the work began. The main structure with its two towers was still standing, and firefighters succeeded in preventing the fire from spreading to the northern belfry. But the spire and about two-thirds of the roof were now gone.

The 850-year-old iconic French landmark held a special place in his heart. Aside from when he was a child, the only time he'd ever prayed was there in Notre Dame. About three months after Claire's death, he'd ventured in, hung over and broken. He sat in one of the worn wooden pews, looked up at the three stained glass rose windows, then down at the gold cross above the altar and asked God to *please make it all go away*. That was it. He would sit there for two hours, repeating his despairing plea. Nothing happened though, nothing changed. There was no great epiphany. No overwhelming, warm feeling of redemption and hope. So, he got up and left the cathedral, resigned to the possibility that God couldn't help him. If He even existed. Over time he'd realized that as things did get better perhaps God wanted him to suffer, that it was a necessary trial and something that would end up making him stronger. Better. Or there really was no God and this is just how life goes. He wasn't convinced yet which it was.

The taxi driver said they couldn't get near the Cathedral, as all the roads nearby were closed. That made sense. Better to visit later, in any case, when he can go on foot and take his time.

Bit by bit the drab gray scenery transitioned to the grand, stoic blocks of old buildings and bridges scarred with varying degrees of soot and weather wear, all of it exuding an aura of history, mystery, and charm. His memory of the city began to clear. It was a slow, steady build of recognition as they turned onto Champs Elysées with the sun now breaking through the clouds.

The transition evoked a moment of happiness, a rare thing he learned to accept graciously whenever it happened. His thoughts then turned to Anne. She was probably still here in Paris, and he would need to get in touch with her. She was the best way to facilitate his first contact with Sharif. Only he would need to do it carefully and thoughtfully. He hadn't spoken with her in years. He felt guilty about that. His personal tragedy was a terrible excuse for ignoring hers. While Sharif and he had some contact, he'd shut Anne out completely. She called him, emailed him, but he never responded. At the time, Dolan thought it would have been too difficult. *I didn't care.*

Anne and Claire were inseparable, best of friends from childhood. As he thought about it more, he realized the tragedy was more hers than his. If he'd paid any attention to her, it might have meant confronting Sharif as well. It was an inexcusable period of weakness on several fronts.

The taxi slowed and pulled up to the front of Hôtel Flambeau. "We are here," stated the driver.

"Merci. Combien?"

"Thirty-five euros," said the man, refusing the invitation to continue in French.

How Parisian, thought Dolan. And he's not even French.

He paid the driver and stood by as a hotel porter quickly approached and began loading his bags onto an ornate brass cart. Once inside he checked in and looked around a bit, noting the relative antiquity of the place. Old, luxurious carpets and Louis XIV-era furniture graced the lobby. Large, gold-framed paintings decorated the walls. A ridiculous crystal chandelier hung from the high, sculpted ceiling. Once in his room he tipped the porter and surveyed the room, a suite. Not nearly as opulent as the lobby. Somewhat Spartan even, but it didn't matter. He would only be here a few weeks.

Dolan put his two suitcases, the backpack, and his duffel bag next to the five boxes lined up against the wall near the door. They'd been shipped and delivered in advance of his flight. He thought momentarily about unpacking. The thought vanished as he realized how utterly fatigued he was. He opened a bottle of mineral water from the mini bar and drank some, undressed and climbed into the plush bed. He drifted quickly into a deep, sound sleep.

That night he dreamt. He was dressed all black and walking brusquely. It was dark, nearing midnight. They were in a city, in the outskirts somewhere. Maybe even Paris. Somewhere in Europe in a park with sculptures. A friend was with him, also in black. Dolan thought it strange he didn't know his friend's name, only that they were close somehow. He could see that his friend looked worried, but somehow his face was blurred, unrecognizable. Suddenly, Dolan was also worried; someone was chasing them. They began to run and turned down a cobblestone path. The pursuer came into view as Dolan looked back, keeping pace with them. As they ran further into the woods, they saw a high fence obstructed their path. Dolan jumped onto the fence and began to climb with his friend close behind. The man stopped and fired a gun. Bullets whizzed by, clinking sharply as one of them clipped the fence wire near his hand. Dolan made it to the top, looking back to hold out his hand but his friend wasn't fast enough. The man grabbed his leg, pulling him down. He lost his grip and fell face-first on the cobblestones, scrambling to get up as his assailant subdued him.

Dolan stopped, straddling the fence and watching in horror as the man pinned his friend to the ground with a knee on his chest. As his friend struggled, the man looked straight at Dolan and smiled sardonically. And though he was looking straight at him, he couldn't discern any facial features. His countenance was enigmatically blurred, in the same way as his friend's. Then, still looking straight at Dolan, he pulled a large knife from his jacket, the blade glinting in the moonlight.

Dolan prepared to jump down and save his friend, but he found he could not move. He couldn't speak. He couldn't even blink. As Dolan watched helplessly, he realized he was dreaming. He could change this. He remembered that he'd had this dream before. Many times. *It's my dream, and I know I'm dreaming.* He concentrated, trying to will the dream to change, to make the aggressor disappear. *It will work this time.* But it didn't work. A sickening dread quickly reached up from the pit of his stomach, through his midsection and engulfed him entirely. He was unable to act, unable to change the course of events.

The man with the knife grabbed his friend's wrist and pulled his arm out, away from his body. His friend struggled for a moment more, then lifted his head, eyes wide and transfixed on Dolan, welling with tears. He said nothing. The man positioned the knife's point to his side near the armpit, and then pushed it to the hilt through the ribcage and into his heart. The ground around his friend began to turn dark, his blood pooling. His friend went limp and the man stood up, looking up at Dolan again with that malevolent grin. Just as he had done a hundred times before. Dolan consistently asked himself the same question at this point in the dream. *Who are they? How could I feel such a close connection with this person and not know who he was?* It always ended the same way. Unable to do or say anything, he would cling to the fence until he woke up.

The sheets were damp. Dolan was breathing hoarsely and sweating. He noted his elevated heart rate. It always feels so completely real. And just as it happened a hundred times before, the fear ebbed.

His heart rate slowed. Once again he felt irritated he was unable to change the ending, to save his friend. He glanced at his watch. Four in the morning. He was unnerved at the realization there was some part of him that actually *liked* the dream. It evoked such strong emotion in him, something he rarely experienced in real life. It was good to feel something now and again, even if it was terror.

The first time he had the dream was after he returned to Florida from Paris. It left him shaken and worried for some time. Then it happened again, and he decided he needed to contain it, wall it off as he did with so many other problems. But with this particular issue, just this one, he was somehow unable.

There were noticeable changes to the dream every time. In each iteration he would see something he hadn't noticed before. A raven atop a stop sign. Someone sitting in a parked car as they ran past. But these were small details, and the plot was always the same. And it always left him seeking answers, searching for meaning. What are the parallels to be drawn between the dream and his real life? *How do I interpret this?* Dolan guessed that the import of the dream was not that a man was being killed, nor was it that another man was killing someone. The significance of the dream lay in *who they were* and that for some reason Dolan needed to see it happen.

He'd heard that dreams are the leftover essences of the day, a random collection of thoughts thrust haphazardly together for disposal by the brain to clear the mind before morning arrives. Cleaning house. Remnants of various happenings. Casual, unimportant clutter the brain just doesn't need anymore. Perhaps this is why one does not remember most dreams—because they are composed primarily of mental trash. But dreams remembered, are they mistakes? Did the brain try to throw out something it shouldn't have? Might that explain why he continues to have the same dream, because these dark and visceral thoughts simply cannot be discarded? Or perhaps it is an attempt by the subconscious to let you know something is wrong. *That there is something I need to fix.*

He'd also heard that one wouldn't dream about doing something they wouldn't do in real life. Not that you wouldn't want to do it or think about doing it. It's more accurate to say one wouldn't ever do something in a dream that they wouldn't dare to do when awake, like committing murder. Which led him to wonder, why was he was prevented from helping his friend? In a real situation he would, without hesitation. Instead he freezes, his friend is killed gruesomely, and he wakes up sweating, eyes wide and heart pounding. It was an evil dream. It scared him. He hated it and wished it would go away. And he also liked it.

CHAPTER ELEVEN

Rolf Haussmann wiped some of the grime from his calloused hands with a worn rag, tossing it on the workbench nearby. He took four five-liter stainless steel tanks labeled *Medizinischen Sauerstoff*—medical oxygen, one at a time from a storage rack and set them on the bench. After connecting a long metal-reinforced hose to the first, he donned a military-grade gas mask fitted with a special filter he designed himself and secured the straps. He flipped a switch under the bench, powering up an industrial exhaust vent installed over the work area. He then took the other end of the hose and attached it to a 10,000-psi pump. Grabbing a second high-pressure hose, he connected the pump to a valve at the bottom of an industrial pressurized reservoir that was standing upright next to the bench. The reservoir was part of a complicated assembly of coiled tubing, electronic and glass elements and five smaller metal cisterns. The entire apparatus was interconnected via a bundle of wires that terminated in a metal box containing circuits that converted analog data to digital. The metal box was then interfaced with a laptop computer using a single USB connection.

Rolf double checked the fittings and went to the laptop to check that the chemical process was complete and assess the purity of the final product. When he was satisfied with the results, he walked to the reservoir and opened the valve. The small pressure gauge attached to the valve dipped initially, and then popped back to its original position. After opening the valve on the first tank he turned on the pump, setting the cutout switch at 2,000 psi. He filled all four tanks in succession. When he was finished, he turned off the pump and slipped on a pair of surgical gloves, carefully wiping each of the four cylinders with a rag. He placed the tanks in an aluminum footlocker, the gray cylinders resting snuggly side-by-side in a form-fitted foam bed. He replaced the lid and closed all eight heavy-gauge clasps, two on each side, ensuring a hermetic seal. Grabbing the hose originally attached to the reservoir, he screwed it onto a valve fitting on the side of the trunk, and turned the pump on once more, creating a vacuum inside. He noted the dial embedded above the valve and annotated the negative pressure measurement in grease pencil directly above the valve and on the lid itself. Any significant delta in pressurization would indicate one or more of the canisters was leaking. He couldn't be too safe, especially considering they will be in his car for several hours.

Rolf went to a storage locker nearby and retrieved a large roll of tape about four inches wide. After wiping down the trunk on all six sides, he wrapped the tape all along the seam of the lid. The tape was red, with the words 'Warnung: Inhalt unter Druck!' emblazoned every six inches or so. Though Rolf surmised there was little risk of the wrong person wanting to open the trunk, in that eventuality a visible warning about contents being under pressure would give pause. He then removed a label from the lid with the 'Vitale, GMbH' logo on it, crumpled it into a ball and tossed it across the lab into a wastebasket.

He surveyed the room to make sure he didn't leave anything lying around that might survive the explosion and subsequent fire. Anything that might incriminate him. He'd already disarmed the sprinklers. Satisfied he'd done a good job, he walked to the corner of the lab where he'd positioned three tall oxygen tanks and carefully loosened the valves one quarter of a turn. The volume of the slow hiss told Rolf it would take at least an hour before the tanks were completely empty. He reached down and pulled the zipper on a backpack he'd placed on the floor against the tanks, exposing a timer. He depressed a button and watched for a few seconds to make sure the device was working correctly. Two hours and counting. It was a small incendiary bomb. Not enough of an explosion to do any real damage, but when combined with that much oxygen and the stockpile of flammable chemicals in his lab he was confident nothing would survive. Even stainless steel would be reduced to slag.

Rolf invented Hemoxin when he was a chemical engineer assigned to the Special Projects Division, a classified sector of the Defence and Security Business Field at the Industrieanlagen-Betriebsgesellschaft, or Industrial Plants Operating Company (IABG) in Ottobrunn, just south of Munich. *That is so German*, he often thought. Such a blasé, self-descriptive name for one of Europe's most important research and development organizations. Much of what the German Defence and Security Business Field had been doing since 1961 was similar to the efforts of DARPA. The Defense Advanced Research Projects Agency, a research and development organization funded by the U.S. Government, focuses on sensitive and evolving technologies that have applications in various government sectors. Unconscionably, IABG quickly shelved the Hemoxin project after determining it had no practical application beyond being an incredibly effective and deadly poison and Rolf was fired for his continued protests and general discontent. He decided to copy all his work onto a thumb drive and took it with him, eventually selling the fabrication process surreptitiously to a contact at DARPA. At the time he felt twenty thousand euros was small recompense for his all his efforts. And it was. Hemoxin was a truly revolutionary substance. But now he stood to make even more money. Far more. He already received one million euros and would receive another two upon delivery.

The demonstration in Marseille went off without a hitch. He rigged a glass jar with a lid modified to attach a small bottle of Hemoxin. He tested the gas on three mice, one after the other. One would have been enough, however Monsieur Blanc insisted on three. Blanc then tested the blood of each to verify the cause of death. After all, Blanc pointed out, Rolf could have just used carbon dioxide to kill them. But then the mice wouldn't have died so quickly. Monsieur Blanc kept the bottle and what was left of the Hemoxin, apparently to do some chemical analysis. Rolf wasn't worried about it. There was no chance Blanc could reproduce the gas by analyzing the sample. It was far too complicated a process and couldn't be reverse engineered. This was important, of course, as he had another two million euros riding on it.

In any case, Rolf couldn't fault him for being thorough. It was a trait he admired. Blanc was just as meticulous as he in planning every aspect of the demonstration. It was a good sign that the deal was going to go through. Neither of them knew anything at all about the other, except for their dark web handles. The residence they used for the demonstration was a vacation home and empty much of the year so it could never lead back to them. Rolf had arrived hours ahead of the meeting to scan the entire house for hidden cameras or other surveillance equipment. They both wore surgical gloves the entire time of course. If only everyone were so thorough. It was probably the only thing Rolf noted about Monsieur Blanc that he liked, however. Blanc was a strange cat and not very friendly. But it didn't matter now. The deal was almost done, Rolf was rich, and he would never need to work again.

He hoisted the trunk up and onto its end, then slid a hand truck underneath while tipping the trunk slightly. After walking back to the bench and shutting off the exhaust vent he secured the trunk with a strap to the truck and paused, taking one last look around his lab. He would miss working for Vitale. Though the work he did for them was far below his level of expertise, he'd been given his own lab and left to do his work unbothered. They realized his value and hired him immediately, giving him special projects and general autonomy. His position with Vitale led to the perfect opportunity to synthesize the gas without anyone poking around or asking questions.

But his career would never recover after what happened at IABG. He would forever be an outcast, forced to work in labs like this one. In the older section and on the sidelines of a large and profitable international company with no real chance of progression.

Once outside the door he shut off the lights and removed his gas mask, trading it for a bright yellow hardhat. He donned loose-fitting, white coveralls over his jeans and a Jack Wolfskin jacket. After tossing the gas mask through the doorway onto the floor of the lab he closed and locked the door. He wheeled the trunk down the empty hall to a service elevator that took him to the ground floor and made his way quickly but carefully across the dark parking lot. He stopped to glance longingly at his BMW X5 parked a short distance away. He would miss that car. Then he navigated his cargo around and behind the lab building into the delivery tunnel where he parked his getaway vehicle. Old but reliable, he'd bought the 2006 Audi in Poland with cash. The plates were stolen. He had a second set of plates to swap them with if he ran into trouble. Rolf loaded the trunk and hand truck into the back, drove out of the tunnel and through the exit gate, looking away from the security guard as he did.

Now he would drive to Zurich to deliver the trunk, concluding his deal with Blanc. Blanc insisted on finalizing the exchange in Berlin, however Rolf maintained that it must be done in Switzerland. It was not too far out of the way to his next destination, and by making the exchange in a different country they made it that much more difficult for anyone to trace it back to either of them. After Zurich he would drive to the Port of Split in Croatia to board a freighter bound for Chile with a new name, a new passport, and a new life. The explosion and subsequent fire at Vitale would erase any evidence of what had been done there, and Rolf would be assumed dead. He'd planned it all out and thought of everything.

In the end the decision wasn't too difficult to make. He'd never found anyone interested enough in him or his work to marry, and his parents had passed. His sister still lived in Munich but the two of them lost contact over the years. There was nothing left in Germany that he would miss. Or that would miss him.

He'd already crossed the line selling classified government information to DARPA, a foreign actor. This was simply the next logical step to ensure he was never caught. He knew in his heart whoever was buying the gas would be using it for nefarious purposes. For what exactly, he had no idea. But no one buys things like this on the dark web if their intentions are good. Ultimately, he knew it was possible the gas could be traced back to Vitale or IABG or both. It could take days, or it could take years. When it did their reputations would be damaged irreparably. Rolf smiled at the thought. Vitale would likely be hit by legal action and serious fines. They could go bankrupt. There would be public outrage against IABG. If and when they traced it all back to him, he'd be on the other side of the world, and no one would even be looking for him. Because he'd be dead. *Screw them all.*

CHAPTER TWELVE

Dolan decided to get up and start his day. Though it was early, he had many things to do before meeting with Stone. He selected three of the five boxes and placed them methodically on the bed. They were packed well, and each item had its place. There was no space left unfilled. The details of his daily schedule were the same; it was a rare day when five minutes went unplanned. Sometimes he had to convince himself that if he wasn't solving, building, or doing something productive it was because occasional rest or leisure was essential in enabling him to do those things more efficiently later. Self-care. But only to a point.

He had always been like that. His parents lived in a comfortable apartment in Boston, having sold their twenty-acre estate in a rural area west of the city years ago. There was a sizeable apple orchard on that property that he enjoyed tending. Trimming the trees, picking apples each fall. His mom would make jelly, applesauce and can quite a bit as well. The rest were given to neighbors and friends. Growing up there afforded him the opportunity to appreciate nature and wildlife. When his homework was done, he'd often go for a run through the forest. There were great trails in several directions. Each time it was an adventure, a search for something new and exciting. If it was snowing or raining it didn't matter. They were welcome variables that added to the overall experience. Though he was moderately content and kept busy, there were some aspects of his childhood that had never been quite right. There was a consistent feeling, a subliminal sensation that something was missing. A muted, unnamable fear with no origin and no reason for being there.

It was that aberrant anxiety that had always propelled him, he determined. Whenever he succeeded at something, whenever he accomplished something significant, it subsided. On occasion, it would disappear entirely. But it was always temporary. As a result, he decided long ago to always remain driven. Always succeed. Always win. This approach enabled and sustained his dreams of doing big things on a big stage in life. And he had, although not everything had gone exactly as planned. Right now he was experiencing some approximation of happiness. Maybe this was the next big stage. Paris 2.0. Much of what he'd accomplished in his career was marred by what happened there. This time he needed to succeed undeniably, with no caveat, no asterisk attached.

He finished hanging his suits and placed his folded clothes in the room's large hardwood chest of drawers. He grabbed his wallet from the desk, removed a worn, folded piece of paper and placed it in his pocket. He donned his running gear and grabbed his earbuds and the iPhone. He'd already downloaded his entire music library. After exiting the room, he took the elevator down to the lobby and headed out for his daily dose of therapy.

He started off down rue Galilée toward Champs Elysées. The streetlights, storefront signs and occasional automobile provided a mixture of incandescent and neon light that clashed with the city's ancient beauty. The full moon was peeking just over the rooftops of the buildings, fighting for attention. It was somewhat eerie seeing this normally crowded, animated part of Paris so empty. Even at this hour he'd remembered it being busier than this. It certainly would be in a couple of months as tourists begin to flood in. But for today, for what he planned to do, he was glad the streets were empty. It was appropriate.

He crossed Champs Elysées and turned left, glancing right for a moment to appreciate the grandeur of the Arc de Triomphe. He planned to run right by the Grande Rêve. Before he begins this mission, he needed to confront his past, his fear. Put it behind him. As he approached the hotel, he could feel the adrenaline begin to flow, his heart beginning to race. His temples throbbed slightly as he allowed select fragments, residuum of that night long ago to squeeze out of its box. Slipping past his defenses and into his cerebral cortex, immediately clashing with reason and structure. He slowed his pace and came to a stop, pulling the headset from his ears. He looked up at the balcony where it happened.

It looked different. He couldn't quite figure it out at first. He scanned the façade, spotting the sixth-floor room from where she fell. The ornate veranda railings looked newer, and higher. He looked down at the sidewalk, remembering her broken form sprawled facedown, the halo of blood. He reached into the pocket of his running shorts and took out the worn paper. He unfolded it and held it at a slight angle to catch the light of the streetlamps and read the words he'd penned so many years ago. It was titled 'Missing.'

He wondered if this little ceremony would do what he wanted it to do. To give him complete closure. Had he let enough out of the box for it to work? Then he reflected on when he wrote the short poem. What he was feeling at the time—totally broken, completely lost. He should be upset right now, perhaps he should cry. But other than self-imposed anxiety, he felt nothing.

At the time he'd been an inconsolable wreck. Though he'd recovered over time he still felt as if *something were missing*. But he'd felt that way much of his life, as long as he could remember. Losing Claire had been like dumping fuel on a slow burn. The result was a fire that raged inside him as the investigation ensued and while he struggled to finish his studies at the Sorbonne. It was almost two years later before he no longer thought constantly of what had happened. He had carried the small remembrance in his wallet ever since. That thing that was missing wasn't Claire. Her death may have exacerbated whatever his issue was, but it wasn't the root cause. Whatever it was that left him so empty inside had been there since he was a child and continued to torment the dark, fragmented pieces of his soul. Regardless, he needed to let her go for good.

He looked around the immediate area for a small rock. Finding none, he reached into the small flower garden hugging the base of the front of the hotel and broke off a single white rose from one of the many bushes. He then placed the poem on the ground where she died, the rose resting on top. Closing his eyes for a moment, he tried to think of an appropriate, short prayer. His lack of emotion made it feel disingenuous, so instead he pictured her in his mind, smiling and happy. Then he turned back down the Champs Elysées to continue his therapeutic run, feeling a little lighter, a little faster. A little better.

As he jogged away, he felt a slight urge to turn and look back, that it might be the right thing to do. A final goodbye. But he resisted. If he had, he might have seen someone step onto the sidewalk in front of the Grand Rêve Hotel, standing over the spot where he'd left the poem.

◆

Stone watched Dolan grow small and merge into the night as he ran. Then he checked his iPhone, verifying it was giving him accurate position data—it was. By his estimation it was locating Dolan to within about a few yards. Better than he'd hoped for, particularly within the city. He looked down and regarded the rose and small piece of paper. He squatted, brushed the flower to the side, and picked up the poem. *Not bad*, he thought after reading it. *How appropriate, to put this sad little piece of history behind him. It will make things easier for now, though he will have to revisit past events along the way.* He folded the poem and tucked it into his wallet.

CHAPTER THIRTEEN

François Martin followed the navigation system's recommendation to take an alternate route around traffic and turned off Highway 3 near Baden. It would add a few minutes to the trip, but he built an extra hour into his travel schedule for this very reason. Hopefully, Herr Schwartz was similarly prepared. He didn't want to spend any more time in Zurich than was necessary. He glanced over at the briefcase in the passenger seat with a disapproving frown. He'd frowned several times during this trip. Schwartz shouldn't profit from this exchange, in his opinion. He was just another infidel. They'd already wired him a million euros. That should be enough. But it wasn't his decision to make. He'd just as soon use conventional bombs as he would this 'Hemoxin' gas. It would be much cheaper, and they wouldn't have any need to deal with an intermediary. He could have built the bombs himself. Sharif went on and on about how there just wasn't anything else on the market that would kill as effectively without leaving so much as a trace as to the cause of death. According to Sharif this was important because neither the public nor the authorities would understand what they were dealing with. It was a silent, invisible killer. It would evoke terror in Europe and in America, the likes of which we'd never seen. These considerations and the fact that it was less likely to lead back to them made the extra expense and logistics justifiable.

François paid no attention to the rich Black Forest scenery as he made his way south. There was too much on his mind. And what a beautiful mind it was. He was certain he was the most intelligent person he knew. His engineering skills had led to several patents for his family's wine business, improving efficiency, quality, and increasing revenue significantly. It wouldn't be long before he was recognized as a leading engineer in his field. He would command respect wherever he went. The ones who talked about him behind his back, about his height, his poor social skills, about his faith. They would be forced to listen to him. To admire him.

Breaking from his family and Christianity, François had truly embraced Islam and the Quran. At least his mother understood him. She'd been forced to accept Catholicism, but he knew that in her heart she was still true to Allah. It's the only thing he held against his father, that he did this to her. And indirectly, to him. His father had done his best to accommodate François' newfound faith, but he'd also made it clear that it did nothing to change the family's allegiance to Jesus.

François also embraced jihad. Even Sharif didn't truly understand that. Sharif's jihadist aspirations were more about revenge than anything else. *After all the facts are weighed,* he thought, *I am the one true and faithful follower best suited to plan and lead this effort.* But Sharif had an expense account that seemed bottomless and Sharif's plan, despite his misgivings, was a good one. It was really his father's plan, but Sharif executed it in any case. It was François' hope that Sharif would eventually see past the superficiality of revenge and understand that it was much bigger than that. It was about jihad and Islam, the one true faith. Once he understood this, Allah would bestow upon them everything they needed in their crusade.

They'd been through it many times, in great detail. These were events that would shock the entire world. No one would see it coming. And when it happened, there would be complete confusion with so many unanswerable questions, like *who* and *how* and *what*. Only the *why* would be answered, and the AMA would deliver their glorious message from Allah to the world. And precisely because the *who*, the *how*, and the *what* will remain complete mysteries, the AMA would strike again, valiantly and without encumbrance. After their victories and as a faithful soldier of Islam François will receive redemption and be filled with righteousness. Less so but still important, Hakeem and Sharif will exact the revenge they have been so patiently waiting for.

Three hours later he was approaching the city limits of Zurich. François cursed the transaction location for the hundredth time. It made no sense for him to travel so far to complete their business, only to turn around and drive for hours with deadly gas in his car. François had argued the exchange should be made in Berlin, or at least somewhere closer to his staging area, but Schwartz had insisted on Zurich.

The sun was low on the horizon as he made his way through the city to Bellerivestrasse, which ran along the eastern shore of the Obersee Lake. Almost immediately François saw the exit for his destination, the Chinese Garden Zurich. After two quick turns he was in the parking lot just outside the park's walls. On a different day he might venture in. Below the colorful, multi-layered dougong roof of the main entrance he noted a few children playing as he parked his car and shut off the engine. Otherwise, the area was deserted. The park was a gift from Kunming, Zurich's Chinese partner city. It belied the city's true nature with its trimmed trees and oriental theme. It was a spurious microcosm of Chinese culture right here in Europe. Out of place. It was a betrayal. It reminded him of Disneyland Paris. Then it reminded him of Sharif, who seemed at times to be pretending he was something he was not. A believer. A warrior of Islam. *Sharif drinks alcohol*, he thought. He is too caught up in the fineries of life. Immediate gratification. He parties too much. As a result of all of it, he wasn't nearly as focused as François on the jihad at hand.

A knock on the passenger window made him jump, and there was Schwartz, standing next to the car looking in at him. He was parked two spots over.

François rolled down the window. "Are there any complications?"

"No," replied Rolf smugly. "Everything is good. Let us finish this."

François helped Rolf carry the heavy aluminum case from his Audi to François' Mercedes. It was smaller than he'd imagined. They put the case in the trunk and François studied it for a moment. Then he pulled a penknife out of his pocket and began slicing the warning tape around the lid.

"What are you doing?" asked Rolf. "The case is hermetically sealed. This is a safety feature. You can't be too careful with this stuff."

François ignored Rolf and finished cutting, then opened each of the eight clasps. He had to pull hard on the lid due to the vacuum inside. Eventually it gave with a hiss. Rolf looked on disapprovingly as François removed the lid and set it against the bumper of the car. Then he reached into the trunk to the left of the case and pulled out a bag containing a small spectroscope, what looked like a glass burner, and some tubing. As Rolf looked around to make sure they weren't attracting any attention François retrieved his laptop from his briefcase. He removed one of the canisters at random, replaced the lid, and assembled everything on top of the case, attaching the apparatus via a hose to the canister.

Rolf's demeanor went from impatient to interested. "I am impressed. You used the sample from Marseille to determine the atomic and molecular species of the gas, and now you are verifying a match using optical spectroscopy."

"I think you know, it's not a complicated process. And I must validate the contents. I am assuming we wouldn't have come this far in our transaction for you to cheat me now." François regarded Rolf seriously. "I would also assume that you would have some level of fear of what might happen to you if I were to find this is not what you say it is." He tapped the case twice.

This made Rolf uncomfortable, knowing Blanc probably had no problem killing him if there were any complications. But then regained his composure. He wasn't cheating him. He did everything they'd agreed on and more. "You needn't worry. All four contain Hemoxin, at high pressure, and the purity is better than 99 percent. I tested it to be certain before I filled them. It would be stupid for me to do anything at this point that might jeopardize our deal."

François booted the laptop, connected the spectrometer to it via a USB cord and opened the valve on the canister for a moment, allowing the gas to flow into the hose. Then he turned it off, ignited the burner and began analyzing the results. It only took ten seconds to verify. "I am happy." François disconnected everything, put the spectrometer and hoses back into their bag, the canister in the case, and replaced the lid. He closed the trunk, grabbed his laptop, and motioned Rolf to get in the back seat. Once inside, François set the briefcase on his lap with the computer on top. Then he looked at Rolf questioningly.

"Yes?" quipped Rolf.

"There is something I need to know before we complete this."

"OK, but we should keep conversation to the minimum. The less we know about each other, the better."

"I agree," said François. "But I must understand. Do you not wonder why I am buying this from you? Do you not worry about what it might be used for?" Depending on his answer, François was ready to kill him, right there in the backseat of his Mercedes. He slowly moved his left hand near the door compartment where he'd stashed his beautiful Glock 18, a gift from Sharif. The Glock 18 is a fully automatic pistol with a firing rate of 200 rounds per minute developed for Einsatzkommando (EKO) Cobra, the elite police tactical unit of the Austrian Federal Ministry of the Interior and responsible for counterterrorism. Martin appreciated the capabilities of the fine weapon and the irony of its original purpose as well. Sharif had somehow obtained five, one for each of them, though three of their team had yet to reach Europe. The serial numbers had been etched away with acid. He was never to use it of course, except if absolutely necessary. *Which could be the case right now…*

Rolf fidgeted in his seat. This was not the kind of banter he expected. It was unprofessional. He wanted to be done with this and to get on his way. "*Es ist mir egal.* I do not care," he said truthfully. "It is not my concern. This is a business transaction, pure and simple. If you are worried about me, you needn't be. As I've told you already, once I drive away, I am a ghost. Whatever you use it for is your business, not mine. I truly do not care." And he didn't.

François smiled. Typical westerner. All they care about is money. In this case, however, that was a good thing. Though Schwartz told him nothing specific about his plans, François made it a precondition of the deal that he would have to leave Europe and change his identity, and Schwartz provided substantial assurance to him in that regard. To his surprise, Rolf told him he already planned it this way and made those preparations in advance. He was confident Schwartz had covered his tracks. He was a scientist, like François. Methodical and thorough.

Still smiling, François began tapping on the keyboard. Within a minute, the financial transaction was complete. He showed Rolf the screen who nodded approvingly, opened the door, and got out of the car. He bent down to see François in the back seat. "Ciao," he said in his thick German accent, then got into the Audi and drove off.

The sun had set as they concluded their business, and the park was closed. The children were gone, and the big red door of Chinese Garden Zurich was closed. The dim yellow lights overhead cast eerie shadows across the parking lot. He was alone. "Ciao, Herr Schwartz," Martin said under his breath. He returned his laptop to his briefcase and smiled again, this time with a great sense of fulfillment. It was the second time he'd felt this way recently. In the other situation the feeling was far more pronounced, back on the fifteenth of April, watching Notre Dame Cathedral from a safe distance as it burned.

CHAPTER FOURTEEN

After Dolan showered, he changed into a tailored charcoal suit and prepared for his first meeting with Stone. They were to meet at nine at a hotel near the embassy. Room 213. There were two CIA safe houses in Paris, but neither were approved for EXCISE. He knew he and Stone should never be seen together, and whenever they met it would have to be done this way. They would arrive and leave separately and at different times. There were just three situations when he was to use a safe house; if he were instructed to, if his life was in immediate peril, and in certain cases of injury. The latter two required approval by Stone beforehand and he was to use the nearest hospital for all medical care except when it could potentially compromise the mission. Otherwise the safe houses were strictly off-limits.

He took the Métro from Charles de Gaulle-Étoile near the Arc de Triomphe, southeast on the yellow line to Concorde, which was near the embassy. On the way he scanned the people in the car. Probably half were tourists. The atmosphere contrasted significantly with that of his commuting to and from the Pentagon. The men, women, and children in this car were from different walks of life and varied nationalities, most talking and smiling. They seemed more alive, more genuine to him than the faceless automatons in DC performing their synchronized, daily routines. A couple people sized him up but for the most part no one seemed to pay him any real attention.

Dolan exited the station, walking up the steps with the tourists to rue de Rivoli at Place de la Concorde, the largest square in Paris and just west of the fabulous Tuilleries Gardens. Concorde was the site of many notable executions during the French Revolution. Now it was a resplendent area with Hittorff's rivers and seas-themed fountains and punctuated by the obelisk of Luxor. Dolan quickly took in the familiar sight and walked southeast toward rue Saint-Florentin, which would take him to their meeting place, the Castille Paris Sofitel.

Once there he walked inside and went straight to the front desk and asked the desk clerk if there was a package for him. The clerk turned and retrieved a white envelope from one of the wooden cubbyholes behind him.

"Merci," said Dolan, regarding the envelope. *M. Dolan* was written on the front.

"Je vous en prie, Monsieur Dolan," replied the clerk as he turned to look for the elevators. Seeing none in the immediate vicinity, he opted for the stairs. He walked up to the second floor and down the hall to room 213, opened the envelope and took out the magnetic-stripe key. He swiped the key, opened the door, and entered the room.

"Michael! Very pleased to meet you. Tony Stone." He moved toward Dolan from the center of the room, his hand extended. Please have a seat, we have a lot to discuss." They shook hands briefly as Stone motioned to one of two Victorian era-style chairs, pulled out to face each other, a small coffee table in between.

"Nice to meet you as well." Dolan noted the expensive cut of Stone's sterling-blue suit. He seated himself, crossing his legs comfortably. His immediate impression of Stone was good. Impeccably dressed, perfect brown hair. Maybe an inch shorter than he, with a fit appearance and casually charismatic. He came across as a young French aristocrat.

Stone sat across from him, leaning forward with his elbows on his knees, his hands moving as he talked as if he were on stage doing a Ted Talk. "Let me say first that I'm thankful to have you on board. The opportunity you represent, to rekindle your former association with Sharif gives us a potential opportunity to break this thing wide open."

Dolan noted he said *association* instead of *friendship*. "I'm glad to be of help wherever I can."

"Good. As you are probably aware, I've looked through your file, and I've read Lauren's report on everything from her debrief with you about your time with Sharif at the Sorbonne. And I am aware of the training you've received. We have one hour to get through some important details, so if you have any questions now is the time to ask."

Straight to the point. *Good.* "Nothing of real concern. The room key, though. Why not just have me come straight to the room? Wouldn't that eliminate unnecessary contact? There's a desk clerk that may remember I was here. And he knows my name as well."

"Ah, well with EXCISE there are certain things we must do differently. If you were a fully trained field officer, we'd most likely be meeting at one of the safe houses. I think you can appreciate the caution needed with those locations. No one can be seen coming or going. As soon as a safe house is compromised, it would be staked out and anyone coming or going would be surveilled and collected on. What we will do instead is, each time we meet it will be at a different hotel. The reservation is made through a travel agency, which requests two keys be left at the front desk, each one in an envelope. One for you, and one for me under an assumed name. The process we've set up ensures you never have to check in or show your passport. It works well and cannot be tied back to anyone. We arrive at different times and are never seen together. I will always arrive first. If I am running late for some reason though, you will still have a key to get in the room. We don't want you waiting around in the hotel looking lost." Stone smiled.

Dolan nodded. "OK, that all sounds logical to me."

"Good. First, let me give you an update on the cell." He reached into his pocket and handed Dolan a piece of paper with two addresses. "The first is Sharif's penthouse address. The second is Anne Bernard's house." Dolan raised his eyebrows as he looked up at Stone. The two of them were already on the same page. "It made sense to me that you would contact him through Anne. It doesn't mean you should strike up a newfound friendship with Anne. If that happens, great. Whatever comes naturally. However, it looks better than going straight to Sharif. We don't want to spook him. Everything must be done carefully."

Dolan nodded again. "What about François Martin? Honestly, I have no recollection of this guy. Lauren showed me his photo. If Sharif was a friend of his back then I think I would have met him or at least heard of him. They couldn't have been close." He wanted to ask who else or how many other suspects were part of the cell, but he figured Stone would get to that.

"You've read his file. He was at the Sorbonne while you were there with Sharif. He had no classes with you or with him. We believe they may have met at a mosque sometime back then, and that the relationship grew from there. There is not much to go on. In any case, Martin hasn't spent much time in Paris since he graduated, having gone back to Metz to work for his father. We received information recently that he's been away from his workplace, but we don't have the assets we need to tail these guys around Europe. If I were to try to task anyone from Paris Station, it would raise all kinds of red flags. We must rely on whatever we can get remotely from Thomas back in DC. I will be able to do these sorts of things from time to time, but when I do I have to make it look like I am doing something else. In other words, my work for EXCISE must align closely with a different, but real, surveillance or other opportunity and I must submit a report on it. This means I must do it solo of course, and the report will essentially end up reading *Nothing Significant to Report.* I can't do it very often for that reason as well. Otherwise I begin to look like an ineffective counterintelligence officer." Stone smirked as if to say *and there is no chance of that ever happening.*

"SO… we have Lefebvre basically in hiding in Algeria, who has somehow funneled millions of euros out of his account in Panama without us noticing. His usual banker there has gone quiet. Sharif's income does not support the opulent lifestyle he seems to enjoy, but we also know he's had an account with Deutsche Bank for years that was set up by his mother, with a substantial balance, though not nearly as much as went missing from Panama."

"How much are we talking about? From Panama."

"Fifty million euros. Enough to buy anything, anywhere. Or to buy anyone. With money left over." Stone stopped moving his hands and leaned a little farther forward, quite serious. "This is the main reason we believe this cell is the real deal. This incredible amount of money, with a radical but intelligent, well-educated leader doing the planning and pulling the strings. This is possibly the preliminary equivalent of another 9/11, with Bin Laden-sized funding."

Dolan began to sense the gravity of what he was being told, and it made him realize how different his role was here than when he was flying missions in Afghanistan. There he was just another cog in the U.S. military machine, replaceable. Here he wasn't a cog. He was still a part of a team, but his role was pivotal to their success. If he failed, it was possible people would die. Many people.

Stone eased back in his chair a bit and continued. "Which brings us to the next, particularly important point. If this cell is going to spend that kind of money, either they are buying a whole shitload of conventional weapons or explosives, or they are purchasing something special. Something rare and difficult to obtain."

The hair on the back of Dolan's neck bristled. "Nuclear material?"

"We don't know. To date there's been no evidence either way. It could of course be biological or a nerve agent, or some other chemical weapon. Or it could be they are hiring another group to pull it off, something we should consider as a possibility. And since it doesn't appear that either Sharif or Martin ever had any kind of military training, that theory becomes more plausible. Our profile on Sharif indicates he won't be readily open to risking his life and lifestyle by getting shot or caught in the act of terrorism. We don't have a complete profile yet for Martin. But a contracted operation leads to other problems. When the contractors are caught, they are likely to fold and turn on their financiers."

"So it is more likely we are dealing with a WMD," said Dolan.

"Yes," Stone said hesitantly. "If I were to guess they are looking to fabricate or buy a weapon of mass destruction. The how, the when, and the where is what we need to determine. It is important for us to find out what it is, but it won't matter in the end if we can take the cell down before they can execute the plan.

"Which takes us to the final point, the cell itself. As you know, Lefebvre is the financier and leads from Algiers. He's on a different continent however and can't risk communicating except via coded, encrypted messages, something we've seen him do with Eduardo Aparicio, his banker in Panama. Sharif is the cell leader on the ground. Martin is an engineer and will likely have a role more central to the device or devices and may handle logistics. We expect that since Sharif's father has close ties with the al-Mulathamun Army, or AMA, that he may recruit some of their members to travel to Europe to help execute the attack or attacks. Or they could already be here. We have been working with Station Algiers to document and assess all Algerians traveling to West Europe. We have some good algorithms that will automatically flag anyone who fits the profile, and then we kick the list back to Langley once a week for analysis. So far no one stands out. Also, it won't catch anyone flying from Algeria to Europe with a stop in a different country if the second leg was purchased separately. And we won't catch anyone who travels by boat.

"So, this is what I'd like you to do." Stone leaned forward again. "Get in touch with Anne. Go have coffee with her, get reacquainted. Tell her about the new job, the language course. Tell her how you didn't contact her or Sharif ahead of time because you felt awkward. So much time had passed. Or something similar. Whatever you tell her, or for that matter Sharif, make sure it is some close facsimile of the truth. If you can't do that, then say nothing. You'll betray yourself if you start lying, you'll end up in a rabbit hole with nowhere to go. Sharif will come up right away; you can ask her for his number. Beyond that, it's up to you how your contact with Anne evolves. It may be she has information on him that might be useful, so if she's amenable to a second meeting, lunch or dinner, go ahead with it. Just remember that she was Sharif's girlfriend. We don't want that to be an irritant to Sharif. Your interaction with him is all that matters, ok?"

"Understood. Honestly, I think it will be more awkward with Anne than with Sharif, as I ignored her completely after Claire's death. We'll see."

Stone looked satisfied. "Alright. Each time you meet with Sharif you'll need to note certain things mentally. His demeanor and state of mind are important. If he is nervous, distracted, easily upset, these are things we will need to know. You should note dates, times, and places he mentions, places he has been recently or will be in the future. If he doesn't mention why he went or will go somewhere, go ahead and ask him if it's not overtly awkward. Who he is associating with is key of course. If he invites you anywhere, suggest he bring his friends. Not right away perhaps, but after things settle down. He's a bit of a party animal. If there's a good opportunity to suggest having a party or celebration, recommend it. At his apartment. Anything for him to consider inviting his friends and associates.

"After a while we hope you will have the chance to meet Martin. We think a party might be the perfect situation to catalyze that. Meeting his mother Salmah, particularly at her home in Marseille, is a high priority goal. We've learned that she has dementia and has an in-home caregiver. This changes our perspective on her possible involvement. She may have some association with the money, but she may be unwitting, and it could be that Sharif has power of attorney, something we are looking into. It also means she might be manipulated into giving away that information quite easily. Also, make sure Sharif drinks. He likes the booze. Loosen him up whenever you can. If he's drunk, he's far more likely to tell you something useful. Just be careful not to get too drunk yourself—we need you to remember what you see and hear."

Dolan shifted in his chair. "That won't be a problem, as I don't drink anymore."

Stone looked at him quizzically. "OK, if that's the case it could make things difficult. We need Sharif to feel comfortable around you, and alcohol is by far the best way to do that. Believe me, I never pay for a drink because the Agency reimburses me for all of it. It's the single best tool in my toolbox. If you don't mind me asking, why did you quit drinking, and is it a permanent thing? Can you make an exception for this *extremely* important operation?" Stone was visibly concerned.

Dolan was a bit irritated at Stone's aggressiveness. "Listen, I'm not under doctor's orders or anything, it's just a personal decision I made a few years ago. I like to be in control, with a clear mind, which is something I believe will benefit our operation. But if it is something I feel I need to do, if the success of the operation depends on it, yes of course I'll play the part."

"OK, that's good enough for me. Just make sure you don't induce any drama or act weird about it. It should look natural. It should feel natural. If it does, Sharif will be content and comfortable and that is where we want him. When we have the evidence we need he will never see us coming."

They spent the rest of the hour going through the finer details of what to collect on and what to ignore, how to notice when Sharif might be lying and various other things. Stone also showed Dolan how to take photos and video with his iPhone surreptitiously, something they discussed back in DC but didn't have time to practice hands-on. Then Stone left. Dolan waited thirty minutes before departing, placing his keycard on top of Stone's on the coffee table. They would meet again in one week at Hôtel d'Orsay-Paris, just across the Seine River in Saint Germain Des Prés. In the meantime, he will have had two significant reunions. He was looking forward to the first, despite the apology he'd have to get through. He hadn't yet fully processed how he should feel about the second, except that if he were normal, he should hate this past friend of his with every fiber of his being. *Not being normal will make it much easier…*

CHAPTER FIFTEEN

François was elated. He'd pulled off the exchange without any complications and Herr Schwartz was leaving the continent. His biggest worry had been that Schwartz might make a mistake or get caught somehow and lead the authorities straight to him. With those worries assuaged he could now move to the next phase.

He surveyed his work area, everything laid out on two large, old wooden workbenches against the side wall of the two-car garage. The gray panel truck he was modifying was parked on the opposite side. It resembled a van more than it did a truck. Finding one with a moon roof in the back proved fruitless, so he'd installed one himself.

He set up his testing kit on one of the workbenches and extracted a small amount of gas from each of the four canisters using the same validation method he and Schwartz used in Marseille. Once again, he took samples of blood from each mouse, and the results were positive. After the spectroscopy test in Zurich it was probably unneeded, but every aspect of this endeavor needed to be checked and double-checked. They could not fail.

Everything was going according to plan. The house was old, in a rural part of Potsdam. François bought the house through a front business he'd created as a subsidiary of Château Group. The business was supposed to invest excess company capital in European properties. Though the house wasn't exactly a logical purchase in that regard, it provided perfect cover for the work he had to do. He already had tenants lined up to move in when he was finished.

François placed each canister back in the case and closed the lid. Then he set to work on the truck. He removed the bench seat from the back and set it against the wall of the garage. Then he used a hand truck to move the heavy cast aluminum base of his launch apparatus in front of the open back doors. The base included a set of two connected gimbals, each to be geared to an electrical motor and controlled by a computer. The gimbals had two functions. One, they allowed François to aim the launch tube with great precision. Two, once the tube was aimed, they enabled minute, automatic adjustments to maintain a perfect trajectory if there was movement inside the vehicle. With considerable effort, he lifted it up against the rear bumper, tilted it forward and pushed it in. François was prouder of this piece than the rest of it, even though it was the simplest. He'd designed and forged it himself and it was a work of art. Every angle, every connection point, everything was exactly to specifications. Once inside he made several measurements and positioned the base perfectly so he could mark where to drill the holes through the metal floor.

After installing the base François attached the motors to the gimbals and ran the wires to a control box, which he affixed with two small bolts to a stationary part of the base. Then he exited the truck to fetch the launch tube. He was proud of the tube as well. He'd spent many days testing tubes made of various alloys before settling on stainless steel. Cold drawn, seamless, and not annealed, its tensile strength was forty percent higher than standard steel tubing. Again, this was probably overkill but he couldn't have the launch tube rupturing. It was a single point of failure, and he didn't have a replacement. In any case, it would take too long to swap out if there were a problem.

François carried the tube to the truck. It was a little over one and a half meters long, with an interior diameter of fifteen centimeters. It was nearly as heavy as the base. He started to curse his small stature and inadequate strength, but quickly rationalized it didn't matter for someone so intelligent. He'd rather be small and smart than strong and stupid.

He moved the rest of the parts into the truck including the thirty-gallon compressor. He had spent some time trying to find the right one. It couldn't be too big, but it needed to put out at least two hundred psi to generate the pressure required to achieve the range he needed. And two hundred wasn't enough, as he'd found in testing, so he compensated by using smaller canisters. This was a concern as it meant he'd have to launch two of them to ensure a 100 percent kill rate, which takes additional time. But it allowed the standoff distance he required. When the canisters fell from the sky, he'd be far enough away that no one would know where they came from, and hence where to find him. A champion of Allah driving away in just another panel truck.

François removed the glass panel of the moon roof and carried it to the workbench. Back in the truck, he positioned the launch tube vertically, inserting it into the gimbaled base. When pointed straight up, the tube extended just above the roof of the truck, visible from outside. He'd fastened the base not in the middle, but to the side of the truck to allow for more of an angle when aiming the tube. He was limited by the width of the moon roof, but not by much. He could get close to a forty-five-degree angle. In any case the standoff distance was going to be determined more by the required entry angle, which he suspected was around sixty degrees. This would ensure the canister hits the ground and not the side of the building. The last thing François wanted was for the canister to hit a window accidentally and go through it. That would ruin everything.

He twisted the tube until the three bolt holes lined up and used a socket wrench to fasten it. Then he ran a braided metal hose from the compressor, which he'd also bolted to the floor, to the base of the tube and used a crescent wrench to secure it tightly. He placed three car batteries in a square plastic tub and daisy chained two of them together, running the wires to the 24-volt compressor. He then ran wires from the two batteries to a transformer and connected the transformer to the battery terminals of the truck, routing the wires under the front passenger seat and through a hole he'd drilled through the firewall into the engine compartment. The transformer would keep the batteries charged so long as the engine was running. The third car battery he wired to the control box on the launch base.

François then booted his laptop and plugged the control box into it and opened the program he'd written to operate the launcher. First, he input the exact coordinates of his position, then the coordinates of a hypothetical target with the desired entry angle. Then he pressed enter. The two motors whirred for about a second, moving the tube. François noted the position of the tube against where it should be generally pointing and was satisfied. Martin understood that maximum range is achieved by launching at a forty-five-degree angle, but this assumes the desired target is at the same elevation as the end of the tube. It also assumes no wind resistance, or drag, which of course there will be. And drag changes with the shape and velocity of the object and with air density. Further, air density changes with the weather and with altitude. The math was quite complicated to code when considerations were made for these variables.

Range was important, but entry angle was equally so. The entry angle, or the angle at which the canister would hit its target, closely approximates the launch angle. In the event one wanted or needed a more vertical entry, range would need to be sacrificed. The computer program he coded displayed the psi required to hit the target with the desired point of impact and entry angle. He would have to do that manually at the compressor, but it was a simple thing as long as it didn't exceed 200 psi. The program also displayed apogee, or the maximum elevation the canister would reach before falling to its target. He made three other entries after noting the readout, entering a ground wind of ten knots from a direction of ninety degrees, and apogee winds at twenty knots from seventy degrees. He also typed in the average air density for the launch location. Elevation variables were automatically selected and inserted into the targeting solution using Google Maps elevation data based on the locations of the truck and the selected target.

Then he hit enter. The motors whirred again, but only for a split second. The tube barely moved but it *did* move. "Oui! Oui, oui, *oui!*" François yelled. He'd been holding his breath, worried that something would be off or that it wouldn't work at all, and he'd be spending hours or days trying to resolve the defect. But it did, and it seemed to be working perfectly.

Finally, François got out of the truck and went to the back-left tire. He removed the valve cap and let about half the air out until the rim settled about four inches lower. Then he went back in the truck and checked the laptop screen to see if the accelerometers in the control box were performing the way they should. Sure enough, the program adjusted the launch tube slightly on both axes to account for the shift.

François exited the truck through the back, used the compressor to reinflate the tire and then walked a short distance away to proudly observe his accomplishment, arms folded across his gaunt chest. Beaming, he walked back to the workbench and opened a cardboard box containing ten burner phones. He selected one, turned it on and fished a small pad of paper from his front pocket. On the pad was a long list of phone numbers. He tapped in the first number on the list and sent a text: *Le Porte-mort vit.* The Deathbringer lives. He waited for notification the message was delivered, turned off the phone, removed the sim card and broke it and the phone in half, tossing the pieces in a paper bag on the floor. Then he took the pencil from behind his ear and lined through the first number on the notepad and placed it back in his pocket.

There was still a lot to do, including launch testing. It would have to wait until the following weekend. He'd been absent from work for some time now and didn't want his team back at Château Group to start wondering where he was. Besides, they needed him. When he was there things went smoothly and efficiently. When he wasn't, people got lazy. Problems accumulated and festered. François was a catalyst for perfection, with no better example than the beautiful apparatus in the truck next to him. He spent six months designing and building it, completely on his own. He looked once more inside the truck. *The Deathbringer.* He couldn't call it that. *François himself* was the Deathbringer.

CHAPTER SIXTEEN

It was a busy day for Dolan. First, he went for a run and then finished unpacking the things he'd need for the next couple weeks. Then he went by the U.S. Embassy to check in with the housing office to see if they'd made any progress finding him an apartment. They told him that because he wasn't a State Department employee or a DoD diplomat, he had no priority whatsoever. But since he was alone and with no family, it would be relatively easy to find him a one-bedroom apartment, so they should have something for him soon. Good news.

Then he went by Lingua Europa to sign in and meet with his tutor. He would begin his French class there the following Monday. La Défense was quite a distance from the city center, about eight kilometers northwest of the embassy, straight up Champs Elysées. At first, he was unimpressed with the school. It was in one of the towers southwest of the Grande Arche, a 110-meter high, very strange looking cubical monument and building dedicated to humanity and humanitarian ideals, as opposed to military victories. The school occupied two floors about halfway up the tower with a nice view of the Arche. The school's spaces and rooms reflected the age of the building, with brown patterned carpet and a suspended ceiling, both stained in places from water leaks. The furniture was 1960s high-school plastic and chromed steel. All of this was overshadowed however by the jovial nature and singular linguistic and professorial abilities of his tutor, Père Aubertin.

They spent about thirty minutes getting to know each other and going over Dolan's curriculum. Father Aubertin was a retired Catholic priest who spent part of his time volunteering in various capacities at the Sacré-Coeur Basilica and about fifteen hours a week tutoring at Lingua Europa. Dolan liked him immediately.

He then took the Ligne Ter train from the Paris-Nord station north to Creil Air Base, where the technical and processing directorates of the Direction du Renseignement Militaire (DRM) are located. The DRM is a military organization created in 1992 to address intelligence shortcomings identified during the first Gulf War. Initially, its responsibilities were limited to military intelligence. Over time the scope of the DRM's activities gradually widened to include strategic and political intelligence that had fallen historically under the umbrella of the DGSE. Lauren and Thomas coordinated his administrative and familiarization meetings with them through DoD, the first at Creil and the second at DRM headquarters tomorrow in Paris. The headquarters was his future workplace.

Dolan did his homework on the DRM. The formation and evolution of the DRM was a good example of the great strides France had taken over the years to create autonomous intelligence capabilities that reduced France's dependence on allies. These capabilities subsequently provided significant opportunity to collaborate and exchange information directly with those allies, particularly with the United States. Dolan's position was within the Current Intelligence Branch and there were similar positions posted for Australia, Britain, Canada, and New Zealand. 'Five-Eyes Plus France' is the term for this group of countries that routinely shares and exchanges highly classified intelligence for the benefit of all.

The train ride took 25 minutes, with another fifteen in a taxi to get to the base. Once there a security guard checked to make sure his name was on the visitor's list before letting the taxi through the gate. The driver dropped him in front of a two-story, newer construction building. The French tricolor flag waved atop a tall pole in the middle of the roundabout in front. He went inside where he was met by a French Army lieutenant who gave him a quick tour and brought him to their administrative office where he spent the next hour filling out onboarding paperwork. There was a form for his personal information, a form for contacting next of kin in the event of an emergency, a form to request classified network access and another for the unclassified system. Fourteen forms in all. When he was done the lieutenant took the stack of paperwork and escorted Dolan to their security office where they took his photo and printed his access badge. It would allow him to come and go unescorted to and from Creil and DRM headquarters in Paris.

They were finished by four p.m. Dolan was now part of the DRM Five Eyes Plus France Office, and would meet his French supervisor tomorrow, a one-star general. He would also meet with David Crowe, the GS-15 he would be replacing.

The lieutenant gave him a parting gift, a lapel pin featuring a circle of six flags, one for each of the countries represented in his office. It was a bit large for a lapel pin, but he'd proudly wear it. He believed in the value of these types of relationships. In his military experience Five Eyes was one that worked well, particularly in Afghanistan. He would perform in this role as he had in any other—to the very best of his ability. And the role may prove to be of benefit to the real reason he was back in Paris. He checked the time on his iPhone again. *Need to get back into town and pay Anne a visit.*

CHAPTER SEVENTEEN

Anne Bernard grew up in Vaux-Le-Pénil, about 50 kilometers southeast of Paris. An only child born to affluent parents, she attended college at the Paris Sciences and Letters Research University where she met Claire and graduated with a degree in Sociology. She and Claire became close friends and decided to attend the Sorbonne together, one of the oldest universities in the world, where she received her graduate degree in Sociology and Applied Human Sciences. Now she worked in the Paris city government public affairs office.

Dolan met Anne the same night he met Claire. He and Sharif were out barhopping that evening and Dolan noticed the two of them at a table against the wall at one of their local hangouts. Only he hadn't seen these two there before. They were both beautiful, each leaning forward towards each other, as if sharing secrets they wanted no one else to hear. Dolan was struck by the auburn-haired Anne, not only for her sublime natural beauty but by how comfortable she seemed to be, how genuinely happy. Real.

When Dolan pointed them out Sharif was immediately attracted to Anne as well. They walked over and introduced themselves and ended up pulling up two chairs. As the night went on, it was evident Claire was more interested in Dolan, and Sharif was completely taken by Anne. And that's how the foursome started. Sharif and Anne began dating, as did Dolan and Claire. Dolan initially wondered if things were somehow mixed up. If he were supposed to be with Anne. But after a while, those thoughts receded, and he and Claire grew close. He would take her out on adventurous dates, sometimes out of Paris to some small town just to try some obscure, Zagat-rated restaurant. They were always exceptional. They visited Versailles several times and ended up making a regular thing of it. Always on Sunday, when the fountains were on. Always a picnic. They'd do the cliché French thing with a blanket, a bottle of wine and a baguette with cheese and some fruit. The same thing every time and it was always wonderful. They'd talk about whatever came to mind and sometimes just lie there quietly, enjoying the sun and the fountains.

But now she was dead. These memories meandered through his mind as he walked rue Fernand Pelloutier into a charming, affluent neighborhood in Boulogne-Billancourt near the Seine on the west side of Paris. *Anne has done well for herself,* thought Dolan. He wasn't surprised. She was probably the smartest of the four. And her parents were wealthy, but you wouldn't know it unless you knew her well. She didn't flaunt it or anything else for that matter. She was humble and kind and not necessarily an introvert. She had a great sense of humor. *She was oddly paired with Sharif,* he thought. Sharif was someone with a proclivity to be loud and demonstrative. He was smart and good looking, but he had never been accused of being deep. Anne was deep. At times Dolan wondered if she stayed with him just to keep the group together. A sacrifice.

Just as Dolan and Claire enjoyed wonderful times alone together, so had the group. Back then they called themselves 'The Fab Four.' They did it all together, seven months of wild and crazy nights and majestic adventures. He counted himself lucky to have been part of it all.

The shadows were getting long as Dolan walked up to her door, a two-story, older brick home that had been painted white. Dolan wondered why anyone would ever paint over the brick, but somehow it worked. Red bougainvillea climbed the right corner of the house and under the eaves, across the top of the doorframe. A small wooden sign hung on the door above a black wrought iron knocker. It read *Petit a petit, l'oiseau fait son nid.* Little by little, the bird makes its nest. So, this was Anne's nest… He reached up and knocked three times.

He heard someone walking to the door. It opened and there was Anne, a curious look on her face almost immediately replaced by a huge smile. "Michael, mon dieu!" she cried, enveloping him in a hug. "I cannot believe you are here, I thought I would never see you again!" She backed inside, motioning him through the doorway, then stopping in the foyer to look at him. "You disappeared. I couldn't reach you. But now, after all these years, here you are!" She turned again and walked in front of him into the living room. As she moved her long auburn hair shimmered angelically in the incandescent lighting. She took a seat on the couch, going on about how surprised she was to see him. The French rolled off her tongue like a sonnet. He remembered these things about her. The graceful gait, her hair. That delicate, perfectly inflected voice and brilliant smile. Dolan sat in an overstuffed chair across from her and looked around the room.

"Anne, first and foremost, I'm so happy to see you. I love your home, your little nest. And you look wonderful." She did. A little older but somehow, more beautiful. As if experience and time had refined her beauty instead of enhancing all the lines and edges. He could tell she was serene, happy. "Please forgive me for not calling ahead, I didn't have your phone number. In any case, I thought it might be better to surprise you. I got your address from your office. I'm not sure they were supposed to give it to me, but I was persuasive."

She smiled big again. "It's OK! I'm glad they gave it to you. I'm sure they realized you were a trustworthy, responsible American, my old friend."

Now Dolan smiled hesitantly. "Yes, an old friend. A friend who needs to get something out of the way. Anne, I wanted to apologize to you for falling off the face of the Earth. For ignoring you, for not reaching out after Claire's death. It's not an excuse, but I was in a very bad place. I was selfish, I was only thinking of myself, and I withdrew. From you, from Sharif, from everyone. It was a terrible period for me. I know as well that losing Claire was extremely difficult for you and I wasn't there. I guess it might have been different if I'd known Sharif was able to help you through it, but he wasn't either. You had no one. And I've felt bad about it for a long, long time." He leaned forward and took her hands in his. "Please accept my apology. What I did to you was unthinkable."

Anne regarded him empathetically. "Michael, please, you need not apologize. I can't imagine how difficult it was *for you*. We all grieve in our own way. It would have been nice had you been there at the time, but I had to respect your need for distance. I just assumed this was what you required. Do not worry about it, please."

Dolan felt suddenly as if a great weight had been removed. The relief was unexpected. *How can she be this understanding?* "Thank you so much Anne. This means more to me than you can imagine."

She got up from the couch and bent down, giving him another big hug as he sat in the chair. It was a little awkward, but it didn't matter. It was real. *"Listen, you!* Everything we have done in life to this point in time has led to this wonderful moment where two old friends from opposite corners of the world are together, smiling and understanding and forgiving. Life is beautiful." It was one of her cute little English witticisms. *Listen You!* She would insert it into French conversation, always at just the right moment.

If Dolan knew how to cry, this would be the moment for it. He didn't deserve this kind of a welcome, for sure. He couldn't have hoped for a better result. He needed a friend right now. Stone wasn't going to be his friend. Stone was his handler. Sharif used to be his friend, his best friend, and Dolan would have to act as if he still were. But he was now Dolan's enemy and a terrorist. Anne might be all he had for a while.

She sat back on the couch, pulled her legs up and wrapped her arms around a throw pillow. "OK Michael Dolan. Tell me your story. What are you doing in Paris, how long are you here, and what have you been doing all this time?"

Dolan told her about the job, as much as he felt comfortable with anyway, and that he'd be in Paris for three years. He told her about his work at the Pentagon and about how he'd left the Air Force. He told her a bit about flying missions in Afghanistan, that it was dangerous but not all that bad. She hovered on that topic for a while, asking questions about what it was like, if he'd lost anyone there, and if he thought the war was justified. She didn't judge or even offer her opinions on it. He remembered that about her as well. A rare and priceless trait. Then Dolan asked about her and her work. If she were still single. She was, though quite a few suitors had come and gone. She was happy. He envied her that—the ability to be content. He'd known for some time that contentment was probably the key. Doing your best and being satisfied with the results, whatever they were. He had never been able to figure it out.

She brought over a bottle of wine, a Syrah from the Rhône Valley. Without much thought, Dolan sipped from the glass as they talked. He marveled at the flavor. It had been so long since he'd tasted good French wine. Any wine at all. When their glasses were nearly empty, she poured them another, and he realized that it was OK. He let Claire go last week. He'd been reset. There was no longer any need to adhere to some self-inflicted abstinence, the reason for which was so far in the past. And it added a warm glow to their reunion. The closest he'd had to a warm glow in the past six years was the regular endorphin and dopamine release he enjoyed after his daily runs. But this was much different.

The conversation finally turned to Claire, each of them taking turns explaining how they dealt with her passing. She was inconsolable for weeks and finally turned to her parents. She took vacation from work and went home to Vaux-Le-Pénil. Her parents knew better than anyone how to help her through tough situations. Sharif made a strangely awkward and insufficient effort trying to comfort her. It only made her more upset, and when she asked him why he was being so short with her, he'd gotten angry. She tried to work through it or around it, but in the end, she left him.

The explanation for why she broke it off with Sharif left him unsettled. That did not sound like him. He wouldn't have let her go so easily. Dolan then wondered again if Sharif felt responsible in some way for Claire's death. That might explain it. Sharif had told her he wouldn't attend the funeral because he was in too much pain, and he didn't think it would bring him any closure. It would make things worse for him. Again, Dolan was surprised. These were the same excuses he had used, though the truth was he was too drunk that morning to show up. Dolan told her about almost failing out of school and how it took him several months to come to terms with her passing. Anne remained silent the entire time, just listening. When he was finished, they made plans to have dinner that Friday. Finally, Dolan came around to his primary objective.

"Anne, do you still have Sharif's phone number? I haven't kept in touch with him either. I'd like to talk to him. Try and reconcile things." All at once he felt guilty, a strange sensation for him. He'd almost forgotten what it was like. He was lying to her now, in a way. But the sensation quickly faded; this was his job. He remembered what Stone told him, that he should always use some facsimile of the truth or say nothing at all. He was comfortable that this was the former.

She nodded understandingly. "I have an old number, not sure if it's still good. Let me get it for you." Anne got up and crossed the room to a small, ornate wooden curio table and took a worn, colorful journal out of the drawer. She read the number to him as he typed it into the contact entry he already had in his iPhone. As he typed, he saw it matched the number Stone had given him.

"Have you been in touch with him at all?"

Her almost perpetual smile faded quickly. "No. He called me a few times after we broke up, but I would never answer. You know Michael, it was never a serious relationship. He was intelligent and humorous and fun, but he wasn't right for me. I don't know what it was, I guess you could say there was too much superficiality in his approach to life. And there was something else. When we were alone, he was brooding a lot. Something was bothering him back then and he would never talk about it." Dolan shifted in his seat, trying not to appear suddenly interested. "I suspect it had to do with his father and all his family problems. It wasn't anything he would let me help with; he wouldn't share. Anyway, we broke up and in the long run I knew it would be counterproductive to give him any opportunity to think he had a way back in. So, I never answered. By the way, here is *my* number." She handed him another slip of paper. "Now you have no excuse to show up unannounced," she said with a grin.

Dolan smiled back, stepped forward and gave her a warm embrace. The residual warmth from the wine combined with human contact made him feel good. Normal. He held her for an extra moment, not wanting that sensation to subside. Then they said their goodbyes as he put her and Sharif's numbers in his pocket, each acknowledging they were looking forward to Friday's dinner. As she closed the door behind him, he was acutely conscious of how drawn he was to her, that it could become a complication with Sharif if it were to grow into something beyond friendship. He quickly dismissed the thought, noting that it wasn't an issue right now and may never be. Even if it were, it was something he could manage. He was a pro at these things. He could manipulate and quarantine situational conflict and emotion better than anyone he knew. If it came to it, this would be no different.

As he walked to the Métro station Dolan glanced at his phone. Almost nine p.m. *Strange*, he thought. He'd made only three short calls today, but his battery was down to fifteen percent. He was sure it had been fully charged in the morning. Then he shrugged it off. Could be he'd lost signal earlier in the day, maybe at Creil. When there's no connection, the battery can get drained quickly. *I should probably pick up a portable charger*, he thought. *Wouldn't want to lose communication with the team. Especially if the shit hits the fan.*

CHAPTER EIGHTEEN

Stone booted up the classified videoconference system and after a couple of minutes he was connected with Lauren back in Clarendon, Virginia. "Good evening, Lauren. I trust you read my report."

"Yes, thank you. We've been having trouble with Intelink lately, but we got it fixed. It's never been exceptionally reliable here, for whatever reason." Intelink-SCI was the Top-Secret intranet used by the CIA to provide connectivity to national, theater, and tactical levels of government and military operations. "It's a good report. I'm glad everything went well in the meeting. Do you have anything to add?"

"Not really. He seems cut out for the job. He's smart and he's reserved. I'm optimistic."

"Good. That's the same impression I got from him."

"I saw that he went to Bernard's house yesterday. Can you give me a breakdown of the visit? I'm not going to see him again until Saturday."

"Sure. First off, in the rush to kick this whole thing off we forgot that no one here speaks French. I had to put in an emergency request for translation services and to make it a standing priority. So, we've got this guy who's assigned to us until the op is completed. He signed the NDA and was able to get us a translation this afternoon. We're looking at about a six-hour turnaround time for an hour of conversation, much less for short translations. Unless of course it's not during normal business hours, and then we must wait until the next day. They talked for nearly two and a half hours, so this one took quite a bit longer. The long and the short of it is, he's rekindled the friendship with Bernard, and she gave him Sharif's phone number. Now he can get in touch with Sharif and ease into it naturally. We could have had him go direct to Sharif, but Dolan seemed to think, or perhaps it was your direction to him, that it was a better idea to contact Bernard first as she might have provided some current information on him, but that didn't pan out. The two of them haven't been in touch since they broke up back in 2012.

"The only other thing to note is, their meeting was more congenial than I expected. Almost intimate, and I'm not sure we want that. When you talk with him next, tell him to keep it platonic with her. In fact, tell him any kind of emotional attachment could jeopardize the mission, Bernard or otherwise. My guess is he understands this already, but these two have history. It could be pretty easy for them to lean on each other and before you know it, they're engaged. He should put off any ideas beyond casual relationships until this is over."

"OK. But she could prove useful later on. She is single and attractive, and the empathy is already in place. Let's agree to let Dolan keep her in the picture, at least to the point where the negatives might outweigh the positives." Stone felt impatience creeping in, wanting to see immediate impact. Progress. But he was enough of a professional to know how to play the long game. "What about phone calls? Did he call anyone?"

"OK, fine. I can agree to that. Yeah, he made a few calls but nothing of importance. He contacted Creil to verify his appointment there and DRM headquarters for the same reason. He did call his parents back in Boston. I guess this one is somewhat interesting. He called to tell them he'd moved to Paris. After the fact. I know what you're thinking, and I'm thinking it too, that it's strange he didn't connect with them before he left. They were both shocked. But supportive. They were happy to hear from him and strangely, it almost sounded like it wasn't out of the ordinary for him to keep them out of the loop like that. As if they don't have much contact in general."

Stone paused to think. "It could be that he's simply continuing an old habit. He wouldn't have been able to say much about what he was doing as a specops pilot all those years. It's probably just ingrained in him. Or maybe he and his parents are just distant. If that's the case, it's a good thing. Less likely he'll tell them anything he shouldn't. Anyway, if our assessment of him is correct we aren't too worried about that happening."

"Be ready for anything. We don't know him well and as good a fit for the job as we think he is, we can't see what's going on in his head. Now, shifting gears. Martin is back at work in Metz, though we don't know where he's been for the last week. There is still no evidence he's been in contact with Sharif either. I wish we could put a tail on both of them."

"Yeah, I wish we could too. I've done a few drive-bys of Sharif's apartment building. Saw him leave early one morning and walk to the Métro, but that's it. Nothing to report."

"Be careful," Lauren cautioned. "We're more likely to get caught by DGSI than to get any useful intel on him. It's not worth it. Once Dolan's in play we'll have a lot of visibility with much less risk. Just remain patient."

Stone chuckled. Lauren was two years older than him but had far less field experience. And the experience she had was not comparable to his. When he was infiltrating terrorists in Algeria, she was hosting cocktail parties in Berlin. "No need to worry, they were drive-bys. I was going that way anyway." It was a lie, he wasn't. But she didn't need to know that. "Listen, on another note we need to find a better place to stash my gear. Especially the puffers. I'm putting myself at risk keeping it all at my apartment."

"I agree. Can't you just stash it at one of the safe houses?"

"I could, but I'm worried people might ask questions that I can't answer, and that it might flow up to Le Pen." Jean-Luc Le Pen was the Paris CIA Station Chief. "It's the puffers. I'm not too worried about the rest of it."

Lauren hesitated, caught in yet another moment where she felt she should have prepared better. "Go ahead and use one of the houses for the gear and keep the puffers at your place for now. I hate to move them back to Berlin; you wouldn't have easy access to them. It was a pain in the ass to bring them to Marseille and we didn't even get to use one. But we might still need them. If we move them back, you'd have to transport them personally, again. And as you know, as soon as you cross the border that black passport means nothing. There is no good solution. You'll have to figure it out and let me know what you want to do. In the meantime, make sure they are kept well-hidden."

Stone knew she was going to put it back on him. She was right, though. Until SCALPEL had its own safehouse in Paris, or until there was an agreement in place as there was in Berlin, they were handcuffed. The two puffers were each about the size of a junior football. He'd taken them out of the storage case they came in and placed them inside two large custom X-ray-proof bronze statues, busts of George Washington and Charles de Gaulle. On display in his living room, they could only be opened by holding a magnetic fob against the base. He kept the fob in his desk at the embassy. It was good, but not ingenious. Nothing was anymore, not in this business.

"No worries, I'll figure it out. Better to risk it and have them on hand than to be safe and wish we had." Then he switched gears. "Listen, I don't know if Dolan is going to try to contact Sharif before we meet this week or not. If you get any hint that he will meet with him, let me know as soon as possible. I need to have my calendar clear for an hour or two on either side of that encounter in the event he needs assistance or finds something actionable. Just call, or text if I don't answer."

"Sure thing. Remember though, our main priority is to identify hard evidence of a terrorist plot, at which point we will notify DGSI and back off. At that point we can send Dolan home, or he can stay and fulfil the term of the intel sharing position if he wants but either way, we cut him loose. We cannot justify taking action unless it's clear to us an attack is imminent, and we have nothing concrete to prove it. And if we do, no guns. For God's sake no guns. That's what the puffers are for, after all. For everyone to wonder how they died."

Stone couldn't help but roll his eyes. "This is the third time you've given that speech, Lauren. I understood the first two times. It's all good."

"Good. Sorry. Sometimes I feel it's better to beat a dead horse than to worry about whether or not it might recover."

Stone laughed out loud at that. It was part of the reason she was in charge, as young as she was. Lauren always said the right things at the right time. And she'd pretty much always done things the right way, for the right reasons. At least to this point. In the end, she and the legacy of the SCALPEL team will be defined by their most significant accomplishment, or their biggest failure. Whichever happens last.

CHAPTER NINETEEN

Michael Dolan was feeling surprisingly good. It was Wednesday morning. He'd only been in Paris a week and things were falling into place. He reached into his jacket pocket, pulled out his DRM badge and looked at the photo. He thought he had smiled; he consciously tried to when Lieutenant Lapointe took his picture. But he failed, apparently. He'd have to make a better effort at being nice. Approachable. He felt that way in general but realized he may not be perceived that way. He'd hardened some in the last few years. It helped him at the Pentagon, to be sure. People's impressions of him were that he was a serious and hard-working member of the team. And he was. But he'd have to loosen up some if he was going to get Sharif to loosen up as well.

He put the badge back in his pocket as the Métro train pulled to a halt at Sévres-Lecourbe station. His stop. He exited the subway car, bumping shoulders with Parisians on their way to work, and an equal number of tourists getting an early start. DRM headquarters was in the 15th Arrondissment, on the west side. It was in a relatively large, three-story building off rue Miollis and not far from Place de Breteuil. Dolan walked the short distance to the building's main entrance, tapped his badge to the reader and pushed through the turnstile, nodding to the uniformed security guard keeping watch.

The FEPF office was on the second floor, a smallish office area with twenty or so cubicles. Not unlike the typical setup at the Pentagon. He showed his badge to the administrative assistant seated at a reception desk that faced the entryway.

"Bonjour. You must be Mr. Dolan from the United States," she greeted amicably, standing and extending her hand. "I am Demeri Fèvre. I have some paperwork for you, which you can fill out later and return to me. But first, let me see if General Barre can welcome you."

"Pleased to meet you, Demeri. I'm excited to be here and to be part of the team."

She smiled and led him to the General's office around the corner and knocked on the glass door. The French one-star looked up from his desk and waved him inside.

His office was of spartan décor—very little on the walls except for a French flag hung above his chair and a few framed mementos from command assignments and deployments. Other than a monitor, an inbox and a jar full of pencils his desk was clean. "Monsieur Dolan, Barnard Barre. Welcome to FEPF." He reached across his desk and they shook hands.

"Thank you General." Dolan sat in an older, rich leather chair facing the General. He noted the visitor's chair was just as nice as the one the General was sitting in. Perhaps the exact same chair. It was a good sign.

"Have you begun to settle in yet? I'm told you are familiar with Paris. That should make things easier for you. Your accent is quite good."

"Yes sir, I attended the Sorbonne back in 2011 and 2012. The French is a little rusty but not bad. I'm brushing up at Lingua Europa for the next couple of months, before I come in full-time. It's at La Défense."

"Yes, I'm not familiar with the school, but your defense attaché informed me about it. It's a good idea though I'm not sure you're in need of it!"

Dolan's first impression of the General was positive. He was clean-cut and fit with a rugged jawline and approachable demeanor. Brigadier Generals tended to be a little more laid back than the full Colonels. After all, they'd made it past an extremely difficult barrier. There were over 3,000 colonels in the U.S. Air Force at any given time, but only about 150 one-stars. A colonel has only about a five percent chance of moving up in rank. It was a difficult transition to make. Many colonels who desired to get to the next level tended to be uptight, demanding workaholics. Only the officer structure in France was different. A one-star in France was the equivalent of a full Colonel in the U.S., and as such there was a five-star rank in the French military that was the equivalent of a four-star in the U.S. General Barre didn't seem like the type of leader who was uptight. Someone he would enjoy working for. If Barre had ever been uptight and demanding, there was no evidence of it.

"Thank you, sir. I suspect that when I'm done at Lingua Europa I should be able to fit in just fine."

"Good. So, tell me a little about yourself. I have some of the details, but I'd like to hear it from you. The U.S. usually sends us intelligence officers for this position. I'm sure you'll do well, but I am curious why you pursued this job, aside from the fact it is in Paris." Paris was not a bad place to be stationed, to be sure.

Dolan gave the general his work history, focusing on his special operations background and U.S.-European strategy experience at Joint Staff. He explained his love of European, particularly French, culture and that he was selected from a very short list. He was chosen over candidates with significant intelligence experience because of his excellent French language skills and keen insight into coalition activities, and because he was a consistent battlefield consumer of the kind of joint/combined intelligence that the FEPF office was responsible for enabling. The general was quite happy with the explanation and impressed with Dolan's accomplishments.

"As you know, what we do here is critical to the success of coalition and other allied activities, particularly those between the nations represented here in the office. We the French take great pride in working closely with the United States to provide intelligence generated by the DRM for the benefit of Five Eyes plus France, and in turn we place great value on the intelligence we receive. Your job here will be to coordinate with the various intelligence agencies of the United States, but mainly with those associated with your Department of Defense: the DIA, the NGA, NRO, NSA, and so on. You do so within the scope of the strategic and tactical needs of FEPF, both for ongoing activities and future need. The future need part is more difficult to assess and is perhaps this office's most important business. We analyze available geopolitical, strategic and tactical military intelligence to forecast what types of currently unavailable intelligence we should have access to prevent conflict and future terrorist activities. In effect, to create 'known knowns' where currently we only have 'known unknowns,' or 'unknown unknowns.' Then you negotiate with your intelligence community to identify that intelligence and work to have it released to Five Eyes plus France.

"You may not be aware of how involved the French military is across the globe. We have troops stationed in Afghanistan of course, and Iraq, Syria, Mali, Mauritania, Burkina Faso, Niger, Chad, and several other countries. Some locations are acknowledged, some are not. This amounts to about 36,000 French troops deployed in foreign territories and they are all collecting for us, the DRM. And though we do not participate militarily in NATO, I'm sure you are aware that we participate in their political councils."

Dolan smiled at the not-so-subtle reference to former U.S. Defense Secretary Donald Rumsfeld's famous *Johari Window* answer to a reporter's question in 2002 about the lack of evidence tying the government of Iraq with supplying weapons of mass destruction to terrorist groups. It made him wonder briefly about how many 'unknown unknowns' there were surrounding the entire EXCISE operation.

They talked a little while longer about what he could expect to begin working on when he started in July, and then the general accompanied Dolan back into the main office area to introduce him to the rest of the staff. Everyone was busy, and he wasn't set to join them for several weeks yet, so the introductions were short and cordial apart from David Crowe, his future predecessor.

David was not the stereotypical intelligence type. Very tall, somewhat gruff, with a serious mustache and passionate about his work, he was jovial and perhaps a little too eager. He was maybe six-foot four with a thick New England accent. He didn't strike Dolan as a good fit for the position, and he wondered if DoD simply 'plugged the hole' with someone who met the criteria without having to sacrifice one of their prime assets for a coalition office they estimated wouldn't be valuable to U.S. intelligence.

They spent a few minutes getting to know each other, made easier by the fact they were both huge Boston sports fans. David had followed a circuitous route to Paris, having been an Air Force intelligence officer for many years. He always wanted to be a pilot, and so he left the service and paid for his own flight instruction, eventually landing a job flying executives up and down the East Coast. After a decade or so he returned to his roots as a senior analyst with the Defense Intelligence Agency, which led to his Paris assignment.

After trading a few war stories and discussing the Boston Red Sox pitching lineup they got around to business. David explained the office protocols and filled him in on the other five team members. They were all intelligence officers, retired from their respective militaries and they all did good work. After the U.S., France, Great Britain and Canada provided the most useful intelligence, in that order. Normally Great Britain would be second on the list, but France was the host country and as such always made sure they were more forthcoming than the others. Australia and New Zealand rounded out the team and delivered what they could, as geographically misaligned as they were.

David seemed wistful about leaving Paris—it had been a great assignment. He arrived at age forty-seven, unmarried and unsure about where his career was going. Now he'll be returning to Washington, D.C. at age fifty, still unmarried and still unsure. He was contemplating going back to flying and had scheduled an interview with NetJets. Dolan began to feel sorry for him until he realized his was a career track that was not so dissimilar.

He talked with David a while longer about the job, finishing with why each of them thought the Patriots might win another Superbowl. Dolan thanked him, said goodbye to the others and turned in his paperwork to Demeri as he left. He didn't plan to come into the office again until his official start date, as he'd only be in the way. And he still had some planning to do for a much more important meeting—with Sharif.

CHAPTER TWENTY

Dolan picked up his iPhone and scrolled to Sharif's number. He was ready to call him. Dolan would have to act naturally and think on his feet if the call went bad, if Sharif seemed suspicious. This was possible if he told Sharif about his intel position at FEPF. Lauren told him he could lie about that; tell Sharif he was working in a coalition office for operations in Afghanistan. But what if Sharif or someone from his cell did some digging on him? It wasn't worth the risk. He decided to tell him about it and to focus solely on the DoD aspects of the job if he pressed. He would tell Sharif that his role with the DRM was to enable joint-effort collection of military intelligence to further common goals in Afghanistan.

He touched the number, and it began to ring. After the fifth ring Dolan began to hope Sharif wouldn't pick up, and he could leave a message instead. That might even be better, he thought.

But then he answered. "Bonjour, Lefebvre."

"Sharif? Hello my friend, it's Michael. Michael Dolan."

There was a pause and then he responded. "Michael? Oh my god, is that really you? I thought I might never hear from you again! I never thought… but, well I'm glad you called. Tell me, how have you been all this time? Where are you and what are you doing?"

Dolan's apprehension dissolved at Sharif's reaction. "I'm doing fine, I've been fine. I think I told you in an email some time ago that I was thinking about leaving the Air Force, and well, I did. I retired. Then I worked at the Pentagon for a while, a desk job, which was OK, and now—brace yourself—I am working in Paris. I haven't started yet, but I'm here and I'd love to meet and catch up whenever you have the time."

Dolan felt dirty acting as if he was looking forward to seeing Sharif. Or maybe he felt that way because he was looking forward to seeing him. Or maybe it was some untenable amalgam of both. Yes, that was it. Dolan felt dirty, but not guilty—it was normal and understandable. Sharif had never done anything to him personally, and he *was* his best friend. Despite everything Lauren and Stone told him about Sharif's involvement in this potential terrorist plot, there still wasn't a shred of evidence tying Sharif to anything. What if they were wrong about him?

Sharif was genuinely happy to hear from him. "Michael my good friend, of course we should meet as soon as possible. I can't believe you are here! This is amazing. Yes, we must catch up and it should be epic, only the best restaurant will do, and then drinks afterwards. There is so much to talk about. What does your schedule look like? My schedule, it's crazy. I'm fully booked today and Friday. We should do this right and I'm so busy. What about Saturday? Are you open this Saturday?"

Dolan was, aside from his meeting with Stone at four p.m. "Saturday sounds great. How about eight? You can choose the place. You always knew all the best places."

Sharif answered with a laugh. "Of course, I know… Yes, eight is great. Let's do this! I am so happy you called."

"I'm happy too Sharif. It's been too long and now we have an opportunity to make up for that. Just text me the location of the restaurant when you figure it out. The number I'm calling from is my cell."

"OK, super. I'll let you know. A bientôt, mon ami!"

"A bientôt, Sharif." Dolan ended the call.

That was easy, he thought. There was nothing in Sharif's voice, nor in what he said that suggested anything was off, that he was any different than the Sharif he knew years ago. Maybe he wasn't involved in this at all? Was it possible the CIA got it all wrong, that there was no plot, or terrorist cell? He dismissed the thought immediately—clearly there is enough evidence, or he wouldn't be here. But maybe Hakeem Lefebvre is running things from Algeria, unbeknownst to Sharif? He frowned, looking out the window of his hotel room. There was a lot he didn't know, what Sharif has been up to and what he might think about Dolan after all this time. There was a lot he hadn't been told about EXCISE as well. And that was fine, to a point. To the point where it impacted his ability to do what they expected of him, where it might put him in danger.

Dolan understood the need for operational security and compartmented intelligence. At the tactical level, there is a need for details related to the actions taken in the field. He didn't necessarily need to know what the strategic game plan was, or how it was drawn up. Methods and sources are the most closely guarded secrets in the clandestine world. Knowing these things, Dolan never expected to be briefed on everything and everyone. But he had this feeling, a gut feeling that he wasn't being given all the information he needed at the tactical level, which would be a mistake. Probably because they didn't fully trust him yet. He had to be patient and as things moved along, they would trust him with more information. He analyzed his thinking to ensure he wasn't being paranoid, something he was only rarely prone to do. *No. I'm not.*

Aside from dinner with Anne, Dolan was free through Saturday. It felt unnatural to have so much unscheduled time, so he set about deciding what to do. First a long run and a workout, then lunch. Then he'd head to Île da la Cité and get a better view of the damage to Notre Dame. Perhaps a coffee, visit a museum. He'd been to quite a few museums in Paris, but not all. There were so many, around 130 if you don't count the small, unofficial ones. The Musée du Vin on rue des Eaux was one he, Sharif, Claire and Anne talked about going to several times. But they'd never gone, for whatever reason. He figured he may as well do it now to brush up on the delicate Francoculture of drinking. He'd never been much of a connoisseur and before the wine with Anne yesterday, he hadn't had a drink in years. It would make sense and help put him more at ease about drinking with Sharif, which he admitted to himself was inevitable. What better than a museum dedicated to the history and finer points of French vintages. On Friday, he would visit Versailles. The fountains wouldn't be running, but that was fine. It would be nice to refresh his memory of the place he and Claire spent so many peaceful, dreamy Sundays.

◆

Dolan woke slowly to *La Mer* playing on his iPhone. It was different this morning though. Painful. The throbbing in his head was old and foreign, but it was unmistakable. He hadn't felt this way in a long, long time. He opened his eyes slowly. The sun screamed through the window, through his pupils and straight to his brain. A hangover. He looked at his watch. Nine a.m. He couldn't remember the last time he slept in this late. Musée du Vin. He had a good time, despite going by himself. The group he paired with was from Norway, a fun bunch. Two younger couples. Not unlike Anne, Claire, Sharif and him. His old clique. They called themselves 'The Viking Clan.'

Together they learned about the different types of French wines. All the reds—Merlot, Syrah, Cabernet. Malbec, Pinot Noir. Zinfandel. They sniffed, swirled, and tasted with bits of bread and cheese. And then, all the whites. They were taught about where the grapes were grown, the difference between varieties and cultivars. They learned how to approximate the acidity, and from that the geographic area where the grapes were grown, by the taste and by evaluation of the 'tears' on the inside of the glass after swirling. All of it. And of course, they drank. After the museum they continued the party, visiting a brasserie for a late lunch and then several bars. Dinner at some traditional French restaurant, then more bars. He finally left the group about midnight, walking alone back to Hôtel Flambeau. He remembered it all, a good thing. He didn't drink *way* too much, just too much. It was a lot of fun. A *great* time, in fact. More fun than he'd had since... *since before Claire died.*

Dolan got out of bed and drank a glass of water, then crawled back in. He never did make it to Notre Dame. He'd have to do that another day. Versailles as well. He was having second thoughts about Versailles anyway. No need to dredge up old memories about Claire so soon after he finally came to terms with her passing. Better to finish sleeping off the aftereffects of his night with the Viking clan, then maybe go for a run and get ready for dinner with Anne.

CHAPTER TWENTY-ONE

Dolan knocked four times on the door to room 117. Their meeting this week was at Hôtel Duc de Saint Simon, not too far from Musée d'Orsay, by far his favorite in Paris. There was so much to see there. Monet's 'Water Lilies,' Van Gogh's self-portrait. He was particularly fond of the second floor with its wonderful array of impressionist masterpieces. From there museum visitors could enjoy a wonderful view of Sacré-Coeur.

Stone opened the door and closed it behind him. The room was arranged similarly to their first meeting. They shook hands and took their seats across from each other. Stone began the conversation.

"Hi Michael. You look well. You all settled in?"

"Hi Tony, thanks. Yes, as much as possible at this point. The hotel is nice. It'll be good to move into a proper apartment though. I talked to the housing office at the embassy. They should have something for me soon enough."

"Good to hear. So, tell me how things went this week."

Dolan recounted his meetings with the DRM, his initial meeting with Anne, his orientation with Lingua Europa and the short telephone conversation he had with Sharif.

Stone showed surprise. "This is fantastic, Michael. I'm glad you were able to connect with Sharif so quickly. Let's talk about how this first meeting with Sharif should go down."

He was cutting right to the chase. *Maybe that's just his version of operational efficiency*, he thought. Effects-based decision making. Dolan understood that. "OK. If you don't mind me starting, I think this is simple. I have dinner with him and see where it goes from there. We have plenty to talk about, everything we've been doing since we saw each other last. I'll employ the techniques we've discussed, provocative statements, quid pro quo, flattery, ego suspension, bracketing, naiveté, oblique references, whatever, at the right moments to try to lead him in the conversation and to give up information that may be useful. I'll pursue courses of action that get him to drink and lead to invitations to his apartment, to meet his mom, and perhaps to meet Martin. I've practiced using the phone to take photos and audio recordings without being noticed. If he leaves me alone in his apartment, I'll see what I can turn up. Beyond all that, I'll have to adjust to the situation at hand and maintain composure."

Stone was impressed. *He's thought this through carefully.* This might be easier than he anticipated. "That's good, actually. Very close to what I was going to recommend. But you'll have to be careful with Sharif. Most of those techniques won't work as well on him because he knows you. The second you accidentally feign naiveté about something he knows you know about; he will suspect something is off. It's okay to pause and think before you talk. Believe it or not, most people take that to be a sign of intelligence. Be very, very careful. And as for the drinking part, it sounds like you're fully on board now. If so, you just made my day."

Dolan cracked a smile. "Yes, I'm on board. I broke the ice the other night. Hooked up with a group of Norwegians. We had a good time. Anyway, I understand to be careful. I'm not going to take any unnecessary risks."

"Alright, good. You have my number. Have you memorized the list of code words Lauren gave you back in Virginia?"

"Yes. 'Pronto' means I need immediate assistance. 'Sunny' means everything is going according to plan. 'Lounge' means to stay back or wait. I have them all memorized. Do you want me to list them all? Honestly, they don't seem like great code words. They are quite similar to the words I would use anyway."

Stone chuckled. "Yeah, they are straightforward. But they work, and they are similar so you can remember them easily. When you are in a tight spot and the adrenaline is pumping, it can be challenging to remember something like 'Black Jaguar.' Anyway, they are words you can easily weave into a short sentence without raising suspicion. No, you don't have to repeat them all."

"Thanks." Dolan was beginning to like Stone. He reminded him of himself in some ways. Should he tell him he has a photographic memory? He changed the subject. "I have a question."

"Shoot."

"What do I do if I find something, some sort of physical evidence, that I cannot simply take a picture of? There could be a large document and I don't have enough time to photograph all the pages. Or an item with someone's fingerprints that we should run through one of your databases, for example. Should I bring it back to my hotel room and hide it?"

Stone wasn't expecting Dolan to lean forward like this. If Lauren were here, she'd vehemently oppose him doing anything of this sort. There was significant risk in lifting physical evidence. "That's a good question. Honestly, I didn't bring that up because you aren't expected to do those types of things. At least, not at this stage. You haven't been trained. But…" Stone paused to formulate the sentence. "*If* you find yourself in a position where taking physical evidence is, in your assessment, necessary and key to breaking this cell wide open, do it. Again, be careful. If it's something that would be missed immediately, note its location and call me. We can then hatch a plan to analyze it or get it when he's not around. If you're going to take something small, use your pockets as long as it doesn't show. For papers, you should fold them and tuck them inside your pants. If it's only a couple sheets you can use your pocket. You can always excuse yourself to use the bathroom and make it more comfortable. A loose-fitting jacket with bulk and large, zippered or buttoned pockets becomes quite useful in these situations. You can also use everyday objects to obscure evidence. For instance, you can use a razor blade to slit the lining of your wallet to hide small papers and thin items. Or in a laptop, inside the battery compartment if it is ejectable. Or inside a pen. Hiding things in backpacks or briefcases is an option but should be avoided unless absolutely necessary. Sharif is likely paranoid about his planned activities and won't hesitate to go through your things when you're not looking or even to confront you directly if he gets leery of you or your intentions. Anything bigger than that, revert to noting its location."

Dolan had already thought about these things, though it was a good point that the techniques he'd been taught wouldn't work as well with Sharif. He thought it strange Stone didn't ask any questions about his meeting with Anne. Perhaps he didn't see any value in it. "Do you have any questions about my visit with Anne Bernard?" He asked.

Stone had already been briefed by Lauren. This was something he needed to remain vigilant about—acting as if he has no idea what Dolan has been doing all week. "Well, I assumed you'd briefed me on the relevant details. From what you told me, she didn't have any additional information about Sharif that might be useful." Then he paused for effect. "You know, and maybe you've already thought about this, but it might make sense to maintain regular contact with her. Your association with Bernard *could* lead to situations that are more convenient for collecting on Sharif. And she might still have information on him that just didn't come up in your conversation with her."

Dolan purposefully left last night's dinner with Anne out of his initial report. In part because it was more personal than anything, and secondly, he wanted to see if Stone somehow already knew about it. It wasn't out of the question to think they might be keeping tabs on him. But there was nothing to suggest in what Stone had said so far that he already knew. Dolan agreed with Stone, and then told him about their dinner. There wasn't anything that came out of it that would help them with the mission, but at the very least his friendship with her was solid. They'd be associating on a regular basis, he was sure. And after last night, which bordered on intimacy, he was wondering if it would grow into something more. But he left that part out.

"Well, any last words of spy wisdom before I do this?" asked Dolan.

"No, I think you're as ready as you can be under the circumstances. This may sound contradictory, but just play the part and be yourself. What I mean is, act natural but within the scope of the mission. Put aside any negative feelings you may have for him regarding his terrorist activities and focus on the friendship. As if it is just as strong as it was before. Let that part of you come alive. You can even give him the benefit of the doubt. In fact, you could look at this as a way to prove that the cell is just Hakeem and Martin and perhaps Salmah. Thinking this way without making assumptions could lessen any stress or anxiety you might have. It's OK to wonder if he might not be involved in the cell at all, as long as you understand that you are looking for proof of his guilt and *not* his innocence. But only do it to a point. You don't want to risk getting too caught up in it because it will blind you to the truth. You don't want to mindfuck yourself."

Dolan thought about it for a minute. It was an approach he hadn't thought of. He wasn't sure it would work for him. His was a rational brain. Logical, cause and effect. Whatever didn't make sense or caused problems for him could be compartmentalized. But why not? For now, there was no evidence linking Sharif to this whole thing, whatever it was.

"I understand. I'll just go with the flow and do whatever feels most comfortable. How about that?"

"Sounds good," Stone replied. "Good luck, Michael. Don't be afraid to call me if you think it's necessary. Just remember to use the encryption card. Never, *never* call me in the clear unless it's life or death. If I don't answer it's because I can't and remember that you won't be able to leave a voicemail when making an encrypted call. I'll see that you've called and will call you right back, so leave the encryption dongle attached and the phone on."

"Got it." In any other circumstance Dolan would feel as if Stone were being overly cautious. He'd gone over these protocols ad nauseum with Lauren and Thomas. But he was a little nervous and this was something he had never done before. It was imperative he get it all right. "Thanks Tony. I'll do my best."

"I know you will. Next Saturday, same time, Hôtel Georgette, rue du Grenier Saint-Lazare, room 115. Got it?"

Dolan made a mental note and filed it. "Yes. See you then."

Stone got up, shook his hand and left the room. He had to wait thirty minutes before he could leave, which would then give him two hours before dinner with Sharif, enough time to get back to his hotel, go for a run and think about things. Later, as he rode the Métro he found himself reminiscing about, of all things, Amy. He realized he was harboring some guilt about the manner he broke it off with her. So sudden, so matter of fact. So sterile. Then he wondered why it might have surfaced now with so much going on. It was a small thing in his estimation. He thought he might give her a call and let her know how he was doing, and to say he was sorry. Had he even apologized when he broke up with her? It wasn't like him to forget details like that, but it happened from time to time. When he'd already boxed something up and subsequently found he might need to revisit it. *Or when it wasn't important to him.* There was something leaking through. But guilt? In situations like this he should go back and do some repair work. Hopefully, that would clear his conscience. He couldn't afford to have anything so insignificant bothering him right now.

CHAPTER TWENTY-TWO

Sharif was already seated when he arrived. Dolan spotted him immediately from the entrance, a table for two set aside near the window. Sharif always requested the best table. The best of everything. Dolan admired him for it. He didn't necessarily flaunt his wealth, but he didn't hide it either. He wasn't overly flashy or ostentatious, he simply enjoyed the finer things in life. And with his resources, who wouldn't? He stood up as Dolan walked over, a grand smile on his face. They embraced each other and Sharif slapped him heartily three times on the back.

"Michael, it is so good to see you! It's been so long, my god. I'm glad you are here!"

Dolan smiled back genuinely and took his seat. "Same here Sharif. I'm sure you have so much to tell me about your success and your adventures. It's good to be back in Paris!" Dolan was surprised how easy it was. He wasn't nervous at all. Maybe because he really was happy to see him. No guilt about that, it was baked into his cover. And they'd been so close.

They ordered bouillabaisse and coq au vin. Sharif insisted on the moules marinières—mussels cooked in an herb-infused white wine broth. They drank a bottle of 1996 Château Rayas Châteauneuf-du-Pape Reserve, a grenache that is unusually hard to find, and expensive. Dolan wasn't sure if it paired well with the meal. For some reason, they hadn't discussed grenache at Musée du Vin.

Their discussion was wide ranging and animated. Dolan told him of some of the more hair-raising combat missions he flew in Afghanistan. Sharif described the details of his Mount Kilimanjaro climb, only six months ago. Lots of catching up, lots of stories. And another bottle of Rayas. Dolan didn't bother to prod him at all, to search for clues of his suspected activities. It was too early. The purpose of today's dinner was to break the ice, to rekindle the friendship. Have a good time and set the scene. To make it easier to get information later.

When they got the bill Dolan's jaw dropped, just over 1,800 euros. Sharif watched his response and grinned. "Shall we split it?"

Dolan fidgeted slightly but recomposed quickly. "Of course." He reached for his wallet.

Sharif broke out in laughter. "Don't be silly my friend! I've got this. You are the guest here and I wouldn't have recommended this place if I thought you'd be paying. For Christ's sake, the wine is seven hundred euros a bottle!" he laughed again, taking the bill from Dolan's hand.

"Thank you, Sharif. I had no idea it would be this expensive. But it was particularly good, I have to say."

Sharif's eyes widened as they were prone to do. "Right! Aren't you glad I ordered the mussels? This was a feast befitting the reconnection of our friendship, was it not?"

Dolan agreed. "Absolutely. Thank you, Sharif." He'd thoroughly enjoyed himself. This was due in part to the ease with which he was able to navigate and direct their conversation on the first try, though he hadn't done it to collect information. To practice perhaps. He had a good time because it had been, well, *fun*. And he knew Sharif enjoyed it as well. He expected it to continue tonight, as these things did normally with him, but it didn't.

"Now I must leave you, my friend. It's eleven thirty and I must get my beauty sleep."

"Sharif, really? Since when do you need beauty sleep?"

"I know, right? But I'm an executive now, you know? I can't be showing up to work on Monday looking like I went on a bender all weekend. Those days are over. Don't worry though, I'm not a complete bore now. We'll definitely find time to party, just not tonight. Work has been pretty crazy recently."

"Hey, I understand. To be honest, I haven't been much of a partier the past few years. In fact, I've had more to drink in the past two days than in a long, long time. Let's get back together soon, though. There are some trips I'd like to take as well, maybe you could come with? We never did make it to Mont Saint-Michel." Sharif didn't mention Anne or Claire at all during dinner. The four of them had planned to go there just prior to Claire's death.

The color drained immediately from Sharif's face, as if he'd just failed to escape the evening without talking about Claire. "Yes. We never did go. You know, maybe going there wouldn't be the best idea," he said morosely. "You know, I didn't bring up Claire as I thought I would leave it to you, if you wanted. If you didn't, then that was fine with me. But I know it's something we haven't talked about, and we can do that, but maybe at another time?" Sharif's eyes were almost pleading.

"Sure, Sharif. Don't worry about me regarding Claire. I was really broken up about it for a while, but I'm good now. It's in the past and I've moved on. If you don't want to go to Mont Saint-Michel, we can go somewhere else." Maybe it was the wine, but Dolan suddenly felt it would be a good idea to tell him about Anne. At the least it would be out in the open and not something he was hiding from him. "You know, I got your number from Anne. I stopped by her place. She is doing quite well."

Sharif didn't know what to say, then looked distant. "Ah, Anne. I'm glad she is doing well. We haven't spoken in so long, since you left Paris actually. If you see her again, please tell her that I said hello. But it is probably for the best that I don't reacquaint with her. We didn't exactly break up on the best of terms."

Dolan regarded Sharif understandingly, nodding. "I'll tell her." Needing to change the mood he said energetically, "Alright my friend, let's call it a night. A good night. I look forward to seeing you again soon. Maybe we should meet for coffee mid-week or so? My treat this time." They both smiled. Sharif paid the bill and they embraced again outside the restaurant, Sharif patting him three times again on the back before hailing a cab.

Dolan decided to walk part of the way back. There was nothing quite like walking the streets of Paris at night. He'd done it quite a bit back in the day. The Métro shuts down at 2:15 a.m. on Friday and Saturday evenings, and the Fab Four were often still going at that time. He took his phone out of his jacket pocket. No messages. The battery was almost dead again, however. He winced. He'd forgotten to get a mobile charger. It was amazing they'd given him a phone that couldn't keep a charge. What he was doing was too important to have to worry about his phone not working. It seemed to be fine during the day, but in the evenings the battery drained much faster.

As European capitals go, Paris can be quiet at night. Of course, it depends on what part of the city you are in. You had to know where to go. Their favorite place to hang out was Dirty Dick, near Sacré-

Coeur. But they closed at two a.m. If the Fab Four were having a particularly good time, they'd usually end up at Little Red Door on rue Charlot. There is a little red door on the front of the building that is hard to miss, but it's not the main entrance. It was a cozy French speak-easy with a loft and a fantastic drink menu. They were open until three. Finally, if they were going to continue, they'd make their way to Prescription Cocktail Club in Saint-Germain Des Prés, near Île da la Cité and open until four in the morning. It was very hip and dark but welcoming and the service was always impeccable.

As he walked, he thought about the evening. The way Sharif acted, his response to bringing up Claire. Nothing seemed out of place. Nothing except not wanting to go out after eating. While that was out of character for him, it was also reasonable to expect he'd matured a bit these past few years, that he'd developed a sense of responsibility.

He wouldn't have much to report except that he'd successfully broken the ice, and that nothing went wrong. *All in all, a successful start*, he assessed. Dolan was eager to get on with it, to show results. But Lauren had told him, and he agreed that patience is key, especially early-on. He may get nothing for weeks, or even months before getting real results. And it might be something small at first. Or, he could hit the jackpot right away. It was a lot like the lottery. Except in this case, he should be able to manipulate the odds in his favor.

CHAPTER TWENTY-THREE

Dolan was agitated. It had been a month since he arrived in Paris, and he was no closer to finding any evidence that proved or disproved Sharif's involvement in a terrorist plot. Without signs of progress his daily routine was getting stale. Get up, run. Then four hours of one-on-one French with Father Aubertin at Lingua Europa. He found a martial arts school not too far from the hotel and was spending most afternoons there. He hadn't done much with taekwondo in the past few years. It was easy to get out of practice while deployed, and he had little time for it at the Pentagon. Getting back into it was a real bright spot during an otherwise uneventful period. There were several adult black belts, and the Sensei there was a sixth degree. Dolan was impressed with the expertise of a couple of them, but none were at his level. He had to tone it down a bit on more than one occasion during sparring when he realized he was close to injuring his opponents.

His relationship with Anne was progressing slowly. A few more dates was sufficient for him to see their chemistry was undeniable. Because of his undercover work with Sharif, he was conflicted about being intimate with her, and she noticed. She told him she assumed it had something to do with Claire. It was too easy to feed that assumption, so he did. And then there was Amy. He wasn't sure if the memory of her was somehow lurking in the background, complicating his closeness with Anne. She'd been on his mind, and he thought he would call her, but he hadn't yet. Dolan made another mental note to get that crossed off his to-do list.

He and Sharif went out a few more times but it was different than back in the day. While it was obvious that Sharif had changed—he seemed more responsible now—he also didn't exhibit any behavior that indicated something was off. That said, there was a slight distance between them. It wasn't blatant, but it was there. He couldn't decide if it was because Sharif now knew he was dating Anne, or because Sharif might be a terrorist and was taking the necessary precautions. Both possibilities were so plausible it kept Dolan from being able to nail down the reason. It also made him wonder if he should break up with Anne, or at least take some time off from her. That might help clear it up.

Dolan pushed their conversations in directions that might shed light on what was going on inside his head, what might be motivating him. He brought up Islam, which seemed to surprise Sharif. He'd been attending a mosque on the outskirts of the city. Going back to his roots, he said. Something he started doing quite a few years ago, after Dolan had left Paris. But he didn't mention which mosque and Dolan knew it would be weird to ask. When he mentioned Sharif's mother and father, he said he'd lost touch with his father years ago, something Dolan already knew. He was in contact with his mom and visited her from time to time, she wasn't doing too well, apparently. Nothing revealing.

When they did meet, they drank. A lot. At least that part was going according to plan. In his review of those encounters Dolan discovered an enigmatic complication. Something he couldn't wrap his head around. He couldn't decide if all this drinking with Sharif was as beneficial as he thought it might be. It might soften him up, trick Sharif into finally telling or showing him something useful, but in the meantime his own psyche, that carefully constructed array of walls and boxes was not as secure. Things were leaking out, thoughts were escaping. Not when he was with Sharif but after, the next day. It was easy to think that meeting Sharif was the reason it was happening, but was it causation or correlation? It was a bothersome irony that while he was with Sharif there was no issue at all. He was at ease. Content. Getting out and being social was allowing him to fill some void not addressable in any other immediate way. To temporarily forget about the infirmity of his compartmentalization. But the next day…

Sharif had evolved since the Sorbonne. He was more serious, more levelheaded. That said, when he and Dolan were together it was much like old times. Dolan assumed that after a while the novelty of their rekindled friendship would wear off, and Sharif would back off a bit with the partying and late nights. But he showed no sign of tapering off. It made sense to think Sharif might be drinking to overcome the anxiety and nervousness of spending considerable time with an American while planning to murder lots of Americans. But Sharif probably didn't see Dolan as an enemy, as an infidel. Or could it simply be the natural extrapolation of their relationship from so many years ago?

Dolan needed to play the part, but he had to do it carefully. He was fastidious in his preparation and worked through dinner and cocktail conversations with his team's goals in mind. He was noting and reporting operationally relevant information, as little as there was. It was likely that Sharif, his former close friend, was a terrorist and his job was to confirm it. But he was enjoying it. *That should bother me.*

The positive relationship he was building with Father Aubertin helped take his mind off these things. Aside from his time with Anne, Aubertin was the only person he could have an open and enjoyable conversation with. Even with Anne, he found himself shaping the discussion at times. Lying, even. Aubertin wasn't privy to his history with Anne, Sharif, and Claire and probably wouldn't be that interested in hearing about it. What concerned him was religion, culture and food, history and politics. They'd even ventured into philosophy, which Dolan found enjoyable. In one of their sessions, Aubertin gave him a worn copy of Nietzsche's *Beyond Good and Evil. Beyond* was a polemical continuation of his better-known book, *Thus Spoke Zarathustra.* Essentially, it was a sweeping attack against philosophy in general. All philosophy but Nietzsche's, of course. In it he accuses other philosophers of being bound to, and thus blinded by the dogmatic decrees of morality. Father Aubertin explained that this is the key—the reason why Nietzsche was right. His premise was that the others were wrong because their philosophies were heavily influenced by rules of men more or less derived from religion. This created a circular logic of sorts and introduced prejudices, thus preventing an accurate understanding of the true nature of man. Nietzsche was a perspectivist—he understood correctly that experience, perception, and even reason will change from person to person based on their individual biases.

Philosophy is much broader than religion, if a comparison can be made. It takes on concepts like metaphysics, the search for truth, knowledge and the meaning of life itself. As such, there is much overlap with theology. Aubertin explained that the conclusions in *Beyond* were difficult to reconcile with Christianity, but that Nietzsche's approach to philosophy is *fundamentally separated* from religion. This makes it easier to objectively explain man's capacity for evil and the innate nature of it. And it also makes comparison to or attempted alignment with any religion a moot point. Other philosophers have no such freedom. "All you have to do is read the title," he'd said, numerous times. The only disagreement he had with the book was in Nietzsche's definement of love. The desire to possess another human being, body and soul, was not love. Nietzsche had confused love with passion, as many do. Other philosophers would say he was forced to define love that way because if he did not, he would have provided basis for others to undermine some of the key arguments in the book. "Love," said Aubertin, "is to desire the ultimate good for another person, unconditionally." Though Nietzsche was philosophically correct, however irreconcilable that was with Christianity, "In the end," he'd said, "it doesn't matter. What and how we think is the best measure of the true nature of man. Those thoughts, that thinking, is persuaded by both good and evil and is both the catalyst and subsistence for all knowledge, experience, and life. And love, by its very nature, foments good. Therefore, if there is love in the world, evil can be kept at bay. Love trumps philosophy. It trumps everything."

It was quite different than what he'd been taught as a child. All the kneeling, standing, kneeling again. The quotidian repetition of archaic prayers of the Catholic church. His parents were religious. Not fanatically so, but strict enough. As a boy he'd come to loathe Sunday mornings and all the attendant activities. Though he did have fond memories of the coffee, juice and donut holes at the get-togethers after mass. Not that he disagreed with the teachings of the church; he recognized the value of Catholicism, however he felt as if the church had held on to too many dogmatic methods and rituals as the world evolved and passed it by.

It was too complicated and too dependent on the waning power of symbolism and mystery. In many ways Dolan felt it used fear as the basis for towing the line. This made it difficult to divine the true value of spirituality, especially for children. Dolan remembered contemplating these things in his parent's orchard. He'd sit under a tree eating an apple and wondering how God could banish a person to a place of eternal fire for committing just one of any number of sins. It was scary. No wonder so many had left the church over the years. Dolan still attended services from time to time and was still working on his own understanding of spirituality. In the meantime, his personal code was quite modest. It had worked well for him, more or less—*do the right thing, to the absolute best of your ability*. It was almost too simple. He felt he needed to add a layer or two to it at some point, some definition or granularity. There were arguments in *Beyond* that helped him understand why he perceived and felt about some of these things so differently than others. He looked forward to more of these types of discussions with Aubertin.

Which brought him full circle. Was he doing the right thing right now? He was fairly certain he was. But was he doing it the right way, and for the right reasons? Was the team doing everything the right way? That's where his certainty faltered. He didn't know enough about what was going on. There was more to it than he was being told. Even if he were successful in doing his part and any potential attacks were averted, would there be blowback from the French government? Could he or someone from EXCISE be hurt or killed? Imprisoned? Clearly, Lauren and Stone were taking risks, operating in a gray area that may or may not be considered legal. And he's caught right in the middle of it.

◆

Dolan's last two meetings with Stone were rather uninteresting. Uncomfortable even. Stone had nothing of real value to report to him.

Dolan had little for him in return, save some questionable responses and obvious deflections whenever Dolan got around to bringing up Islam or Sharif's mother and any new friends Sharif might have. In both meetings Stone seemed anxious. They were each accustomed to getting results and thus agitated at the air of uncertainty that pervaded. Stone was beginning to push Dolan hard to get to Sharif's apartment, to do something that would make it more likely for him to meet Martin, or to accompany Sharif to his mother's house in Marseille.

Well, he's in luck, thought Dolan. Sharif invited him to his home for dinner two weeks from now and would be preparing a traditional Algerian meal. If Dolan could be so lucky, Sharif would invite Martin or others somehow involved with the cell. It was unlikely, however. As long as he's associating with Dolan, Sharif would probably distance himself from anyone else involved, particularly as the attack became more imminent. And perhaps Martin wasn't even a friend but instead just a jihadist colleague, some kind of a brother in arms. Or a disciple. *Who knows.*

CHAPTER TWENTY-FOUR

"Alright team, please bring me up to speed. I have a hard stop at the bottom of the hour." Phil Dittrich had assembled the team via secure teleconference, including Lauren, Stone and Thomas.

"Well sir, let me start by summarizing what we already know…"

"No," interrupted Dittrich. "I don't need you to regurgitate what we already know. I've been reading the reports on Dolan. What I want is your assessments, your analysis. Is it working? That's the key. We're a month into this and as far as I can tell we don't know one fucking thing more than we knew in April. Prove me wrong."

There was an uncomfortable five seconds of silence as neither Stone nor Lauren were prepared to cut right to the chase. Lauren finally addressed him. "Sir, my assessment is that Dolan has done everything we've asked him to do, and he's done a good job. A surprisingly good job, actually. What you don't know is that he's finally been invited to Sharif's apartment."

"Finally!" Stone said in an overly relieved tone.

"OK, now we're getting somewhere," said Dittrich. "Stone, you need to meet with him before that happens. What are the pros and cons of having him place a bug?"

Lauren cut Stone off. "Sir, I would advise against that. As you know, we decided at the beginning that we wouldn't put Dolan in a position where he'd be performing high-risk activities for which he wasn't trained. The probability his cover's blown, or that he's compromised would increase drastically, and then we'd have to revert to Plan B, which no one wants." Plan B called for Stone to actively surveil Sharif and Martin full-time, alternating from week to week. It would mean notifying Chief of Station Le Pen that Stone was going dark, under an authority that was above him. And he wouldn't be briefed in on it. Stone was good, but constant surveillance activities like this with no backup were always under significant threat of being counter surveilled. They were currently operating under the assumption that the French already knew Stone was CIA, and that they were likely surveilling him periodically. This meant that any time Stone needed to conduct any clandestine activity there were numerous and complex precautionary measures he had to take. Not a good situation.

"OK, let's revisit this. Please tell me the rest. What else."

"Well," continued Lauren, "as you know we have insight into Algerians travelling to West Europe, looking for anyone we could tie to Hakeem Lefebvre and Sharif or to Martin. Yesterday we got a hit. Three men, two in their twenties and another who is thirty-five. They flew on the same flight from Algiers to Berlin. One of them used to work for Lefebvre's oil company, and the younger two are brothers though we don't have any background on them. The tickets were purchased in a single transaction. Unfortunately, the tickets were bought on the same day as the flight, so by the time we figured out they were a match they'd already landed and now they're in the wind.

The return flight is next Tuesday. We'll know for sure there's something to follow up on if they miss that return trip."

"That's good news, good work!" Dittrich went immediately from sour to cautiously optimistic. "If they are in fact part of the cell, their travelling to Berlin could mean they are in the latter stages of planning, or close to execution. I assume you're already set up to find and track these three? It is likely they went dark as soon as they landed and won't pop up under their real names. We need to check anyways of course. Hotels, car rentals, credit cards, ATMs."

"It's already set up sir," Thomas piped in. "If they perform any kind of monetary transaction using their real identities, or if they get pulled over by the local police, we'll be notified immediately. At least in Germany."

Lauren closed her eyes, knowing what was coming.

"What do you mean, at least in Germany?" said Dittrich, visibly irate. "What about France? Why shouldn't we give these three to the DGSI?"

"Sir, as you know the Bundesnachrichtendienst has worked closely with us for quite some time. But the DGSI, and well, the DGSE too, both have been hard nuts to crack." Lauren paused, not wanting to sound patronizing. "There is strong political pressure to prevent any perception that French intelligence is somehow collaborating with or dependent on the U.S. You know, because of the drone attack in Algeria."

She held her breath.

Dittrich backed off a bit. "Yeah, the drone operation. What a fuckup. That's going to haunt us for years. OK. Get whatever else you can on those three. Known aliases is probably a pipe dream but try anyway. In the meantime, make sure German federal intelligence has all their information and photos. Should we assume they'd be travelling immediately to France? Our initial assumption was that the U.S. Embassy in Paris was the most likely target. The other likely target was the U.S. contingent in the stands during the Bastille Day parade on 14 July. Any updates or analysis on timing and location?"

"Sir, if I may." Stone was tired of waiting his turn. "If these three suspects are travelling now, the timing aligns with the 14th. The fourth of July is probably too close. They still need time to do casing, walkthroughs, and whatever training might need to be done. Based on our profile of him and what I've seen from Dolan's interaction with Sharif I'd say he won't take part in the actual execution of an attack. I think he is the enabler, the leader. I believe he thinks his cell will launch the attack and he'll just keep living his pretty-boy executive life after all the investigations are complete and closed. In that respect, I think he's a novice in this and is simply a pawn for his father. Lefebvre is using his own son to fulfill his vengeance, and that vengeance is enough motivation to put his son's life and future in jeopardy."

Dittrich thought about it for a moment. "Lauren, what's your take?"

"I think we're grasping at straws sir. We assume the attack will be in Paris because that's where the largest concentration of Americans is. But let's be honest, it's only the largest concentration of Americans *in France*." She paused to let that fact sink in. "Just because Martin and Sharif are French, that doesn't mean the attack will happen in France. It's premature for us to think the target is anywhere in particular. We have consulates in Bordeaux, Lyon, Marseille, Rennes, and Strasbourg with less security. Paris is a stronghold. With our current suspects having no previous ties to terrorism and no known training to that effect, why would they take the most difficult approach? Sharif and Martin are intelligent and successful. My guess is they won't leave anything to chance and have been impeccable covering their tracks along the way. And getting back to my original point, the fact three new suspects from Algeria flew into Berlin makes Germany a possible location for the attack. I know that would be poor planning on their part and kind of flies in the face of what I just said, but we shouldn't assume they will think of everything. Again, they are novices at this. Outside London, Paris and Berlin are the largest embassies in Europe, with fourteen consulates and posts between them. We have forty other embassies in Europe, and the U.S. Missions to NATO and the EU, which are arguably busier than any of them. And then our military bases."

Another, less uncomfortable five seconds of silence passed before Dittrich answered. "Lauren, I want you to draft a cable for immediate release, to all European missions and posts. Keep it simple—something like 'current intelligence indicates credible threat against U.S. personnel in West and Central Europe, effective immediately. Recommend increased security at all U.S. installations in Europe until further notice.' Draft a second requesting any reports from countersurveillance at U.S. Missions in Europe that indicate increased or significant suspicious activity. We should get everything from Berlin and Paris, however insignificant. I think those two are where we focus our energies, with Paris being the top priority. But let's not rule anything out. Make sure the Defense Intelligence Agency is notified as well.

"Stone, can you surveil Martin, in a limited way, and still take care of Dolan? My thinking is that if the attack is going to be in Paris, Sharif isn't going anywhere. But Martin could be making a move soon. And as you've reported, he's already dropped off the radar a couple of times, for days at a time. If Sharif is the leader of the cell, Martin probably has a role that is closer to the actual execution of the attack. If this is true, communication between our three new suspects may be with him. In fact, it may have already begun. And I'm much less concerned about you being counter surveilled in Metz than I in Paris."

"Sir, I can definitely pull it off but may need a directive from you to Le Pen, so I don't catch too much attention."

"OK I'll get that out to him tomorrow. As for Dolan, go ahead and give him a bug to plant at Sharif's apartment. Brief him on how to activate it and where to hide it. But tell him to do so only if he's left alone. And only if he can place it somewhere where the chances Sharif might find it are near or equal to zero."

Lauren quickly shook her head in disagreement. "Sir, I don't think…"

"Listen Lauren, it's my call. If this blows up, it'll be on me. The fact is, we need to take some risks if we are going to break this cell open, and we need to do it now. They might be close to or already at operational readiness. And we are still very much in the dark. Dolan seems to have a knack for this work, and we should begin to lean on that more and more as we move along."

Stone took advantage of a break in the conversation. "Sir, it would help if we could somehow give me access to the live feed from Dolan's phone. I'm the only one on the team who's fluent in French, and Lauren wouldn't have to wait hours or days for an interpreter. I could just call her and fill her in. The way this is set up is backwards, frankly."

Lauren felt the meeting getting out of control. She needed to reign everyone back in. "Wait, everyone, please wait. Tony, I've told you before that it won't work. And there are good reasons for why it's set up the way it is. The first is, and this is currently out of our control, there is only one server that can receive the encrypted feed, and once it's decrypted, it absolutely must be transferred to a closed system, which we have here at the Pit. The system is an asset that is not acknowledged in the Agency outside SCALPEL." Dittrich was nodding in agreement. "This is not so much to protect us against foreign adversaries, but from our own NSA. Do I need to explain the implications of that, or is it clear?"

Stone looked unconvinced but conceded. "OK I get it. But if we're going to use this capability operationally, it needs to be improved. And that means enabling our officers in the field."

"Listen," said Dittrich, "there's nothing we can do about it now, Lauren's right about the feed. It shouldn't be much of an issue if the team is communicating well."

Stone was silently fuming. Anything having to do with Dolan should have been delegated directly to him. What was he there for, anyway? And now he's being assigned to surveil Martin, which was progress in his opinion, but the priority should be with watching Sharif. Only he can't because it would be redundant with Dolan in the mix. His presence on the team was beginning to feel like a hindrance. The only saving grace was his imminent visit to Sharif's apartment and Dittrich's concession on the bug. *If Dolan has the balls to plant it.*

They were running out of time, and Lauren needed to hit on one more topic. "Sir, have you had time to read the transcripts?" She assumed he hadn't.

"I've scanned them. Pretty dry stuff. What's your take?"

"Yes, pretty dry stuff. But there are two things I've gotten from them. One, Dolan probably needs to drink less when he's with Sharif. He's doing an incredible job actually, everything we've taught him, but I think he might do better if he backed off a bit. It's not evident in the transcripts, but when you listen to the recordings, it is. Stone, you can pass that to him the next time you see him. Second, Dolan did push him on key information, particularly about his religion, attending mosque services, etcetera. He pulled it off by acting interested in

Sharif's life changes and sharing details about his own search for spirituality. But the point is, Sharif was evasive. He didn't say which mosque and changed the subject each time it was brought up. He did the same with Dolan's inquiries about his mother, and about who Sharif was hanging out with these days. These are all red flags."

"No, I didn't get any of that from a brief review. So, it is not evidence per se, but it builds toward confirmation of our assumptions. Listen, I am out of time. Last thing. We have some open items from Marseille. I haven't seen anything yet on decryption of the network data you collected from the laptop in the house. Any progress from Thomas?"

"I haven't reported anything because he hasn't been able to crack it, sir. I'd say it's a dead end," Lauren replied.

"OK. What about the license plate on the SUV down the road from the house? That should have been an easy one."

Lauren couldn't believe she'd overlooked that. *Shit*. Dittrich had mentioned it almost in passing during the operation and she never made a note of it. She guessed that Thomas hadn't either. "I'll have to get back to Thomas, sir. I'll send you an email later. It's something I haven't followed up on yet, with everything else going on."

Dittrich regarded her through the monitor, incredulous. "*You haven't followed up on it?* What does that mean, exactly? Listen, I shouldn't have to remind you to check every detail, to filter through every scrap of potential evidence, however small. I mean, how many times in our work is it the most insignificant, innocuous detail that breaks a case wide open? Holy fuck almighty." Dittrich was rolling his eyes. "Yes, please do check on that and get back to me soon.

"Alright team, I have a meeting with the Director. *Do good things.*" Lauren and Stone winced in unison as Dittrich's square on the screen went black.

"Stone. Before you go." Lauren had to set this straight.

"Sure, what is it?" he replied.

"I don't care what Dittrich just told you. Under no circumstances will I allow you to let Dolan try to plant that bug. Using him to execute tradecraft like that is going to ruin this op and could put him in serious jeopardy. We will continue with the plan as-is. With Dolan on Sharif and your surveillance of Martin we'll have double the opportunity to get something valuable. We'll let you know what happens at Sharif's apartment. Please tell me you understand."

Stone paused before answering. "Sure Lauren, I understand. Don't worry about it."

Lauren nodded, satisfied. "Thanks Stone. I hope you know I'm grateful for the work you're doing."

"Just doing good things." He smirked at her kiddingly and signed off. Then he sat there in his Savile Row suit, staring at the black screen and thinking. Lauren was too conservative to be leading a black unit like SCALPEL. He could *feel* it—the cell forming, its members planning and casing. They were in the latter stages of preparation, and it was all going to go down soon. In his estimation, and given the French were dead set against collaborating with them on anything related to Algeria, they were going to have to take this cell out themselves. Which meant him. He'd been offered the latitude he needed, and Dittrich was right—Stone needed to consider taking some risks.

CHAPTER TWENTY-FIVE

Dolan had just finished his run. He couldn't remember ever having needed a workout so badly. He was carrying extra adrenaline today and it was making him anxious. Six miles had almost done the trick, but the process wasn't complete. He moved the ornate coffee table against the wall of his hotel room and laid down on his back on the carpet, waiting for his heartrate to slow. Once it reached sixty beats per minute, he did five hundred crunches: two hundred crossover crunches and three hundred straight up. Then he flipped around and did a hundred pushups. His normal routine consisted of running five or six times per week with three additional anaerobic workouts added in. He hadn't been doing the workouts regularly since he arrived in Paris. He was OK with that since he'd taken taekwondo back up. But it just wasn't enough.

He had the dream again last night. Only this time it was different. On any other day he would have shaken it off and quickly forgotten about it, but not this time. It was less surreal, but darker. More foreboding. Shocking. The pursuit at the beginning was all the same, but as the assailant was straddling his friend and pushing the knife between his friend's ribs and into his heart, his friend's visage had become unblurred. Dolan was now able to see his face for the first time, a face he recognized. A face he saw every time he looked in the mirror. In his dream, the same dream he'd had a hundred times, he'd been watching his own death and unable to do anything about it. He couldn't call it a dream anymore. It had become much more personal—a bona fide nightmare. He wasn't just a spectator; he was the victim. It was abominable in a way he hadn't experienced before— it was ugly and odious and *seemed so real*, both cognitively and physically. Where before he'd accepted and even masochistically liked the reoccurrence of the dream, now he would fear it. And it wasn't something he could compartmentalize. Clearly, these dreams were not the *leftover essences of the day*. This was his subconscious trying to tell him something. Something important, unavoidable, and terrible that he did not want to hear. It was affecting him now in ways it hadn't before, and he didn't know what to do about it.

When he was finished working out, he showered and dressed for language training. That meant jeans and a polo, which was nice. Or maybe shorts—it was beginning to get warm in Paris. He should enjoy it while he could, as he'll be back to wearing a suit soon. Just as the real summer heat begins. At least Paris wasn't quite as hot or humid as DC. He'll be moved into a proper apartment before long. The housing office at the embassy already found him a place, but he turned it down as it was out on the northeast side, almost all the way to Aubervilliers. It was too far away. Once he starts work at FEPF he'll have to manage his time very carefully. Commuting that much would be counterproductive to the operation. Since he wasn't a diplomat, the embassy was doing him a favor in finding him a place. Turning it down meant he was on his own now—he'd have to locate housing himself. Ideally, he'll want something near Sharif's luxury apartment on rue des Ecoles in the Latin Quarter. He even discussed it with Sharif the previous day on the phone. Sharif had said "living near each other would be awesome." He even recommended a few neighborhoods he thought might be in Dolan's price range.

On the Métro he thought about his meeting tonight. Stone sent him an encrypted text, the first time he'd done that, telling him to be at the Hôtel de Petit Moulin on rue de Poitou at eight p.m. The suddenness of it worried him a bit. He hadn't yet told Stone of his upcoming dinner at Sharif's apartment. He planned to brief him about it at their normal Saturday meeting. Something must have happened, or Stone needed to update him on some development. He'd have to cancel his dinner plans with Anne. Or reschedule. He was upset at this, and relieved at the same time. His relationship with her was evolving, they were becoming closer. But he'd continued to resist her somewhat and kept telling himself the reason was related to his undercover work. He felt he couldn't let it get too serious. It would create a conflict of interest. But deep down he knew that wasn't the reason. It was already a conflict and becoming more so each time he saw her. *So, what was the root cause of it?* It's not Claire. He'd already put her behind him, he was sure of it. It couldn't possibly be Amy. But she kept popping into his mind, and he still hadn't called her. Or his parents, not since he first arrived. Maybe he didn't want to have to hurt her? Or was he worried Sharif might do something to her if he began to suspect Dolan? He couldn't pin it down. Overall, he felt the extra worry was strangely unsubstantiated and unwelcome in the aftermath of his dream. Thus, the additional need for a workout today.

He wasn't used to dealing with these thoughts. He walked over to the dresser, grabbed a bottle of cognac he'd bought the day before, opened it and poured himself a small glass. That would calm his nerves. His hangover this morning wasn't quite as bad as the last time, and the workout took the edge off. He downed it in a single gulp, poured another and drained the glass. Feeling better, he headed out the door certain these bothersome feelings would pass. *Even if the dream is now a nightmare, a nightmare is still just a dream.* Everything would work itself out with Anne, and his focus on the mission would drown out the rest.

◆

"Good afternoon, Tony."

"Good afternoon, Mike! Have a seat."

Stone seemed in an unusually good mood. He took his seat and leaned forward. Dolan thought he looked different. Yes, his outfit. It looked more like a vintage Men's Wearhouse suit, and dull gray. No tie. It made him appear older, less attractive. Less successful. *He's getting into character.*

"Thanks for rearranging your schedule on short notice. As you may have suspected, I have some updates for you that were important enough for us to get together early this week. But why don't you tell me about any updates you have first."

Dolan was curious to hear what it was but remained stoic, controlling the direction of the conversation. "I suspected as much. I don't have a whole lot to report; there is one significant thing. Why don't you tell me what this development is first—I'm eager to hear."

Stone was irritated but he capitulated. "OK, sure. The first thing is, we have decided based on your performance so far and because of our confidence in your abilities to ask you to take on more of an operational role. The success you have with these additional responsibilities will dictate how far we go with that, but for now I have a couple of things to give you."

He opened his brown leather attaché and produced a small manila envelope. He opened it and removed a flat, brown, circular object, about the size of a nickel but thinner. He handed it to Dolan. "This is a listening device. A bug. It activates once you peel off the backing and adhere it to a flat surface."

Dolan held it up to the light from the window and regarded it closely. The bug was quite thin and had a woodgrain finish. Other than that, there were no discernable features, not even a seam.

Stone continued. "It does not record, it only transmits. The range is about fifty yards, give or take. I've already planted the receiver within range of Sharif's apartment. All you have to do is plant the bug. It only transmits when it registers a certain level of sound. This enables the battery to last quite a long time and negates the need to swap it out at regular intervals."

Dolan put the bug back inside the envelope. "So, I'll be expected to plant this, and to retrieve it as well? And then, I suspect, to replace it when the battery dies?"

"You'll have to plant it. Whether or not you retrieve it will be decided later. The device self-destructs when the battery gets low. That is to say, the electronics inside are fried to the point an electrical engineer would be unable to forensically determine its purpose or capabilities. And it does this without smoke or smell. Over time we'll review what's recorded and combined with what we already know, if we get enough to show Sharif might be involved in planning a terrorist attack, we'll provide that information to the DGSI. At that point the DGSI will want a detailed download of everything we've collected. We'll decide what to tell them, and essentially, the op will be over. They'll pick it up and arrest Sharif and whoever else they can tie to the cell.

"But let's not get ahead of ourselves. You should only plant this when Sharif is not in the room and you're sure he won't walk in on you while you're hiding it. And it needs to be hidden in a place where it would never be found, realistically. It's wood colored, as the best places are usually inside or underneath furniture. You can always recolor it using white-out, fingernail polish, or something else if you need to. So, the most important thing is how well it's obscured. The second most important thing is that it's hidden in a place where Sharif will do most of his talking. In this era of cell phones, that's usually somewhere between the television and wherever he keeps his computer. The bedroom is also a good place. Any questions so far?"

Dolan was not the paranoid type; he was quite the opposite. He detested the illogic and general lunacy of conspiracy theorists, and even in the tensest situations when information was lacking, he was always able to keep his head until he was able to make sense of it all. Such was the position in which he currently found himself. Stone was going on as if he already knew about his dinner at Sharif's. He hadn't mentioned it, but Dolan could see no reason why today's meeting couldn't have waited until Saturday. Was it possible Stone was spying on *him*? Sure, he could understand Lauren and Stone wanted to keep tabs on him, at least until they were sure of his capabilities. But they already knew they could trust him—the polygraph they made him take was the best measure of that. And how better to do it than using the iPhone they'd given him? The battery problem could be related to it.

Then Dolan's caught himself. He'd allowed his instincts to override logic. He had no proof they were watching or listening to him without his knowledge. And they are the good guys… Better to continue ops normal until and unless future events dictate a change. But he would hold off a little on telling Stone about the invitation to Sharif's. To test the theory.

"No questions," replied Dolan. This is a relatively simple thing. I'll either have the opportunity or I won't. Either way, I'll let you know."

Stone nodded, maintaining eye contact with him, as if to tell him 'OK, but don't you have something to tell me?' "Good. A final note on this—if you have any contact with Lauren, don't tell her about the bug. She didn't want to expose you to this level of risk. However, the Deputy Director approved it, in my presence. In fact, he instructed me to do it. I'm confident in your ability to carry this out without complication. So, I don't have any problem with it. Do you?"

Another interesting development. Internal disagreement, insubordination even. These are the types of things normally found as the root cause in an error chain analysis. Human error is the origin of most catastrophic aircraft accidents, by a wide margin. And one could extrapolate that across most types of failures, systemic or otherwise. What it meant was that Dolan would need to be extra vigilant, more careful even than he'd thought previously. There were problems within EXCISE beyond his control.

Dolan shook his head. "No, no problem at all. If it's too risky, I won't plant it."

"OK, great. Now to the second item. I know you already know how to use this from your time in the service." He reached back into his attaché and pulled out a black handgun, offering it to Dolan. "This is a Beretta APX. It's a great multi-caliber weapon designed for military and law enforcement use. It's loaded with seventeen rounds, nine-millimeter. That should be what you're used to. Now let me be clear— the Agency is not issuing this weapon to you. The Agency doesn't know that you have it. In fact, the Agency denies its very existence. And there is no serial number on it. That doesn't mean it's been removed; it means there never was a serial number. It's untraceable in that respect, but if the authorities get their hands on it, you don't want to be in possession at the time, for this and other obvious reasons. But it should never come to that. If you are in a situation where you need to discard it, and you cannot get it back to me, break the weapon down and throw the components into the Seine, each piece in a different area.

"You don't have to take it." Stone then handed him a small cardboard box from his case, just larger than the Beretta. "It is my professional opinion that the cell is farther along than the others believe. If we find ourselves in a situation where we know an attack is about to go down, and if we are unable to hand operational control over to the French, we will have to take the cell down ourselves. This weapon is for your self-defense. I suspect that if it comes down to it, I will be on my own. And I'm fine with that. But during the takedown you could be exposed. If that happens, I want to be sure I've given you the ability to remain alive. Should you decide to accept it, my instructions are simple. The first rule is, keep it well-hidden, always inside the box, in your hotel room. You should have easy access. The hotel safe is the worst place. I recommend you keep it inside a large wad of dirty laundry, in a suitcase on the floor of your closet. Believe it or not, if someone breaks in and goes through your room, it is probably the last place they will look. And the maids won't touch your dirty laundry. You know, you wouldn't have to worry as much about hiding it if you'd taken the apartment the housing office offered you."

Dolan froze. He did his best to act as if nothing was wrong, but Stone just confirmed one of his suspicions. Either Stone was checking up on him at the housing office, or he somehow knew that he'd told Sharif about turning down the apartment. And he hadn't come back around yet to ask him about his 'significant thing.' Dolan expected Stone to be more eager to hear his updates, especially if it was considered important.

Stone continued. "The second rule is, do not ever remove it from its hiding place unless you are sure you need to use it. For the sake of clarity, that means you are in a situation where you expect to discharge the weapon in your defense." Stone paused then, as if contemplating whether to go on. "There is a slight chance I may need help. It's difficult to predict what 'slight' really means, but it could happen. If it does, can I count on you for backup?"

Another surprise... Dolan held the weapon, feeling its weight. It was a little bulkier than the Beretta M9 he'd trained on and carried in Afghanistan. "Yes, of course. Can I assume I am to say nothing of this to Lauren as well?"

Stone regarded him seriously. "Yes. Only you and I know about this, and it needs to stay that way. When this is all over, you will return the gun to me. You'll probably never need to take it out of the box, to be honest. But I've been doing this work a while now, and if there's one thing I've learned it's that it's better to be prepared and not need it than otherwise. Here." Stone handed him the attaché. "You can keep the case. It's nice."

"Thanks Tony, it is nice." Dolan put the Beretta in the box, and the box in the case. Now he was sure Stone was tracking him, spying on him. Which is why he showed no interest in Dolan's report. He already knows about dinner at Sharif's. And he would be suspicious if Dolan weren't eager to tell him about it... "I appreciate that you're concerned about my ability to defend myself. I'll keep it hidden as you say. Listen, I'm eager to tell you. Sharif invited me to his apartment for dinner on Monday, July first at seven p.m. It will be a good opportunity to plant the bug." Dolan watched him closely.

Stone went wide-eyed. It was difficult for Dolan to determine if his reaction was genuine or contrived. Dolan also knew that as a seasoned operative it would be easy for Stone to maintain composure and to feign surprise. But it should also be just as easy for him not to screw up the way he just did by mentioning the housing office.

"Outstanding Mike! Yes, and maybe our only opportunity, so do your best. And beyond that, collect whatever you can. Once you activate the bug, I'll be recording everything audible in the vicinity. Just remember to keep an eye out for anything that might pass for useful physical evidence. And if there are others who show up at the dinner, it is possible they could be involved with the cell somehow. Shape the conversations and get as much as you can without raising suspicion, as we've discussed. We'll debrief Tuesday morning. I don't have the location or time yet—I'll have to send that to you via secure text." He sat back in his chair expectantly, almost as if he'd gotten everything he wanted and was now just waiting for the conversation to end. "Go ahead and tell me the rest. What else have you gotten from him?"

Dolan recounted the two conversations he had with Sharif since his previous meeting with Stone, from Saturday night at Little Red Door on rue Charlot and the other, their phone conversation on Sunday about the dinner. He noted the situations when Sharif deflected his questions, and the unease he displayed when Dolan brought up his religion. He gave a normal, good report as if nothing were out of the ordinary, watching Stone the whole time for any tells.

"That's a good report, Mike. We are finally getting somewhere, and not too soon. I'll pass this on to Lauren tonight. "Oh, and one last thing. Make sure that when you two are out drinking that you don't overdo it. Pace yourself. As you may know, your ability to do this work well has returns that diminish proportionally to the degree to which you overdo it. A few drinks are good to take the edge off and get loose. After that it's all downhill."

Almost as if he had been there himself on Saturday night. "I understand Tony. I won't do anything to jeopardize the mission." Dolan got up from the chair, shook Stone's hand, and moved to the door. He half expected Stone to say something else, but he didn't. He felt that the way the conversation went Stone might have guessed that Dolan was aware Stone was surveilling him. If so, he was probably hoping Dolan would interpret it as a protective measure for both him and the operation. And Dolan suspected this was probably something close to the truth. But it all ran counter to his personal code. It was dishonest. Stone wasn't doing the right thing, to the best of his ability. Not with him, not with Lauren, not with Excise. He had the option to tell Lauren about all of it, certainly about Stone giving him the weapon and enlisting him in a second level of operational involvement without her knowledge. Dolan wasn't trained for this, but he believed that even as capable and experienced as Stone is, he might not be able to pull it off by himself. He was only one person. Could Dolan risk blowing up the operation at this point when the cell might be close to operational readiness? Probably not. Dolan couldn't trust Stone, not completely, but he could go along with Stone's plan. And even though Stone seemed to be somewhat of a loose cannon, it could be that surveillance on Dolan was ordered or managed by Lauren, or even the Deputy Director. If he didn't cause friction about his suspicions or report the apparent fracturing of the team, they might still be able to pull it off. And he could use what he now knew to his advantage along the way. *Time will tell.* The only thing that was perfectly clear at this juncture was that he couldn't trust anyone.

CHAPTER TWENTY-SIX

Martin left the main office parking lot of Château Group in his Mercedes. He had some of his favorite snacks in the passenger seat for the long drive to Berlin and a trunk full of supplies for his brothers who awaited him. If he had looked toward the office entrance as he drove off, he might have seen Stone making his way through security, on his way to plant a bug in Martin's office computer. But Martin was unaware of who Stone was or what he was doing. In fact, Martin was feeling quite confident, happy even. With only a week to go, everything was falling into place. His warriors from Algeria had arrived and were safe at his property in Potsdam. They were to hole up there until he arrived with their instructions.

Exactly seven hours later he was pulling into the gravel driveway. He drove the car up to the house, then turned right onto the grass and parked next to the tree line at the edge of the yard. He walked a few yards into the forest and retrieved a cloth car cover from under its rock, unfolded it and draped it over the front two-thirds of the car, leaving the trunk uncovered.

No one was allowed to enter or exit through the front or back doors. Only the garage door was to be used. If there was ever a knock, or if the doorbell rang, they were to remain silent and out of sight. Martin entered the code into the keypad and the garage door opener whirred, revealing the drop cloth he'd spread across the inside of the opening. He pulled it aside and quickly assessed the interior—the truck and everything else as he left it. *Good.* Then he closed the garage door and went in to meet his warrior brothers for the first time.

They were all standing when he entered the living room, a Bundesliga soccer match playing on the television. Martin paused inside the doorway, having prepared himself mentally during the long drive to play the role of the teacher, the leader, the seer. *I must boost their spirits, validate their faith, and give them courage*, he thought.

One of them pressed the mute button on the TV remote as Martin held out his arms, as if he were about to hug them all at once. "As-salaam 'alaykum! Welcome, my brothers! I am François, and I am happy that you made it here safe and sound. Karim, Mehmet, and Ebrihim, welcome. Tell me, did everything go as planned? Did you encounter any trouble?"

"Wa 'alaykum salaam," they replied in unison.

There was a moment of silence as the three waited to see which one of them would answer. Then Mehmet spoke up. "Mr. Martin, we did as we were told, and everything went fine. The flight was uneventful, and we all took separate buses to get here. We walked the last two kilometers, did everything as you instructed, and have spoken with no one. We await your orders."

Mehmet, the oldest, was the only one with any education having completed two years of high school. He was unusually quiet with a slight frame overcome in part by his gritty, weather-worn face. He looked older than his thirty-five years. Mehmet was injured in the drone attack on Lefebvre's forces. He almost died and ended up losing a kidney. He was fond of showing off the long, gnarled scar that spiderwebbed the right side of his back. Karim and Ebrihim were brothers, twenty and twenty-two years old, respectively. Both thin and short, they could easily pass for twins. All three were fully indoctrinated into the al-Mulathamun Army. They were trained in hand-to-hand combat, small arms, bombmaking, and subterfuge. Skills that, in accordance with the will of Allah, would help them succeed in Paris. They were handpicked for this mission. None were married or had any strong familial ties back in Algeria and they were fully dedicated to jihad and even martyrdom if necessary. The final and critical prerequisite was that they were all fluent in French.

"Brothers, the mission we are about to embark on is a holy one. No man can say otherwise, and nothing anyone says after we succeed can make this untrue. Only Allah can judge us, and it is for Allah that we do this, because it is his will. The Americans invaded our lands and attacked our people. They did so without even showing their faces like the cowardly dogs they are. They hide behind money and technology and false religions while they propagate their evil culture across oceans and borders. Our jihad is a just one, and one that will send a message across the world that the United States will pay for these sins, and they will continue to pay as there is no hope for them. Do not misunderstand, they will not stop until they've inserted themselves everywhere, dropped bombs on everyone who disagrees with them. Until the entire world is drinking Coca Cola, eating at McDonald's and watching pornography and fornicating in the streets, and all our women are walking around half naked in the markets!"

Martin was getting caught up in his speech, emotional even. And why not? He strongly believed every word of it because it was all true. His voice was getting louder as he took a few steps farther into the room, closer to them. "They will not stop until they are met face to face with jihad—with pain and death. Only then will they pause. With jihad we can cause them to withdraw their forces from our Islamic homelands and retreat within their own borders. And even then, our jihad will rage on until they have repented for their sins and embraced Allah. Only then will there be peace! This is our jihad, brothers! This is why we are here; this is why we were born, and we will be rewarded both here in life and in death for our sacrifice toward such a noble goal. Allahu akbar!"

What started as a softly spoken speech had risen gradually both in volume and urgency as he delivered it, and his holy soldiers were feeding off it. He could see their eyes opening wider, each of them gaining energy and anticipation for what was to come. As soon as he finished, they began repeating "Allahu akbar!" together, over and over. This gave Martin a great sense of pride and accomplishment. It was working. This sort of thing had always been hard for him; his father always told him he wasn't leadership material, that he would be better off being the more intelligent, quiet person in the room so that when he finally did say something everyone would listen. His father was wrong about a lot of things but in this, Martin believed he was partially correct. Being a leader *was* difficult for him. But people were listening to him now, and when their mission was completed, the whole world would be listening.

The four of them brought in the supplies from Martin's car, mostly foodstuffs and bottled water. Martin finished putting the car cover on and cinched it tight. Then they went to the garage. Martin could tell they were eager to understand the details of the mission and to become familiar with the gear and weapons. Up until this point they had been told nothing of what they would be doing. Martin was sure they were contemplating the possibility that they would be required to wear suicide vests, as this is part of their standard training. It was a positive sign that none of them seemed to be having second thoughts this close to the execution of their attack, knowing they may be martyred. They could be trusted to carry it out to the end, Martin was sure.

He lined them up side-by-side near the wall so he could stand between them and the panel truck. "I am only going to explain this once, and I don't want any discussion or questions about it after this. I am sure you've had time to look inside the truck and wondered what the machine inside is for. Perhaps you thought you would be using this machine in our jihad. You will not. This truck and its contents have nothing to do with your mission. As I mentioned to you in my message, you are not to touch it, ask about it, or discuss it. As far as you are concerned, it does not exist. Have I made myself clear?"

"Yes," they all replied quietly. Martin saw various combinations of confusion and disappointment on their faces. But they quickly hid their emotions, which was good.

Martin walked over to the workbench where an assortment of stacks of papers and boxes were arranged. He pulled the chain on the fluorescent lights and took a Paris Métro map from one of the stacks, unfolding it as he turned around to show to them.

"OK. Now that we have that settled, let's talk about what you will be doing. There is another vehicle not far from here. It is hidden in the woods. You will be driving this car to Paris on the third of July. You will stay the night at a hotel that is already reserved and paid for, near a subway station called Concorde. You will not check in at the front desk. In fact, you should make every effort not to talk to anyone or to be seen at the hotel. To make this possible, the hotel keys will be mailed to this house in one or two days. The hotel has an underground parking garage, the hotel key will open the garage gate for you to park there.

"The United States Embassy is having a large celebration on the fourth of July, which is a big holiday for them. It is their day of independence from Britain. There will be hundreds, maybe thousands of Americans in Paris who will go there for the celebration. The party is not just for those who work at the embassy; many Americans who live or work in, or who are visiting Paris will be going there. The celebration begins at six p.m. You will launch your attacks as close to five forty-five as possible. You will do this inside the subway cars as they approach Concorde Station. There are three different trains that stop there. Each train is named after a color—one is yellow, one is purple, and one is green. Mehemet, you are responsible for the yellow train. Karim, you have the purple train. And Ebrahim, yours is the green one. Each of you will be carrying a canister of deadly gas…" Martin walked over to one of the two workbenches, reached into a cardboard box and pulled out one of the four smaller tanks he'd filled from two of the larger canisters from Monsieur Schwartz.

"You see, the gas must be contained for it to work well. This means if you release it out in the open, like in a city square, only a few people will die because the gas will dissipate quickly. But when it is discharged in an enclosed area, like a room or in this case, a train car, it has nowhere to go, and everyone inside will die. And they will die quickly.

"You will dress nicely, like businessmen. I have suits for you in the hall closet. You should try them on to make sure they fit. I also have briefcases for each of you, big enough for everything to fit inside. Each of you will get on your subway line one stop prior to Concorde and release the gas as soon as the doors close and after the train has left the station. You should choose the subway car that has the most people in it. Mehmet, it is especially important that you get on the yellow line at the Champs Elysées station. There are many embassy workers who have apartments in that area, and they won't be on the train if you get on from the other direction. You will all be given these…" He placed the canister back in the box and pulled out a gas mask and one of the Glock 18s Sharif procured. "If anyone suspects you, or if they try to stop you after the doors close, shoot them." He held out the weapon for them to see. "The mask will protect you. However, as soon as you put it on, people will know there is an attack happening. Wait until the doors close and the train leaves the station. Then open the briefcase, put the extra ammo clips in your suit pockets, put on the mask, and release the gas. Protect yourself with the gun and hold onto the canister until it stops hissing. This means the gas has been completely released. Once it is empty, you will leave it and the briefcase and move into the next car and begin shooting people. Especially if they look American. Do not waste your time and ammunition shooting people until you move to the next car. The gas takes a little while to kill but believe me, once they take a couple of breaths, they are dead. Keep moving though each car, shooting, until you run out of ammo or until the train reaches the station at Concorde.

"Everyone will have five ammo clips, one in the handgun and four more. This means you will have 85 rounds. Make your shots count. Do not wound them, kill them. But you must do it quickly as you will only have a couple of minutes. Once the doors open at Concorde you will remove the mask and drop it with the gun and ammo clips inside the train and run out of the station. You will pretend to be scared like everyone else so the police will think you are just another survivor. If anyone tries to stop you for any reason, run right by them as if you don't notice them, as if you are scared for your life and will stop for nothing. Finally, do not worry about shooting the women or the children. In Allah's eyes they are all infidels. And our message is louder, our victory sweeter when the enemy realizes we do not make these distinctions.

"You will not be able to fly back to Algeria, as the authorities may already know who you are and could be looking for you. Instead, you will go back to the hotel, get in the car and drive South, all the way to Port-la-Nouvelle where there will be a boat to take you home. We have a few days to go through all the details, study maps and photos of the subway, and discuss your getaway. But this is basically it. It is a good plan. Once you are safely home, we will attribute the attack to the al-Mulathamun Army in a video that Monsieur Lefebvre plans to release on the internet. Are there any questions so far?"

Mehmet, Karim and Ebrihim each shook their head, visibly relieved this wasn't planned as a suicide mission. He wouldn't tell them the truth, of course. There would be no boat waiting for them at Port-la-Nouvelle. If they were to somehow make it out of the subway it is likely they would be killed or captured within minutes, if not seconds. If they were extremely lucky and made it to the car, they'd be apprehended long before making the southern coast. But they wouldn't make it out. The gas masks would give them an extra ten seconds, tops. They would not protect against the Hemoxin. His soldiers would get through one clip, maybe two before they collapsed and died. It was the only way. Once they were dead there would be nothing at all tying them to him or Sharif. It was the only way to ensure he and Sharif could continue their work without risk of being caught. The only way to continue their jihad. It was the will of Allah.

CHAPTER TWENTY-SEVEN

Stone watched from his car as Martin made his way out of Château Group headquarters and into the parking lot. *He looks happy. I wonder why...* He surveyed Martin as he weaved between the first few rows of cars, hoping he wouldn't need to get out of his own car to take a photo. But he stopped at a big, black Mercedes about fifty feet away and Stone was able to zoom in on the license plate. In a couple days he'd return and plant a GPS tracker on it. Ideally, he should have already done it but there had been no time. He came straight here from Paris.

Martin got in his car and drove off slowly. Stone got out of his car, affixed a Château Group security badge to his lapel and walked purposefully to the front door. He made it through security without issue and moved to the elevator, which he took to the fourth floor. Pretending to look busy reading from a sheaf of papers, he exited the elevator to the right and walked down the hall. A small group of employees conversed as they strolled past him. On top of his file was a hand-drawn map that pointed him to Martin's rather large office, where he stopped near the door. Stone casually leaned against the wall as he continued to pretend to read. Without moving his head, his eyes darted left and right. No security cameras were immediately evident. He waited until the last employee turned the corner, leaving him alone. Taking a small electronic device from his pocket, he inserted the attached keycard into the reader on Martin's door, quickly hacking the lock. After another quick look up and down the hall, Stone went inside. He shut the door quietly, moved quickly to the windows and closed the blinds.

The office was well appointed with expensive leather furniture and art deco paintings and accoutrements. Stone nodded approvingly and wondered if Martin truly appreciated the global impact of French art deco, the elegant and exuberant fusion of circa-1920s style with fine craftsmanship and good materials. It was a celebration of luxury, glamour, and faith in the technology of the time. Based on what Stone knew about him already, Martin probably didn't even know what art deco was.

He made his way quickly to the desk and tapped the spacebar on the computer keyboard. The screen promptly came to life, revealing a password entry window. He took a small USB key from his pocket, so small that once inserted into the back of the desktop, it protruded less than a millimeter. It was essentially invisible. The key contained a program that would open a back door over the internet, allowing Stone to remotely view and download any files that might be useful. It also contained a microphone. Like the bug he gave to Dolan, it was sound activated; however, this device did not require a receiver. Instead, it enabled conversation in the room to be recorded on an Agency cloud server. If remote access were suddenly denied, or if it were physically removed from the computer, the bug would self-destruct, rendered inert with the chip inside melted. He could also deactivate it remotely if needed. It was unfortunate he couldn't use the same device on Sharif's personal computer. The probability of him discovering it would be much higher though, particularly if it were a laptop. Likewise, he couldn't do anything like this in Sharif's office. Francopharma's security was much tighter than Château Group's. There was too much risk.

He began going through all the paperwork in Martin's office, snapping photos of anything that didn't appear attributable to the wine distribution business. He was also looking for SD cards and flash drives, anything that might be used to hide important data. He then moved around the room, snapping photos of each wall and area of the office until every square inch was captured. His work complete, he grabbed his lock hacking device and sheaf of papers and exited toward the elevator as if nothing interesting were happening. *Too easy*, he thought.

Once in the car, he reached under the passenger seat and pulled out his Agency field laptop, booted up and accessed the remote server. The bug was already connected. He set it to upload all documents, presentations, spreadsheets and similar files, along with Martin's browser history and bookmarks from the hard drive. Any future changes to the current files and history would be uploaded automatically. Once Stone got back to Paris, he would parse the upload and narrow it down using a proprietary Agency program that automatically searches for coded messages and several other things based on criteria he would select. It could also decrypt most files, though the amount of time required to do that sometimes made it a warrantless effort.

Turning out of the lot, his mind moved to the next task and his mood soured. Lauren had instructed him to drive to Hamburg and get everything he could on Rolf Haussmann, the owner of the BMW X5 that was parked down the street from the house in Marseille. By all accounts he was dead, having perished in a huge fire where he worked at Vitale, an industrial chemical company. But there was something shockingly odd that came up as they ran his name through their various databases, something that made it an immediate necessity to follow up. Haussmann's name was associated with a report within DARPA that was shared with the Agency. Stone shook his head at the incredulity of it for the hundredth time. Apparently, this guy provided DARPA with the method for processing Hemoxin after working for IABG. He was the inventor. It wasn't developed by DARPA at all. Instead, it was an international black-market acquisition. There could be no coincidence that Haussmann was in the vicinity of the Marseille meeting, and it was highly likely that Sharif and Martin's cell were at some stage of weaponizing the gas and preparing to deploy it.

Of course, the entire team scrambled on the news to get as much information as possible. Lauren pitched the possibility that they might have enough to bring DGSI into the loop, but Dittrich cautioned against it until they were able to somehow verify Haussmann had actually transferred the gas to the cell. His death could have preempted the exchange. Dittrich also fired Thomas for never running Hausmann's plate in an expletive-laden tirade, then reversed course almost immediately as there was no one qualified to replace him in short order.

They were flying in senior directors from IARPA and another from DARPA who was involved in the purchase. They'd be briefed on every aspect of the chemical properties of the gas, how to detect it, and how it could be defended against or rendered inert. Another cable was sent out to U.S. embassies in Europe clarifying the probable nature of the threat. Their embassies and military installations were placed on high alert and security was tightening everywhere. They still assumed that U.S. Embassy Paris was the most likely target and that their Fourth of July celebration was the terrorists' most likely candidate for mass

American casualties. The U.S. consulates and posts in France had no comparable Fourth of July plans, not on that scale. The only other event of considerable size was in Berlin. They were expecting over two thousand at the Paris celebration.

Stone had read the security announcement, released this morning. The Independence Day party was to be much more controlled than originally planned with extra marine guards assigned and metal detectors in use. Only clear bags would be allowed inside, and everyone would be searched. It was Stone's opinion that with these added measures, if the terrorists were planning to attack inside the embassy gates they would have to do so by force. The standard chemical threat detectors were already in place, but until they knew more about its composition the SCALPEL team had to assume they were worthless against Hemoxin. And without more details, without confirmation of an actual impending threat they couldn't cancel the celebration. Doing so could risk exposure of EXCISE, and it might tip off the cell. They'd immediately halt all preparation for their attack and replan for later, or they would run. Either situation would make it much more difficult if not impossible for them to be caught or killed. Both Martin and Sharif would immediately become overly cautious, destroy any evidence and cease all communication. Stone would have to proceed with *extreme* care from this point forward to avoid upsetting the applecart.

It was an unimaginable irony that the cell planned to use the very weapon Stone came so close to using on them first in the Marseille operation. The perfect scenario would be that he was still able to do that—the opportunity to open up George Washington's or Charles de Gaulle's head back in his apartment, take out one of the puffers and use it to execute Sharif and Martin and the others in one fell swoop. *The one in Washington's head of course, not de Gaulle's,* he mused.

They would realize in their final, waning seconds that their own jihadist tool of destruction had been used against them. Shortly thereafter, they'll be even more unhappy to find the 72 virgins they'd been promised are nowhere to be found. Stone had read that this passage in the Quran doesn't mention that number, or any number, or even virgins. One acknowledged interpretation states that jihadist martyrs would receive 'raisins' in heaven. *As false martyrs, they won't even get the raisins.* A crowning example of karmic justice.

CHAPTER TWENTY-EIGHT

"Something is worrying you," Père Aubertin observed.

They chose to take class outside, as it was such a beautiful day. They were seated on a bench along voie des Sculpteurs, each drinking a Coca Cola and facing the tree-shaded courtyard that stretched from the Grande Arche at La Défence to the Esplanade Métro Station. Beneath the trees in front of them four older French men were playing a game of pétanque.

Dolan was caught off guard; it was a statement rarely directed at him over the years. "Is it that obvious?" He smiled at Aubertin. In the short time they'd known each other, they'd developed a bond. Friendship was probably too strong a word; there was an old-world recognition of respect for seniors that the elder generation in France still observed, and Dolan always did his best to honor it.

"Well, you seem tired. And as a rule, you don't seem to smile much, but you do smile. I haven't seen one from you in a while. If I had to guess, I would say you are dealing with an issue or problem, maybe one that is difficult to resolve. If I am intruding, please tell me. But if I can be of help, tell me that too."

Dolan stared at the Frenchmen, so serious about their game. It was much like curling, except with steel boules in place of curling stones. There was one ball made of wood, called the *cochonnet*, which was the target ball. And it was played on a hard dirt surface, instead of ice. Without a broom of course. *I guess it's not so much like curling, in reality…*

"Michael?"

Dolan broke out of his reverie with a wry face, turning his attention to Father Aubertin. "I have history here. In Paris. Some of it…a lot of it was good. But some of it was bad."

"Aahh," he said, almost under his breath. Aubertin's deep-set eyes searched inside his for a moment, then he looked toward the trees and continued. "And so, years later you find yourself here, where on any given day the tune of *La Vie en Rose*, the site of the Tuilleries Gardens, or even the smell of baguettes from the boulangerie can be the thing that dredges up painful memories."

Dolan, not necessarily seeking guidance, said nothing.

"You know, and I'm not insinuating that you haven't already tried this, but I've found that it helps to treat time as it is—a continuum. That is to say, there is no such thing as the past. And likewise, no such thing as the future. 'Past' and 'future' are just monikers for concepts invented by man to simplify the processes and order of life. The truth is, time takes place continuously in the present. It helps to envision the creation of a painting. The only action, ever, is in the strokes. Once the tincture is laid down, it dries and there it is, the color, the shape. But do you see the paintbrush anymore? Well, it is in your hand of course at a different place, changing pigments, making new shapes, building on what's already there. If time were not a continuum, we'd be able to revisit the past, or to see into the future. To undo the stroke, clean the slate. Or to observe the finished painting when we are just halfway through with it. But we cannot, can we? There is only now. Things we have done and said and experienced, or things that have been said and done to us, those are dry. They are recorded. Facsimiles of a bygone present. It's data, more or less. What we do with that data, with that information, has impact on how we feel and what we choose to do in the now."

Dolan was beginning to get interested in what he was saying.

Aubertin went on. "We can choose to use that information in ways that help us make the right decisions. A clichéd summary would be that we can learn from our mistakes and from our successes to ensure we remain continually happy and content, and to help others do the same.

As a man of God, in my younger years I was certain I would never have any need of this area of thought. In fact, I never bothered with this intellection at all because I already understood what God wanted of me. I knew what my role was in life. But even with the sacrament of reconciliation, with penance, I found I was haunted by certain things recorded long ago. It seemed they should remain dormant. But to me, they did not. I would say that most people don't worry about things like this, but I was not like most people. You are not either, I believe. So, I understood full well that I needed to learn acceptance. That I could not change the past, that I should study and learn from it, but I lacked a simple mental paradigm in which I could arrange it all. To reconcile everything. Time, structured and rational without all the complexity of a philosophy or a grand equation. Once I was able to figure this out, I was free. And it was so uncomplicated! I quite literally became a different man. A better man. I am not saying this was any easy thing to do, no no. Saying that something is simple doesn't mean it is also effortless. It took thought, prayer, and action. What those actions are for you, I cannot say. It will come to you. But it takes practice. It's an art, really. Once you get it, once you understand, the past becomes the dry, finished quantum of a composition for your regard and analysis, and the present is empty canvas. The palette is in one hand, the brush in your other. From there, the future is as much an unknown masterpiece as your mind, imagination, and conduct can fashion."

It was pretty deep. But straightforward as well. These were things Dolan appreciated about the man, that he was intellectual but also wise; that he was well-spoken and at the same time, unassuming. Genuine and kind.

Sure that he'd spotted a flaw in Aubertin's counsel, however, Dolan jokingly attempted to poke a hole in it. "But one could always just paint over what's already there."

Aubertin observed him warmly. "Yes, of course. But the original paint remains underneath, does it not?"

◆

Dolan purchased a portable charger for his phone, then spent much of that evening trying to work out the most logical way to proceed. If Stone or Lauren were tracking his movements (and worse, his conversations) using his mobile, he had to decide how that affected his role in Excise. He understood it, but it wasn't right. He had to eliminate unknowns, level the playing field. Reduce or remove any catalysts for anxiety. He needed to plan when to turn it off or simply leave it in the hotel. He could always put it in airplane mode. He needed to handle it in a way that wouldn't raise suspicion. For this meeting, he decided to leave it behind.

Anxiety was an emotion he wasn't used to dealing with and that left him concerned about how it might affect his performance. The bottom line was he needed to purge or at least mitigate it significantly. That meant being more in control. The phone was part of that. It was true that the issues surrounding Claire, Anne, and Sharif still left him unsettled, but he concluded these were lesser worries. He was sure the team hadn't told him everything he needed to know. Better understanding the facts surrounding the AMA, Lefebvre, and the French and U.S. governments would make a significant impact. Creating knowns from all the unknowns that were continually dominating his thinking. It was time to pay the DRM and David Crowe a visit.

Sporting a slim-fit navy suit and his oversized FEPF lapel pin he opened the door and stepped into the office.

"Demeri, good afternoon. How are you today?"

She put down a file she was reading and beamed. "Mister Dolan, how nice to see you! Do you have a meeting with the General?"

"No, I'm here to see Mr. Crowe. Is he in?" Dolan had come unannounced. He felt it was better if Crowe didn't have any time to mull over what he was about to ask him to do.

"Yes, I believe he is. You just can't wait to get started, can you?" She winked at him. "You can go right in of course."

"Thank you Demeri."

He walked the long way around the connected, modular cubicles, to the left in order to avoid General Barre's office window. David was there, hunched over his keyboard and tapping away. He looked up as Dolan stopped in the entrance to his cubicle.

"Oh, hey Michael, I didn't know you'd be coming in today. Good to see you." He motioned behind him while swinging around to face the empty chair. Dolan sat down.

"That's because I wasn't planning on coming in. It was sort of a last-minute thing."

Crowe settled back into his seat. "Well, what can I do you for?"

Dolan rested his forearms on his thighs, leaning in a little and lowering his voice just enough to let him know he didn't want anyone else to hear their conversation. "I have a favor to ask. And I'm not sure there's any protocol or precedent for it. But it's important and to be honest, this is the ideal place to get what I need."

Crowe looked confused. "OK. Well why don't you just tell me what you need then. Hopefully, I can help."

"I need information. And I can't tell you why. Further, I must insist you don't ask me any questions about why I need the information, or what I will do with it. Lastly, you can't tell anyone about this conversation nor confirm that it took place."

Crowe's facial expression shifted slowly from confusion to guarded suspicion as Dolan spoke. "OK…How about I agree to all of that on the condition that I may not be able to give you what you are asking for?"

"That's fair. You may or not be familiar with a terrorist group called the al-Mulathamun Army, the AMA. They are an Algerian offshoot of the al-Mulathamun Battalion, which in turn was once part of al-Qa'ida in the Islamic Maghreb." Crowe was nodding his head in recognition. "The main financier and defacto leader of the AMA is a man named Hakeem Lefebvre who is in hiding in Algeria. He has an estranged son who lives here in Paris. His name is Sharif Lefebvre. What I need to find out is whether French intelligence has reported at all on Sharif and whether he might be involved in his father's terrorist organization. Is this something you might be able to package up as a request to the DRM for release to the U.S.?"

Crowe's eyes were wide open at this point. "Wow. OK, so I've gotten requests from a couple of U.S. agencies for information related to the AMA, but nothing specific to this Lefebvre guy, or Rashik…"

"Sharif."

"…Sharif. Right. But you must understand, this isn't how it works. A request must be generated from a U.S. intelligence office or agency, and that is what I use as the basis for a request. Yes, part of the job is to analyze current geopolitical situations and conflict zones, and to make recommendations for release of certain types of classified information, but those recommendations usually go out to analysts in the intel community first so they can weigh in on their value or usefulness. Only after the recommendation has been vetted would I take it to the team, or to the DRM."

Crowe paused, shifting a bit in his seat, waiting to see if there were any questions to this point. Noting Dolan's silence, he continued. "So, that's only the beginning of the process. The DRM still must review the request to determine if it has merit. If it does, they hand it off to analysts who scour their intelligence systems to see if they can find a match or matches. Overly sensitive hits are discarded straight away. If there's something that looks promising, they'll submit it to their foreign disclosure office whose job is to determine if it's releasable, what parts to redact, and so forth. Finally, it must be approved. Only after that do I get it. And about half the time, I get nothing at all. Chances are improved if I execute the request on a quid pro quo basis. So, I get something that is related to my request released from the U.S. agency for disclosure to France, or to Five Eyes Plus France, and attach it with my DRM paperwork. That takes even longer, as you can imagine, but the success rate goes up significantly. The whole process is similar if requesting information from the group, FEPF, and yes that takes even *longer*."

Dolan remained stoically quiet as Crowe laid it out, but the wheels were turning. "This would be a request just for the DRM, from France. Isn't there some kind of escalation or high-priority status you can use to speed it up? I would imagine that if, for instance, the requested information had the potential to save lives or to prevent armed conflict, they'd skip a lot of the red tape and get it to you quickly."

"Yes of course. It's not used very often. The last time was immediately after the November 2015 attacks right here in Paris. They killed 131 that day and there was a barrage of requests, mostly outgoing from the DRM, but some from the U.S. as well, and everything was shotgunned and approved overnight. But…" he looked at Dolan seriously "if I don't know what this is for, there's no way I can justify it. Seriously, how can you come in here with this kind of request when you aren't technically part of the team yet and insist I can't ask you about the source or reason? As far as I know, you are just a language school student right now. You shouldn't have any reason to be asking this of me."

Dolan smiled understandingly, and realized Crowe wasn't going to go along with it unless he gave him something. He purposefully let out a guarded sigh of surrender. "That is all true. So, let me give you some background then. Sharif Lefebvre is an old friend of mine. We both went to the Sorbonne several years ago and we were close. I left Paris, we lost touch over the years, and now I'm back in town. Of course, I've linked back up with him and we've kinda picked up where we left off. Only, he's told me certain things, these things about his father and the AMA, and it doesn't feel right. I am worried about him, and about the possibility that he may no longer be estranged from his father. That he might actually be involved. If this is the case, of course I need to distance myself from him.

"But like I said, he is a close friend. I am not going to ask him directly about my suspicions of course. Coming to you is the best course of action, in my opinion. And if he is actively engaged with the

AMA, I have no problem taking what I know directly to the French authorities. But I can't do that without knowing for sure, and if there's nothing on him in that regard, I'll know my suspicions were likely false and our friendship won't be affected." Now Dolan shifted in his seat, to get more comfortable and to pause long enough so he could think of how best to put out the bait and get Crowe to bite.

"When I was in Afghanistan, there was a lot of talk about the AMA by the French there, I guess a bunch of them got wiped out in some attack outside Algiers. They wouldn't say much to me about it, and an intel guy let me know they were instructed not to discuss anything with the U.S. My guess back then was that we may have had something to do with the attack and pissed off the French government. As a probable result, they've been tight-lipped about the AMA ever since. So, here's what I propose. Send an all-agency request to the U.S. intelligence community for anything releasable to France regarding the AMA, Lefebvre, and his son Sharif here in Paris. To give the DRM a reason to open up. Make it clear in your analysis the French will probably release key AMA intel to the U.S. if what we give them is good enough. Then let's see what happens.

"I have a lot of former pilot friends who now fly for the airlines. You said you were going to interview with NetJets. If you are willing to do this for me, I'll get in touch with a good friend of mine who's quite senior at NetJets and maybe make it a little easier to get you on board with them. What do you think?"

Crowe took off his glasses and looked at the floor as he thought about what Dolan had just said. He raised his head after a moment with an odd look, appearing caught halfway between puzzlement and gratitude. He put his glasses back on and grabbed a pencil and notepad from his desk. "OK. First, give me their names again."

Dolan spelled them out for him.

"Thanks." He tossed the notepad back on the desk and kept the pencil, twirling it between his thumb and index finger. "This is what I think. It is unlikely this will get anywhere while I am still on the job. So essentially, you'll be getting your own request after you've taken over. I don't see that as an issue. As far as the reason for the request, well, obviously I'm not going to use the one you've given me. I'll come up with something. Listen—I do appreciate the connection. While this job in Paris has been the highlight of my career so far, in the back of my mind I've always wanted to be an airline pilot. It means a lot to me." He held out his hand to shake Dolan's.

"David, it's nothing. I wouldn't recommend you if I didn't think you were a high-caliber person and a great fit for the company." He stood up and moved to the cubicle entryway. "One last item. If DRM releases anything, I would like to see it before it's sent to the U.S. I'll need some time to extricate myself in the event there's any dirt on Sharif. I don't want to be caught up in any crossfire. You have my number; call me the second you hear anything."

Crowe waved at him. "I will, don't worry. But like I said, these things don't happen quickly."

Dolan nodded, waved back and left. *Ah, David Crowe. Something tells me you will be surprised.*

CHAPTER TWENTY-NINE

"OK team, bring me up to speed." Dittrich was in a good mood, and it showed as he smiled at the live images of Lauren and Stone on his secure Intelink console. Things were starting to come together.

Lauren began. "Sir, first an update on Salmah Lefebvre. We've spent a lot of time digging and we are confident she has no witting part in any of this. She's in the latter stages of Alzheimer's and has a live-in nurse. We found evidence that a healthcare power of attorney does exist, and yes, Sharif is the legal agent, but it has nothing to do with her financial accounts or property. And we still have no idea why Martin visited her house that night after the Marseille op.

"Overall, I think we are close to the point where we can contact DGSI and hand this off. Until now, we haven't had enough solid evidence that a real threat exists. Now that we believe we know what the weapon is, and that the weapon is indiscriminate, we feel the French Government may have no choice but to work with us. They wouldn't think of pushing back and risking the lives of French citizens because of a tense working relationship. All that being said, I believe there are four things we need to wait on before pulling the trigger. First, Stone's analysis of Martin's work computer data. Second, Dolan's dinner with Sharif on July first. Third, the existence of and our possession of Hemox is Top-Secret. We need to come up with an innovative way of telling them what it is and why we know the cell has it without admitting we have it ourselves. Though we've kept details about the gas from Dolan due to the obvious sensitivities, he does know that the weapon *could* be gaseous. And fourth, we need a couple of days for us to process what Stone found on Haussmann, the inventor of the gas who allegedly died in a fire at Vitale in Hamburg a few weeks back. He's joining us from Berlin."

"Hello sir," said Stone.

"Tony, good to see you. I hope you're not making yourself too visible there in Deutschland. Be careful, you're out of your diplomatic jurisdiction—the BND would be all over you in a second."

"Thanks, good to see you as well. Not to worry, I'm laying low at the safehouse and I'm leaving tomorrow. I'll be heading back to Metz to tail Martin and finish analyzing his desktop, then back to Paris for my meeting with Dolan after his dinner with Sharif. In the meantime, I have some interesting things to report on Haussmann."

"OK, let's hear it," quipped Dittrich.

"I've found evidence that indicates Haussmann may have staged his death. I mean, how unfortunate would it be for him to cash in on the deal of a lifetime, only to die in a fire at work a short time later? Clearly, he was aware that he'd be found out eventually, no matter what precautions he took. And he did take precautions. I searched his home, and it was squeaky clean. No computer or phone in the house; he probably brought those to Vitale and let them burn in the fire. But I did find something interesting, a receipt for an automobile oil change. He just left it in his wastebasket." Stone paused to see if either of them understood where he was going.

Lauren bit. "Let me guess, the oil change was not for a late model BMW X5."

"Exactly. It was for a 2006 Audi sedan with Polish plates, three days before the fire. Haussmann has only the BMW registered to his name and the Polish plates are stolen. Mike is helping me with the research. We're combing through the German traffic camera database now to see if we can get any hits. My guess is he'll be careful to avoid risking a traffic violation, so we don't expect to find anything there. Once we're through with Germany we'll tackle the bordering countries."

Dittrich interrupted. "Mike Collier? Tell him I said hello. We need to catch up on a few things."

"Yeah, Collier, my old mentor who almost got us killed in Algiers. I'll tell him. As an aside, I've only told him what I needed and not why, though he's already voiced his assumption that Haussmann is somehow connected with the three Algerians. Team Berlin is doing everything they can to shed light on where *they* might be as well. But no one is being too nosey. As a former SCALPEL operative Mike knows what we do obviously, and why. He gets it. We both suspect that Haussmann's not going to fly commercially anywhere, at least not until he's out of Germany. If I were him, I'd get as far away from Europe as possible before using *any* public transportation. We have good images of him and are checking facial recognition systems throughout the European Union. If he enters a major airport, we should know quickly. Of course, we're monitoring his financial accounts to see if there is any activity. Nothing so far. He left about six thousand euros in his bank account, and there were no odd transactions leading up to the day of the fire. He wouldn't have faked his death without first creating a false identity, so we're not wasting too much time tracing his name or driver's license. The BND is working with us on both efforts. I'll let you know as soon as I hear anything of significance."

"Good work Tony. Tell Mike to let me know directly if there's anything I can do to help. If you locate the Algerians, let the BND run point but make sure someone from the embassy is right there with them. As for Haussmann, wherever he is we'll rendition him back here for interrogation. No one will miss him since he's already dead, and it'll help us justify keeping the Annapolis safehouse in play. Did you bring Washington and De Gaulle with you?"

"Yes sir, they are tucked away at the safehouse."

"Good. Switching gears—Lauren, you mentioned a while back you'd be doing some handholding and calling Dolan now and then. Have you been doing that?"

Lauren realized she hadn't. Another oversight? "No, I have not. To be honest, Dolan has exceeded my expectations so far, and in my estimation Tony's meetings with him have been sufficient in that regard. No need to add risk where it's not needed, I think." Inside, she felt as if she'd somehow let Dolan down. But what she had just said was correct. Dolan *has* been able to take care of himself, and Tony seemed to be giving him what he needs.

"OK. Tony, you agree?"

"Yes, I agree. He's done exceptionally well and I'm confident he'll get something useful out of this dinner with Sharif on Monday." *Wink wink.*

Dittrich went silent for a few seconds, putting his thoughts together. "Alright, let's think about the timeline. We don't know when the attack will happen, but we suspect now it will be on the fourth. Let's drive to that. If it turns out to be the fourteenth, then we'll be well-prepared. I want you to submit two satellite tasking requests with the NRO, one each for Berlin and Paris that we can access at any time over the next week. I will approve it. Then make sure the Pit is surveillance-ready and that our usual techs are prepped and available.

"We must be ready to notify the correct authorities no later than the third. And by correct authorities, I mean the French DGSI, but let's stay open to the possibility the attack may happen somewhere else, or that there will be multiple attacks. We must be ready to recommend cancellation of public activities at all embassies, consulates, posts and military bases. Lauren—make sure those cables are drafted and ready to go out. That gives us four days. Four days Tony, to finish analysis on Martin's computer and get whatever you can get with surveillance. See what Dolan can get from Sharif on Monday and draft a threat description of the Hemox gas for the French with a credible explanation of how we came to know about it. Then, to collect Haussmann and extract everything we can out of him. Though I would not consider that a priority at this point. Finally, we have nothing new on these three Algerians who flew into Berlin ten days ago. Stone, I expect you to analyze Martin's hard drive data closely with that point in mind. Dolan should know about the Algerians before the dinner. Did we brief him on the Algerians?"

Lauren felt as if she were making mistake after mistake. First Haussmann's license plate, not calling Dolan to ease him into his role, and now this. She should have already told Tony to brief him. "Not yet sir. Tony had a meeting scheduled with him for tomorrow, but they met earlier this week instead, on Tuesday. Tony has been on the road. Maybe this is a good opportunity for me to touch base with..."

"Not necessary, Lauren, I got this," interrupted Tony. "He's used to working with me now, and we have our protocols worked out. Better to let me do it."

"Um, ok that's fine Tony," she replied hesitantly.

Dittrich was irritated at the banter. "OK well it doesn't matter to me who does it, just get it done. All in all, a short timeline for a team this small to get everything accomplished. You'll have to work through the weekend obviously, collaborate closely with the BND, prep the safehouse in Annapolis and notify our French translator he's on call round the clock and until further notice. And if I were you, I'd be listening in live to Dolan's dinner with Sharif. Keep me apprised. Anything else?"

"No sir. Dolan should have the phone with him at Sharif's and we'll have the translator with us to get real-time feedback." responded Lauren.

I'll be listening in as well this time, Stone quipped to himself.

"Great. The satellite tasking will be a big deal, I may have to kick it up to the director. Submit the request today. Thanks guys." Dittrich hung up.

He didn't tell us to do good things, thought Lauren. It almost made sense. She was beginning to feel they may have to do some *bad* things between now and the Fourth of July.

CHAPTER THIRTY

Dolan rang the doorbell at Sharif's apartment as he glanced down the hallway in each direction. He was ever-so-slightly nervous. Stone had sent him a secure text just thirty minutes earlier with information about three Algerians who flew into Berlin recently. The team believed they were part of the terror plot. Things were beginning to go down, and he was in the thick of it. His work tonight could be instrumental in undermining their efforts. His first *real* attempt at clandestine work. After a moment, Sharif opened the door and beckoned him in with a broad smile.

"Michael my friend, welcome to my home!" Sharif held one arm out in a sweeping motion as they moved inside, as if to say *look at all this…*

His apartment was huge and luxurious. Nothing Dolan hadn't expected. It was an open floorplan on the top floor of the fifteen-story building. The main living area had expansive floor-to-ceiling windows on the northeastern wall. They provided a glorious view of the spires of Sainte-Chappelle, the blackened towers of Notre Dame, and the city beyond.

"Wow, Sharif. This is amazing. And the view!" Dolan walked to the windows.

"Wait until it gets dark. I've been lucky my friend! Let me get you a drink."

"Well first, I brought this." Dolan handed him a stylish rustic gift bag made of burlap. The bag cost almost as much as the wine, a moderately expensive California Pinot Noir.

Sharif pulled the bottle out and read the label carefully. "Ah, California. This is nice, thank you. You know, a lot has been said about the equality of California wines with the French vintages. But you must know, nothing is ever as good as the original. Your grapes have our roots, but the California vines, well, who knows what they are. They are close, don't get me wrong. Anyway, this is nice." He looked again at the label, then walked over to an elaborate wooden bar complete with a diverse selection of spirits displayed on backlit mahogany shelves, a custom built-in refrigerator, sinks, and everything else a bar might need. He opened the bottle and poured two thin-rimmed glasses, handing one to Dolan.

"To the future," Sharif toasted.

"To the future." Dolan clinked his glass to Sharif's and they both took a sip. Dolan swirled the wine a bit with his tongue, relishing the hints of cherry and truffles, savory sweet. Remembering all the pertinent details from his visit to Musée du Vin.

They moved back to the windows. "Such a shame about Notre Dame," said Dolan.

Sharif frowned. "Yes, decidedly so. I didn't agree with it. I don't know why anyone would want to destroy such a historic monument to God."

Dolan was taken aback. "Agree with it? Do you mean, it didn't agree with you? Anyway, I'm fairly sure they believe it was an accident. From some faulty wiring or something."

"Yes. I meant it didn't agree with me—it made me sick. And you're right it was probably an accident, but someone should be held responsible. Faulty wiring or not, these things happen when someone isn't doing their job well enough. I had to stand here in my living room and watch her burn. I was very angry." Sharif abruptly caught his arm. "Come on, let me show you the place, then you can help me set the table. Everything is about ready."

He gave Dolan a tour of the flat with its two bedrooms and a master bath nearly as big as the bedroom itself. The cedar sauna had room for six as did the circular, zero-entry whirlpool tub. Sharif took him through French doors off the side of the living room and opposite the bar that opened into an expansive study. Dolan made mental notes of everything in the room before Sharif quickly whisked him away to the kitchen. White granite countertops, a stainless commercial-size refrigerator and dual ovens. The cupboards were mahogany as well. Everything was top of the line, yet fashionably understated. Sharif had always had an impeccable sense of taste.

Dolan helped him set the table and bring the dishes of food. He'd prepared a soup called chorba, made with chickpeas and chicken. There were lamb and rabbit dishes with couscous and Shakshouka—a dish of eggs poached in tomato sauce and flavored with chili, garlic and paprika. He'd also baked his own khubz at-tajin flatbread. *Quite a feast,* Dolan observed.

As they were eating the conversation wandered. Sharif asked more questions about his combat experiences in Afghanistan. These questions were different than their last discussion about it, however. What it was like and how he felt about killing other soldiers. To some, the answers to questions like that would be difficult. But not to Dolan. It was a relatively impersonal task taking out the bad guy with the AC-130 Spectre gunship. They were flying thousands of feet above the target. Dolan never saw any blood. No bodies. Just the glowing figures and trucks and houses on his screen. Yes, he flew the plane into position and pulled the trigger, but it was the fire control officer and gunner doing the real aiming. He was defending freedom, removing a pestilence. It was legal, easy to justify and easy to do. Dolan wondered if these questions were Sharif's way of trying to assess how he was going to feel after his attack went down. *If he was even involved.* What did they have on him yet, other than him being the son of Hakim Lefebvre? *Time to change the direction of the conversation.*

"When's the last time you heard from your dad?" asked Dolan.

Sharif kept eating, looking at his food as if the question didn't bother him. "I haven't heard from him in nine years. I know I didn't talk much about him when we were at the Sorbonne, but that's because I was angry back then, if you remember. My mother became sick, and he just turned his back on us. He hasn't been a part of her life and he hasn't been a part of mine. In any case his political views have made him an outcast. He'd never be able to come back to France even if he wanted to." He wiped his mouth with a napkin and looked at Dolan dead-on. "I can forgive him for leaving me. But not for leaving her. I'm still angry, but I've learned to deal with it. To channel it. I'm close to acceptance. I'm getting some more wine."

Dolan thought Sharif might come to tears just then, but he didn't. No one Dolan knew was as stoic as he, but Sharif had always made a good effort at it. They'd already finished the Pinot Noir and a second bottle from the bar. He opened another red, a Malbec from Bordeaux. Then they talked about his mother and the progression of her Alzheimer's, how she barely recognized him now. He didn't know how much time she had left. The nurse he hired to live with her kept him abreast of her condition. It left him worried most days, as his work prevented him from moving there. She'd always said she would never leave Marseille, and he respects her wishes. He drove down to see her about once every other month and was planning to visit with her in the next few days.

Dolan tried to seize on the opportunity. "Is there anything I can help with? I can go with you if you want. They like me at Lingua Europa, I can take a couple days off."

Sharif answered without looking up from his plate. "No, thank you. It wouldn't be interesting for you, and I'm not sure there's much you could do."

"OK. Well, if you change your mind let me know."

They cleaned the table together. There were lots of leftovers, some of which Sharif packaged up for Dolan to take with him. Then they moved back to the living room where Sharif poured them some cognac.

"I don't know Sharif, we've already killed three bottles of wine," cautioned Dolan.

"Ridiculous!" said Sharif, holding the glass out. "If we can't drink here, we can't drink anywhere."

"OK, thanks, maybe one." They both took a sip.

"Martell Creation Grand Extra," he said while holding his snifter at eye level, swirling the rich brown liquid in his glass. "It is made from Ugni Blanc grapes, exceedingly rare. But it's not as expensive as you might think."

Dolan wasn't interested in the price. He was beginning to wonder if he'd have an opportunity to plant the bug. Sharif hadn't left his sight. "I guess you aren't working tomorrow? All I have to do is talk to an old French priest for a few hours. You have to run an empire."

"Like I said, ridiculous. No one will blink an eye if I show up a little late, and besides, I have something for you that will help in the morning." Then he looked suddenly surprised, as if he'd had a small epiphany. "Actually, it will help tonight too." He took a quick sip and set his drink down on the coffee table as Dolan sat on the couch. Sharif went back behind the bar, disappearing for a moment as he ducked down to get something from underneath. It was an ornate wooden box with a mirrored glass top. He brought it over with a guilty smile, sitting opposite Dolan and opening it. He removed a small pestle, a crystal dish with matching lid, a thin aluminum tube and a razor blade. He set them down on the coffee table and looked at Dolan seriously.

"We've been working on a new antidepressant at Francopharma. It's revolutionary, really. If you are familiar with bupropion, this is something similar."

Dolan watched as Sharif removed the lid from the crystal dish and removed several white tablets. "Are you talking about Wellbutrin? Isn't it a drug to help people quit smoking?"

"Exactly. Wellbutrin is one of the brands, and you may have heard of Chantix or Zyban." Sharif put the jar back in the box and closed it. He placed the pills on the mirrored top and used the pestle to grind them into a powder. "But it is a stimulant and is also used as an antidepressant. We developed a drug that is molecularly close to bupropion, but it is more effective in preventing depression and it is safer." He laid the pestle down and used the razor blade to refine the powder. "It's gone through most of the testing, and we are maybe a year out from getting it approved for the market. As it turns out, if you take it the right way the effects are similar to cocaine. We haven't yet formulated the extended-release version, which would negate that completely. We are thinking about calling it Nupropion."

Sharif then used the razor to form the powder into four lines. He seemed engrossed in the effort, not saying anything or bothering to look at him. Maybe because he was afraid to hear Dolan's opinion on doing drugs on a Monday evening just prior to starting a new job with the U.S. government. Dolan's nervousness had disappeared before they started dinner but now it returned, and in no small way. "Sharif, I'm going to use the restroom."

Sharif looked up and grinned. "Go for it."

Dolan made his way across the room and down the hall to the bathroom. He closed the door and took his iPhone from his pocket, noting that the battery was down about twenty percent since he left the Flambeau. They had to be listening in. Could they see through the camera too? No time to get paranoid. The alcohol had helped initially, but now he was losing his edge. They'd killed three bottles of wine. And the cognac. *Drugs???* Dolan was still in control of his faculties, but he drank too much. He was putting the mission at risk. He still had to get into Sharif's study and plant the bug. The right moment hadn't presented itself yet, but Sharif had to use the restroom soon. He would do it then. The right amount of stimulant would heighten his mental alertness, improve his effectiveness.

He'd absolutely have to turn off his phone first. *Shit,* he thought. *They are certain to figure out a way to ask me about it without admitting they've been spying on me.* He could always tell them the battery was low, and he wanted to make sure there was enough juice left to call them if needed. *It could also be a good test of my theory…* Except that it was more than just a theory. He was sure of it. He turned it off and put it back in his pocket. Then he used the commode, washed his hands and went back to the living room.

Sharif was waiting for him, four lines neatly arranged on the small box.

"Will this drug show up on a toxicology screen?" asked Dolan.

Sharif's head went back as he laughed, clearly intoxicated. "Oh Michael, you are worried about getting into trouble. The answer is no, because screens are designed to look for certain things, and this certain thing doesn't exist yet, as far as the world knows. Now, it might show up on a toxicology *report*, depending on how extensive it is, but this type of test is usually only done to determine the cause of, or factors contributing to death. Unless you plan on dying soon, I wouldn't worry about it."

"You never had a thing for drugs before, though. How long have you been doing it?"

"No need to worry, it's just recreational. And like I said, it's very safe. At the right moment it is worth its weight in gold. It's helped me numerous times. Making impossible deadlines, working all-nighters. Why not? Anyway, people change Michael. I've changed. I have more important things to worry about now, responsibilities. Goals. These things only happen with change. You must know that."

Dolan did know that. "In case you were wondering Sharif, no, I've never done this sort of thing before. In fact, I've never taken any drugs in my life aside from prescriptions. But I'm open to it." That was it. It was decided, and he couldn't take it back. He was going to do it. He had to.

Sharif chuckled. "I was assuming you hadn't. *Tenez bon la rampe!*"

He'd been studying French idiomatic expressions recently with Père Aubertin. *Hold on to your hat!* And then they did it. Dolan had never felt anything like it before in his life. An incredible surge of euphoria came over him, a rewarding sensation so intense it eclipsed even how he felt crossing the finish line of his first marathon. All nervousness, any anxiety he had was long gone. He was as confident as he had ever felt, as if he could solve multiple complex math theorems in his head while having a deep conversation. *It was the right thing to do.*

Sharif looked as if he was having the same experience, laughing, talking very fast about how inept some of the other executives were at work. Dolan heard every word but none of it was important. And then the moment came.

"Brother, I am visiting the little boy's room. Don't go anywhere."

As soon as he turned the corner out of the room Dolan noted the second hand on his watch, sprang from the couch and went directly to Sharif's study. Not needing to bother with taking pictures, he left the phone off. He would memorize anything that looked important or out of place. *Anything about the AMA or jihad, fatwahs or bombs or gas or an attack. Anything about the United States, or embassies, or the three Algerians or Algeria in general, anything about Berlin.* Recalling where everything was from before, he went directly to the desk, ignored the laptop and took mental snapshots of all the papers on his desk, quickly leafing through them and then he moved into the drawers. He found and quickly memorized the files that looked important, mostly tax and financial papers. When he was done, he went to the large bookcase on the opposite wall and quickly felt behind all the books, grasping for anything hidden. Not finding anything, he reached into his pocket for the bug and peeled the backing off while looking at his watch. Twenty-eight seconds. He affixed the bug to the underside of one of the shelves at knee-level, left the room and sat back down on the couch. *Forty seconds total. I might have done more. Fuck.*

As he waited for Sharif to return, he began to analyze what he'd seen. The financial and tax paperwork was probably nothing, though he wasn't surprised to learn that Sharif probably didn't make enough to support such a lavish lifestyle. One thing immediately caught his mind's eye, a sticky note stuck to the inside of the front face of the file drawer with an address written on it. Nothing else. Out of place, hidden. Potentially important.

His sense of accomplishment was almost too much to bear. As Sharif reentered the room Dolan was laughing to himself.

"What's so funny?"

Dolan laughed even harder at that. He *really* felt like sharing what he'd just done with *somebody*. But then, he realized he already had. Tony was undoubtedly somewhere nearby, waiting the last four and half hours for a connection once the bug was activated.

"Nothing, nothing. It's just that I haven't felt this good since…well, since we were all together. Back then."

The smile fell from Sharif's face. Dolan thought it strange. Just as quickly it came back, but muted. "The Fab Four. Yes, I miss those times. But it's in the past now. Let's not talk about Claire, OK?"

Dolan didn't know what to say. From the absolute pinnacle of elation just a few minutes earlier, a switch was flicked and now they were in this very weird place. Dolan's head was still swimming with surplus dopamine, yet his brain was suddenly telling him to feel bad. It wasn't working.

"Sharif, I wasn't going to, just…remembering, that's all."

"Yeah, I know. And with you seeing Anne now, it's just not a good subject."

Dolan had told him a few weeks back, but he'd been OK with it. Why the resentment now? What is going on? Was it Claire, or was it the thought of him dating Anne that was getting him down? It wasn't the first time they had mentioned Claire. Dolan didn't like this turn of conversation. He wanted his brain to go back to happy mode.

Then Dolan caught himself. Had he done his job tonight? Had he gotten Sharif to say anything revealing or useful? Dolan had planted the bug, but Sharif wouldn't even be here for the next few days since he was leaving to visit his mom. He knew that there would be things said tonight that professionals like Lauren, Thomas and Tony would be able to parse for useful information, things that weren't readily apparent to him. But had he asked the right questions? Did he get Sharif to slip up anywhere? The weirdest thing he said all night was his response to the mention of Notre Dame. But that had nothing to do with their mission. And bringing up Claire, that was strange. Again, nothing helpful. The timing of his trip to visit his mom might be something. Was he going to Marseille, or was it an alibi for what he'd really be doing in the next couple days? *No, I've done it right. I planted the bug, and I have a lot of data memorized, some of which could be useful.* And he wasn't qualified to judge the intelligence value of their conversations.

"Listen Sharif, I've had a great time tonight. But it's about midnight and I want to make sure we are both able to function tomorrow, at least somewhat. I'm going to head out."

Sharif smiled at him without speaking for a few seconds, as if evaluating whether to push him to stay. "OK my friend. It is getting late, and you are right. We both have things we are responsible for, things to get done. Here."

Sharif held out the small crystal jar, still nearly full of pills.

"What? No, I'm not going to take that. Anyway, you probably have more use for it than me."

"Rubbish, Michael. I get it for free. Anyway, as I said, it's the absolute best thing in the world for a hangover. You are going to wake up tomorrow and your head is going to feel like it's about to explode. Then you will take this, and you'll be right as rain. Believe me. Just take it."

It had worked well for him tonight. It might come in handy again. *I wonder if the bug is picking this up.* If so, he could explain it away.

"Fine, thanks Sharif." He took the jar and latched the lid. Then they hugged each other. Sharif grabbed the leftovers from the fridge, put them in a paper bag and handed it to Dolan as they walked to the door.

"Sharif, thank you so much for tonight. The food was amazing, and it was a lot of fun. Very grateful. And do let me know about Marseille, I'd be happy to go down with you if you change your mind. Just let me know."

Sharif looked at him wistfully. "I'll be fine Michael, thanks. I had a great time tonight too. Be well my friend."

Be well. No one says that unless they are saying goodbye. Really saying goodbye.

"Goodbye, Sharif."

CHAPTER THIRTY-ONE

He came to with a fire raging in his forehead. Thirsty. Dolan grabbed the bottle of mineral water on his nightstand and drank it dry, then tapped the stop button on his iPhone, cutting off the song just as it ended. *An rien peut arrêter moi konin la.* Nothing can stop me now. His affirmation. To go with the hangover, he was immediately confronted with an unreconcilable mix of guilt and success from the night's activities that left him wondering if he still had the right to call it an affirmation. *Holy shit, it's seven thirty.* If he hurried, he'd still be on time for his meeting with Stone.

He got out of bed quickly and the rage in his head exploded. He was off-balance and dizzy. He reached for his bottle of cognac and drank straight from the bottle. Maybe too much. He couldn't show up like this. He looked in the mirror and saw the bags under his eyes, then looked down and there it was, the small crystal jar next to the bag of leftovers. He had forgotten to put them in his minifridge. The smell of the food made him feel even worse. Without hesitating he unlatched the dish and took two of the pills, washing them down with a glass of water from the bathroom sink. The pain subsided after a few minutes and suddenly he was good to go. Like magic. Then he put the jar in a drawer and looked at his watch. Ten minutes to get presentable.

After a quick shower he got dressed, looked at his phone as he was walking to the door and realized he'd missed a protocol. He went back to the dresser and pulled out the top left drawer, setting it aside. He reached inside the opening and fumbled for the Ziplock bag taped to the support from inside and pulled it out. After inserting the dongle, he opened the chat app and saw two messages. The first from Tony. *Tried to reach you last night. Meeting still on in a.m. Sharif tore up his apartment after you left. Yelled a lot. Talk soon.* There was no reason for Stone to call Dolan last night. Sharif messing up his flat was something that could have waited for the meeting. It had to be because he shut his phone off. He checked his call log and there it was, Stone had called him three times. He'd slept right through it. No voicemail. Dolan was getting increasingly pissed off.

The second, unencrypted, was from Crowe. *You need to come by the office ASAP. Time is of the essence.*

Dolan's eyes went wide. *Could he have gotten what I asked for that quickly?* He should run by there right after meeting Stone. But that meeting could last a while—he had a lot of information to download. *Time is of the essence.* The information had an expiration date. Tony would have to come second. Perhaps he would confront Stone directly about the team surveilling him with his phone. He had enough on Stone to do it, between the bug and the Beretta. It would give him leverage.

Dolan sent Stone an encrypted text, saying he'd just woken up and was running an hour late. *Probably more than an hour. But he will wait, I'm certain of that.* He replaced the Ziplock and the drawer, then headed out.

Going through security at DRM Headquarters, Dolan took his iPhone out of his suit jacket pocket as usual and placed it on the conveyor belt. Then it hit him—if they are tracking him, he just gave away his real reason for being late to the meeting with Tony. Once on the other side he put the phone in airplane mode. The GPS receiver would still be doing its thing, but whatever software was sending his conversations, and perhaps his location to the EXCISE team wouldn't be working. They might know where he went, but he could come up with an excuse. And they wouldn't hear his conversation with Crowe.

At the FEPF office he waved and smiled at Demeri and proceeded to the left again to avoid General Barre. Crowe looked up from his desktop computer as he entered the cubicle.

"Just in time. I have maybe an hour before I must send what I have back to the U.S."

Dolan took the chair behind Crowe's and swung around. "So, let's hear it. Anything interesting?"

"Interesting doesn't begin to describe it. I mean, the reaction on both sides. The information itself, well, I don't know if it's going to be helpful to you. I'll let you read it, I printed out a hardcopy. But first, the reaction. I submitted the recommendation the way you asked, to the entire community. I got a response about five hours later from the Department of Homeland Security. It came from a high-level, considering the quid pro-content they attached for submission to the DRM. The message said there was an urgent need for information pertaining to the AMA, particularly to any intelligence that indicated possible activity in Europe and particularly in France. They attached a memorandum, classified secret and releasable to France that acknowledged U.S. involvement in a drone attack in Algeria on the AMA some years back—the same attack you mentioned in your last visit. The U.S. government was aware this was in violation of international law and that it had negative impact on the French government and French interests in the region. It contains an official apology from the Director of National Intelligence himself! There is a caveat though, that the memorandum remains sealed and classified and should only be released to…and then there is a list of specific French individuals and offices. It is strange to me that the response is coming from Homeland. In my opinion, it should be coming from the CIA based on what the DNI is apologizing for. Someone is trying very hard to keep certain facts buried. And the French will notice that too, but I don't think they'll care. This is a real coup for them."

Dolan maintained his composure, despite wanting him to get to the information he needed. "Wow, that is something, isn't it? And how did the DRM respond?"

"Well, this is where I almost lost control of the exchange. The DRM told me they were going to respond directly back to Homeland given the gravity of the information provided. But I contested that approach and cited our own Memorandum of Understanding that lays out the protocol specifically and is signed by both countries. So, they capitulated. Here is what they gave me." He handed Dolan a sheaf of papers.

Crowe began to summarize but Dolan cut him off. "Hold on, just let me scan these first." There were twenty-eight pages in all, entirely in French. Mainly intelligence reports from the DGSI, DGSE, and from the DRM itself. Some pages were highly redacted, others less so. Sharif was mentioned in only one of the reports, and only to the extent that he was Lefebvre's son, living in Paris, and was estranged. Nothing else. The same report also mentioned his mother Salmah, a French citizen who was also estranged. Lots of information about web 'chatter' that was potentially linked to AMA supporters and apologists throughout Europe. Then, the jackpot.

The final report in the stack was four pages long. And it was all about François Martin. Most of the content was obtained from the Direction Générale des Finances Publiques (DGFIP), the French equivalent of the IRS. It looked as if they suspected criminal activity outside their jurisdiction and subsequently looped in the DGSI. The DGFIP noted significant real estate purchases by the wine distribution company Château Group. Mainly in France, but some in other countries as well. The purchases raised a red flag when the money trail didn't all line up. Martin was identified as the leader of the investment effort, and they started looking into him. It turns out that a large chunk of money used in some of the acquisitions came from a numbered account in Geneva that belonged to none other than Salmah Lefebvre, and that Martin had obtained power of attorney as sole executor for the account. *Holy shit. This is why nothing on funding for the attack could be found on Sharif—it was Martin instead...* The DGSE was now involved, and the investigation was ongoing and sealed.

The last two pages was a list with locations and descriptions of the properties Château Group had invested in since the time of the financial discontinuity. Dolan read quickly and stopped abruptly, two-thirds of the way through the list. It was an address he knew. The same address that was penned on the sticky note hidden in Sharif's desk. In Potsdam, *just outside Berlin.*

Dolan looked up at Crowe. "I have to go. Now. Contrary to what you might think, this was very helpful."

Crowe was flustered. "But how does this help you with your friend Sharif? It doesn't necessarily clear him, and it doesn't indict him either. It's a nothing burger."

"I'll have to explain later, David. Let's just say there is other information I have, and this helps put a lot of context around it. I really do have to go. Thank you very much." Dolan handed the pages back to

Crowe. "Oh, and just to let you know, I've already contacted my buddy at NetJets. I'll forward you the email so you have his contact information. They are excited to hear from you."

Dolan turned and left as Crowe, still flustered, was left saying "Thank you Michael, see you again soon..." to an empty cubicle.

He quickly navigated out of the office, nodding on the way at the Australian intel officer who looked up and nodded back, probably expecting him to drop in for a chat. No time. On the Métro Dolan began putting all the pieces together in his mind, seeing linkages, drawing conclusions. Without a doubt, Sharif was involved. The note with the Potsdam address proved it. He had weaseled a way to keep the heat off himself by having Martin handle the money, and probably a lot of the planning as well. The three Algerians flew into Berlin, right next to Potsdam. The Potsdam address was not commercial, it was a house and the only German property on the list. It could be their base of operations and staging area.

Dolan checked his watch and remembered to take his phone out of airplane mode. No new calls or messages. Then he began to think about how the team was proceeding and what would probably be done next once he passed this new information to Stone. It was unclear. He couldn't even make an educated guess. But he had to take it to Stone. It was game-changing intelligence. Shouldn't he? Was there an alternative? He didn't trust any of them, and rightly so. They'd left him out of the loop on so many things. Heck, he just learned yesterday about the three Algerians, and they'd arrived in Germany several days earlier. If EXCISE had any intel on what type of weapon might be used, they hadn't told him. Why were they marginalizing him? Why were they spying on *him*? A new plan began to form in his mind. *Ordnung muss sein.* One that might just take down the terrorist cell faster, and in a manner that he could control. On *his* terms. He was being used by his own team, in a way he didn't fully understand and that troubled him. He shouldn't have to worry that he was being lied to, surveilled by his own people, or unknowingly put in harm's way by an irresponsible field officer.

At the next stop he exited the train, put his phone back on airplane mode and walked around to the far platform to board in the opposite direction. He was making a decision that in hindsight could be particularly good, or it just might be the worst possible decision he'd made in a long time.

CHAPTER THIRTY-TWO

The box was where he left it, in the closet and wadded in a ball of dirty clothes inside a suitcase. Dolan opened it and took out the Beretta, checked the breech, the clip and the safety, replaced it and put the box in the chic leather attaché Stone gave him. He grabbed the Ziploc bag from inside the dresser, opened it and placed the jar of pills inside with the encryption dongle. He grabbed his half-empty bottle of cognac and shoved it with the Ziploc, his phone cord and portable charger into the attaché. Then he packed some clothes and his vanity kit into his black Tumi backpack, shoving the leather case in last. It was raining, and the weather looked to be poor across Europe for at least the next few days. He went back to the closet and donned his black overcoat. Looking around the room to see if he'd forgotten anything, he noticed Sharif's leftovers still sitting on the dresser. With a disgusted look he grabbed the wastebasket by the desk and tossed the bag of food in, then carried it out of the room and into the hallway, placing it just outside his door. Then he slung the backpack over one shoulder and with a determined step, he walked out of Hôtel Flambeau.

◆

Anne looked surprised to see him at her work. Dolan could feel others in the office staring him down, the seeds of water cooler rumors being planted. She was standing near her desk as the receptionist escorted him over. "Michael, what a wonderful, unexpected surprise!" As he got closer, she continued in a lower voice. "Why are you here *mon canard*, is everything alright? You look tired."

"Things are fine Anne, but I have a favor to ask and it's important. Can we talk in the hall?"

"*Mais oui*, let's go."

She led Dolan past her gawking public affairs coworkers, through a doorway and into the main hallway. As the door closed behind them, she pulled him to her and gave him a quick kiss followed by a bright smile. "I'm so happy to see you."

Dolan dropped his backpack to the floor, gave her a warm hug and kissed her back, a little longer. He held her hands in his and admired her. She was so beautiful, both on the outside and within. He hadn't noticed just how truly beautiful until now. "I'm happy to see you as well Anne. I wish it were under different circumstances, but it's not. Did you drive your car to work?"

"My car? No, I always take the Métro. The car is at home. Do you need to borrow it?"

"Yes. It's important. And I might be gone for a few days."

"A few days? Where are you going?" A slight frown broke through her smile.

"I must go to Germany, for my work. I can't talk about it. You know, classified stuff. But I should be back by the end of the week. I would be so grateful—I'll make it up to you."

Anne pursed her lips. "*Listen you!* Of course you can borrow the car. I hardly ever use it anyway. It's in the garage. The keys are on the wall by the front door, and there's a spare housekey under the rock to the left of the door. But I will miss you. I haven't seen enough of you lately. After this, you *better* make it up to me. Call me."

"I will. Thank you, Anne. And I'm late, so I have to run."

She pulled him in close again and kissed him sensually, withdrawing just far enough that they could focus on each other, eye to eye. Softly but with conviction she whispered, *"I love you."*

Dolan didn't know what to say. How do you leave that hanging out there? But he didn't want to say it if he wasn't sure. And he wasn't. He wasn't certain he even understood what love really was, or if he'd ever felt it before, even with Claire. All he knew was that he cared for her deeply, and that any uncertainty or caution due to conflict of interest with the operation that existed before was now gone. And that it was only now, as he was walking into a complex, unpredictable and dangerous situation where his life was going to be on the line, that he was able to put the true value of their relationship into context. At that moment, she was everything to him.

"You are everything to me."

Anne looked at him, pausing to judge her satisfaction with his response. With a flush, she grinned playfully and poked him in the chest. "You bring my car back in one piece!"

"I will, I promise. Thank you so much Anne." Dolan grabbed his backpack by the strap, slung it over his shoulder and strode down the hall, glancing back to take a mental snapshot of her angelic form as he left through the front door and into the Paris rain.

CHAPTER THIRTY-THREE

"WHAT THE FUCK IS GOING ON!" yelled Dittrich. Thomas, who had done his best to be invisible since his run-in with Dittrich over the license plate fiasco slid as low and deep into his chair as he could. No one else moved in the Pit. Dolan had missed his meeting with Stone and was off the grid. The phone call with Lauren had been short, and Dittrich drove straight over to the Clarendon office.

Lauren cleared her throat and glanced at the notes she'd written on a yellow pad of paper. "Here is what we know so far, sir. Dolan went to Sharif's apartment for dinner last night. We had our translator listen in live and we were able to glean some useful information from their interaction. But the connection dropped about three and a half hours after he arrived, so we don't know what happened after that. Dolan sent Tony a secure text the next morning, saying he was running an hour late for their huddle, but he never showed up. We checked his movements, and it appears he went to the DRM Headquarters building, arriving there about the time he was supposed to be meeting Tony. Then the connection was lost again. It came back on about forty-five minutes later. He was heading in Tony's direction when we lost him a third time, and the connection's been dead ever since. We've tried calling him multiple times and continue to do so."

Dittrich turned to the bank of monitors set up beside the conference table. "Tony, do you have anything to add to this mess?"

"Yes sir. Dolan was successful in planting the bug. I was able to listen in after Lauren and Thomas lost the connection. It was faint, as if they were speaking in another room, but I could make most of it out. Dolan didn't stay long after that. Nothing of real value was said during that time. But after Dolan left, Sharif began muttering to himself, then began shouting. Mostly curse words. It sounded like he began throwing things around the apartment. I heard glass breaking and a lot of noise. One thing he did yell was of interest. He was cursing his father. *'Goddamn you father! Everything is fucked up now. You left me, I made a good life for myself despite you, and now you've come back to ruin things again. Fuck you!'* That's essentially the translation. It indicates he's had recent contact with him. It could also mean that things may not be going as planned."

Lauren was livid. She wanted to call him on the carpet right then, but she couldn't. Dittrich is the one who had told him to go ahead with the bug. Dressing him down for this would have to wait. For all she knew, Dolan's disappearance was somehow tied to it. *Shit.* "Sir, what we did hear was that Sharif is leaving for Marseille, to visit his mother Salmah, or so he said."

"As of two a.m. last night, he was still in his apartment. I waited around to see if he would leave after trashing his flat," remarked Stone.

Lauren continued. "Our timeline is getting short, and we just lost control of a key asset. Tony can't cover both Martin and Sharif while searching for Dolan by himself, and until we figure out what's going on with him, we shouldn't hand this off to the DGSI. There are significant developments Dolan is unaware of, and he could have already been rolled up. If he does get detained, he'll be held indefinitely if they find the encryption dongle or do any forensics on his phone. Then we'll have to disavow him, and I'm not prepared to do that. The bottom line is, he could pop back up at any time, but we can't rule out the possibility that his cover was blown at Sharif's last night. It might explain Sharif's tantrum, and perhaps even why Dolan was turning off his phone. If he suspected Sharif knew he was spying on him, he would know Sharif might try to call him to get his location so he could take him out or have him taken out. What it doesn't explain is why Dolan wouldn't reach out to Tony or me for help." *Dolan might be dead…*

"One thing to add, Tony you don't know this yet. The Five Eyes Plus France office in Paris, the very office Dolan is set to begin working at in a week or so, sent a recommendation out to the intelligence community on Friday, asking for releasability of anything to the French that might get them to return intel on the AMA and Sharif. One of our foreign disclosure analysts passed it on and we were able to get the DNI to provide an apology of sorts that will remain classified and releasable to a small handful of French government offices and select individuals. We are hoping to get back information that will help us with this operation. Knowing what the French know could also prevent missteps on our part. This is most likely Dolan's doing and would explain why he was at the DRM office instead of meeting Tony. If so, he was keeping it from us, which doesn't make sense as he should know it's probable we'd be involved in the process given the content of the exchange. Either way, we are still waiting on a response from the DRM."

The deep red in Dittrich's face subsided slowly as Lauren spoke. He hadn't considered that they may have a casualty. It was starting to get ugly, and he was getting a bad sense of déjà vu, Algiers all over again. Back then it had been Michael Collier who went rogue, taking risks he shouldn't have. Those risks ended up being key to the success of the mission, but he was compromised as a result and both he and Tony barely escaped with their lives. Overall, it had been a mixed bag. They critically weakened the AMA, but the French uncovered what had happened and shared at least some of the details with Algeria. Thus the icy trilateral relationship. After much handwringing he'd decided to reward Collier with the Berlin Chief of Station post instead of punishing him. He was one of the best for so long...

Dittrich nodded. "Call the DRM Lauren, find out why he was there. Call his language school. Create a timeline of all his activity the last few days, it may give you a lead. Just find him. Tony, you're on Sharif now. Let's not ignore the possibility he might be unstable. Sounds like he's got daddy issues and he's pissed about the state of things. He could behave erratically. We want to know about any visitors or phone conversations he might be having. Listen in on him, follow him. If he's not there you have the green light to check his flat. Get inside and find whatever you can, document it all, then locate him and stay on him. And let's not forget about Martin. Did you bug his car and house? Anything useful from his work computer?"

"I was getting to that. I finished analysis of his hard drive. There is nothing on the Algerians, nothing at all that would indicate he was directly involved in a terrorist plot. There were a lot of invoices to get through, the vast majority of which looked like your everyday wine distribution stuff. He did buy some strange hardware a few months back, but I couldn't rule out that it was probably just equipment for their business operations. It looks as if Martin has some financial clout in the company. He made a lot of what looks like corporate investment or expansion purchases for the company over the past two years. Mainly exclusive business properties and real estate, most of it in

France. Lastly, and this one caused me some concern, from January and leading up to the time of the fire he did extensive online research on Notre Dame Cathedral. He investigated the companies that were involved in the ongoing renovations, service schedules, when it would be open and closed to the public, everything. If I were a betting man, I'd say he was either planning an attack at the church, or that he was involved with the fire somehow. I have an analyst here at the embassy reviewing everything. He's not read in of course, but I've told him what to look for."

"Holy shit," remarked Dittrich. "Notre Dame? The news said it was an unfortunate accident that started the fire I thought." Lauren was shaking her head in disgust.

"Yeah, holy shit. It could also be that Notre Dame was a potential target for the gas attack. If that was the case, it probably isn't any longer. Anyway, when I got back to Metz Martin was nowhere to be found. He wasn't at home and he lives alone, so I had my run of the place. If he has a computer, he took it with him. I planted a few bugs. I'll have to go back at some point to collect the receiver with the recordings. Not sure I'll even have time for it if I'm on Sharif full-time. And I went through every piece of paper in his house. Again, I found nothing immediately helpful in determining their timeline, attack locations, or methods. Nothing about our three Algerians, either— where they are, what their orders are. But I did find quite a bit of Islamic fundamentalist-type pamphlets. Some in French, some in Arabic. I photographed it all and my analyst is on it."

Dittrich looked at Lauren seriously. "OK. This whole thing started with a major fuckup in Marseille, and it looks to be finishing the same way. We don't know where Martin is, and the Algerians are in the wind. We don't know where Dolan is or why he's gone dark. We have bugs planted that are essentially useless. We don't have a credible list of targets and we don't know the timeline. Either you get it all figured out, and I mean now, or I'll have no choice but to turn everything over to the French regardless of how prepared we are for that. At least they have the resources to deal with it. As of right now, we do not."

Lauren knew what she had to do; she'd already made the decision before calling Dittrich. She felt responsible for whatever Dolan was going through. They hadn't kept him in the loop, and she'd made certain assumptions about him that were convenient for the rest of the team. *He's doing fine, he can handle himself.* They pulled him into an extremely dangerous and dynamic operation without proper training or sufficient mentorship. Perhaps they shouldn't have brought him in at all.

It had been a while since she'd been in the field, but she was certain it was an old bike she could just get on and ride. Nothing can undo what had happened so far, but it may not be as bad as they were all thinking, and she could influence how things evolve from this point on far better in person than from half a world away.

"Sir, I'm going to Paris. This morning. Thomas will handle things here; Tony can locate and stay on Sharif. We'll send out the cable to cancel all public Fourth of July events across Europe immediately." She shifted her attention momentarily to Thomas. "Get the techs and translator here now. Put the Berlin sat feed on Martin's house in Metz, and I want the Paris feed switching between Dolan's hotel and Sharif's apartment every hour. Monitor for data from Dolan's phone continuously. If any of them pop up, stay on them and keep Tony apprised. Once I'm on the ground everything goes through me. I'll find Dolan. Tony, send a courier to Metz to collect the Martin recordings and invite DGSI to the embassy for a data dump tomorrow evening, let's say, eight p.m. That's two p.m. here. When you contact them do *NOT* ask if they have any U.S. citizens in custody. If they don't have Dolan, it would tip them off and they will be all over us. We'd be immobilized. Plan to have everything analyzed, packaged up and ready for them. Thomas, if for some reason I haven't found Dolan by then, I will call you with instructions. You will probably need to manage the meeting remotely and transfer everything electronically, as there will be no one there to meet them at the embassy. Make sure you stay in close contact with Tony's analysts." Thomas nodded.

Dittrich approved. "That's what I like to hear. Good stage management. It's a solid plan Lauren. Listen up everyone. If I must tell my people what to do to succeed, it means I have the wrong people. I should never need to get in my car and drive over here. Ever. I'm heading back to Langley now. Believe it or not, this isn't the only rodeo in town. There's a situation in Syria that is burning more and more of my bandwidth." Dittrich got up from his chair and walked to the door. Without looking back, he strode out, waving one hand and issuing his standard directive, "Do good things!"

CHAPTER THIRTY-FOUR

There was a lot of time for Dolan to think during the long trip to Berlin. He couldn't get there too soon, and the monotony of the drive was killing him. Several times he considered ditching his plan and turning around, but with each kilometer that ticked off his resolve strengthened. The effects of his hangover had subsided, but to his great concern they were replaced by mounting anxiety and a slight case of the jitters. He thought this might happen. It was the only reason he'd brought the bottle and the pills along with him. He felt guilty about it, of course. *Desperate times, desperate measures…* If there were *more* time, or a *better* way he'd be all over it but there just wasn't.

He realized he hadn't eaten yet today; that could be part of the problem. He gassed up the car and grabbed a couple bags of nuts, three protein bars, an energy drink and a liter of water just outside Mons, Belgium. He ate while driving and waited about a half hour. He felt better but it wasn't enough. He had to be on an even keel. Not just when he arrived, but now—while he was refining his approach. Thinking, weighing alternatives. Planning for contingencies. He drove further and pulled the old Peugeot over in a remote area with vast, rolling fields of rapeseed on either side of the road, as far as the eye could see. The gray clouds and soft rain gave the amber landscape an exquisitely forlorn quality. *Rapeseed. What a terrible name for something so beautiful,* thought Dolan. Most just take canola oil for granted. It was one of those things where people don't care or even wonder about where it comes from, only that it's useful to them.

He pulled the attaché out of his backpack in the passenger seat, opened the bottle of cognac and took a swig. After hesitating he took another, larger drink and put it back. Then he opened the crystal jar and swallowed two of Sharif's *Nupropion* pills while glancing in his rear-view mirror. No sign of trouble. He packed it all back up and continued driving.

After twenty minutes he was as right as the rain pelting the windshield. While he drove, he went through everything he knew, all the details to-date. He prepared himself mentally for the various situations that could ensue upon his arrival, determining courses of action for each one. Hours later and with an enhanced vigor, Dolan felt altogether resolute and prepared as he passed Hannover into the homestretch towards Potsdam.

◆

It was ten p.m., very dark and still raining as Dolan slowed Anne's Peugeot to a crawl in front of the address from Sharif's sticky note. The house was set back from the road and largely obscured by trees. Lights on inside. He kept driving for another quarter kilometer until he saw what appeared to be a trailhead leading off into the woods. He turned and drove in just enough that the vehicle would go unnoticed, then turned off the lights and ignition. His heart was racing, perspiration on his brow. This was different than flying in combat. Different at least from the combat he had seen. Taking out the bad guys from thousands of feet above, high enough that they don't even know you're there, that was surgical. It was precise, well-planned and he always had the advantage—good intel, infrared video, protective distance. He lacked all of that right now. But he did have cover of dark and the element of surprise.

He buttoned his overcoat, swallowed two more pills to steady his nerves and took the Beretta out of its box. After checking the magazine, he chambered a round and flicked off the safety with his thumb. Dolan then got out of the car, locked the door and began backtracking along the side of the road. It was a rural area. No streetlights. No sidewalk. He tried not to look too suspicious in the event a car passed by. He imagined he'd look out of place in any case, walking along a backwoods street late at night in a downpour.

He reached the driveway and hunkered down, just inside the line of trees and very slowly stepped closer to the house, being careful not to make any noise. The constant rain was a benefit; it was less likely he'd be seen or heard. As he neared the edge of the front yard he was startled as the garage door began to rumble open. *There's no way they saw me…* Dolan's heartrate quickened as he crept quickly behind a rock, peering over the top to see a large drop cloth hanging in the entryway with lights on and ghostly silhouettes moving in the background. Holding the Beretta with both hands at the ready position, he waited.

The left side of the drop cloth was moved aside momentarily as three men wearing black raincoats walked out carrying what looked like suitcases. *Three Algerians.* Dolan caught a glimpse of a vehicle inside, a panel truck with a strange paint scheme. Then the cloth fell back in place and the three walked toward the left edge of the yard and into the woods as the garage door closed. *What the heck?* Dolan moved out from behind the rock and moved along the tree line to where they had disappeared and saw there was a path. The Algerian in the lead turned on a flashlight as they made their way in front of Dolan, allowing him to track them while following at a safe distance.

The rain was coming down harder now. The overcoat wasn't enough—his shoes were already waterlogged, and it was becoming more difficult to see. *A baseball cap would have been perfect for this.* After a short distance, the path intersected a much broader, straighter one that looked to be an old railroad, the tracks and ties removed. He could just hear the three men, catching words here and there. Arabic. A short distance later the bobbing yellow beam from the flashlight lit up the mouth of a tunnel as the three men walked inside with their cases.

Dolan waited until they disappeared from view before leaving his cover and approaching the opening. He could see them exiting the other side, perhaps forty meters away. Should he follow them further, or head back to the house? If they double back before he gets through there would be no place to hide. *The cases could contain explosives or weapons.* He could head back to the house afterwards. Dolan walked quietly inside the tunnel, his gaze fixed at the other end and ears peeled for sounds of their return. Halfway through he stopped to listen closely, the Beretta in his right hand at his side. Nothing.

He picked up his pace and made it to the exit only to stop abruptly as an additional light appeared directly ahead. They were there, about a hundred meters away, three silhouettes lit by the trunk light of the vehicle they were loading. Dolan slid along the inside wall and around the opening, slipping a bit but catching his balance as he moved quickly down the embankment and into the trees without being seen. Shortly thereafter they finished loading the car and began walking back towards the tunnel, speaking in hushed tones. *They'll probably be back with another load.* Or were they just prepositioning, to leave later? He needed to find out what was in those cases.

Dolan waited two minutes after they'd reentered the tunnel and climbed back up to the trail, approaching the vehicle. It was a large, black, late model Citroën. Dolan noted the vehicle details and plate number, put the Beretta in his left pocket, fished his iPhone from the right and turned on the flashlight. He held it close to the front and back side windows. Empty. Everything must be in the trunk. He walked around to the back of the car and pressed the button under the lid. *Unlocked? Amateurs. They are going to be back soon*, he thought. Three carryon-size suitcases and a silver aluminum case lay illuminated by the trunk light. The case immediately drew his attention. *This is not luggage.* He turned off his phone flashlight and put it back in his pocket, pulled the case closer and opened each of the eight clasps, opening the lid. Inside were three two-liter sized pressurized canisters. Gas. But what kind? Probably chemical. Biologicals were usually delivered with aerosol dispersion or via a submunition. It was highly unlikely they'd transport a bioweapon under pressure, particularly if it weren't frozen. Under such conditions a biological agent would lose its viability. Dolan's mind was racing, remembering all the details from his deployment training. But what to do?

He closed the case, lowered the trunk lid and glanced quickly over the top of the car. It was too soon for them to return. Raising the lid again, Dolan made a decision. First, he went through the three carry-ons. Each contained a suit and undergarments, dress shoes, a belt and vanity items. *And a military grade gas mask.* He closed the three suitcases and reopened the aluminum case. He removed two of the canisters and set them on the ground near his feet. Then he held his breath and grabbed the valve of the third still in the case, closed his eyes and turned it ever so slightly. A barely perceptible hiss came from the canister and he quickly closed the case lid, refastening just the two clasps that were visible from the trunk opening. Then he pushed it back to its original position and closed the trunk. Grabbing the two canisters, he jogged about halfway back to the tunnel and opened his eyes. He set the canisters down and bent over, grabbing two fistfuls of mud and began rubbing his hands vigorously together. After rinsing them in a large puddle nearby he picked up the canisters and walked brusquely into the tunnel and back towards the house, pausing every few meters to look and listen. If everything went according to plan the terrorists would get in the car and die before getting very far. If they don't die, they'll at least be disabled, and they won't have their chemical weapons. He'll deal with these three first, then enter the house to gather as much intel as possible and decide whether to call Tony. And that was assuming there was no one else inside. He had to proceed with caution and be ready for anything.

Dolan's heart rate had slowed by the time he was back to his original hiding place in front of the house. He felt confident he now had the upper hand and he was fully in his zone. He hadn't felt this way since Afghanistan, and he welcomed it like an old, dear friend. He was calm. Precise. Lethal.

CHAPTER THIRTY-FIVE

Lauren went straight from the airport to the embassy to meet with Stone. It was shortly after midnight in Paris, July third. She had only a small carryon and her purse, nothing to weigh her down. The entire building was ominously quiet, only a few Marine guards going about their business. Their meeting was quick. Sharif was gone and Stone had gone through his apartment. He hadn't had enough time to collate everything yet, but the bottom line was he didn't find much of any intelligence value other than an address written on a post-it that appeared to be hidden in his desk. The courier had been dispatched to Metz. Still no word on the whereabouts of Martin or Dolan.

Then the kicker. Tony sheepishly admitted giving Dolan an unregistered, non-serialed handgun. *In case things went bad.* She nearly lost it. He defended the move strongly, describing all the precautions he provided and his directions for its very limited-scope use. She told him they'd deal with it later, but this was strike two and maybe three as well.

She spoke to David Crowe yesterday before her flight, who was surprised to receive the call. She told him she was with DoD resource management and had some important information to pass on. She got what she needed, verification that Dolan had been there and talked to him, and that they were working on an official intelligence exchange. He was in the process of sending the DRM's response when she called. Thomas would have it as soon as it processed. Dolan hadn't shown up to Lingua Europa on Tuesday and hadn't called ahead to let them know he'd be absent.

After their meeting Stone left for Salmah Lefebvre's house in Marseille, attempting to catch up with Sharif. If it wasn't Sharif's actual destination Stone would be useless to her for the next fifteen hours. But it's all they had to go on.

She was hoping she'd have more information or good news by the time she reached France, but no such luck. Lauren left the embassy and took a taxi to the Flambeau. After verifying Dolan wasn't at the hotel, she rode the Métro west towards Anne Bernard's house in Boulogne. Hopefully, she would be able to shed some light on Dolan's location. *Maybe he was there.*

Completely alone as she navigated in the dark from Billancourt station to rue Fernand Pelloutier, Lauren admired what she could see of the quaint, pricey neighborhood. She double-checked the address on her phone and pushed the wrought iron gate open at Bernard's home, then walked up to the door and knocked firmly four times and waited. Hearing nothing inside, she used the wrought iron knocker. A light came on and she heard movement. *Thank God, she's home.* Then a quiet voice, coming through the door.

"Oui? Qui est là?"

Lauren spoke loudly. "Hello Miss Bernard, my name is Lauren Rhodes. I apologize for the late hour. I am from the United States and a friend of Michael Dolan. I need to speak with him." Lauren crossed her fingers.

A moment later the door opened a few inches, Anne's concerned face coming into view. "What is the matter? Is everything OK?" Wearing a long, white cotton robe, Anne opened the door wide upon seeing Lauren.

"I work with the U.S. embassy, and Michael has a family emergency. I can't discuss the details, but we've been unable to get in touch with him for the last twenty-four hours. Michael has you listed as an emergency contact. Is he here?"

Anne opened the door completely and stepped aside. "Please come in. My God, I hope it isn't too terrible." Lauren could see the genuine concern on Anne's face. "No, Michael is not here. I loaned him my car yesterday morning, he needed to go to Germany for work. Have you tried to call him?"

Lauren stepped into the foyer, the door still open. "Yes, we've tried calling him, several times. It seems as if his phone is turned off or out of service. We checked with his language school and with his office, but no one knows where he is. Did he say where in Germany?"

Anne bit the tip of her forefinger, trying to remember. "No, he didn't say where, he just said Germany. But if his office doesn't know where he is, why would he tell me it was for work?"

Lauren had anticipated the question. She thought about creating a believable story about why he might be missing but decided against it. Better to stick with the truth, keep Anne worried. She'll be more likely to try to locate him. "I don't know Ms. Bernard. Did he seem anxious or upset when you saw him? Do you have any reason to think he might be in trouble or need help?"

It was working. Anne went from concerned to visibly worried. "Please, call me Anne. No, not at all. I mean, he was acting perfectly normal when I saw him yesterday morning. But the trip to Germany did seem last-second. I was thinking at the time he should have told me earlier, but I didn't push. He said he couldn't talk about it. That it was classified. Maybe this is why his work said they didn't know where he was?"

"What time was that, when you met with him, and what was he wearing?"

"Umm, about ten in the morning? It was at my office. He was wearing a black overcoat, dark pants, and black shoes. He still had to come back here to get the car though, since I use the Métro for work."

"OK, this is all helpful, thank you. Do you have something to write with? It would be good to get a description of your car and the license plate number. You know, in case we don't hear from him soon. We can ask French and German authorities to keep an eye open for him and get back to us."

Anne ushered Lauren inside. "Yes of course. Just a moment." She walked to a small desk between the living room and kitchen, wrote down the details and handed the notepaper to Lauren.

"Thank you, Anne. Here is my card. It is a U.S. number, my cellphone. If you remember anything else, or if you hear from Michael, please let me know immediately. Have him call me at that number." She began moving back to the front door. "Again, I apologize for the late hour."

"Of course, thank you for letting me know. I'll call you if I learn anything."

"Thank you so much. Good night."

"Ms. Rhodes?"

Lauren stopped and turned. "Yes?"

"If you hear anything before I do, will you please call me?"

Lauren could see she was on the verge of tears. *She is in love, poor girl.* "I will Anne, I promise."

"Thank you."

"You're welcome. Good night."

Lauren tried calling Dolan once more as she walked to the Métro station, but again it went straight to voicemail. *He may not have his encryption dongle.* She decided to leave a message. "Michael, hello. This is Lauren. I'm in Paris and I've been unable to reach you the past couple of days. It's supposed to be overcast again tomorrow and we may have to cancel our plans. Let me know, pronto." *Overcast* was the code word *for things going badly. Pronto* meant *in need of assistance.* The good news was she was able to rule out that Dolan might be burned, at least for now. What she needed to determine next was why he went to Germany, where exactly, and why he went dark. Those answers would give her a better feel for just how bad things really were.

Lauren chose the safe house near the airport. She signed in with the attendant, walked down the hall to her assigned room and threw her bag on the bed. Then she called Thomas on a secure line.

"Thomas. Hello, it's me. Please tell me you've gotten somewhere with the analysts here in Paris."

"Hi Lauren. Yes, we've kept a videoconference going the entire time. The courier returned with the Martin recordings. They are all blank. I guess he hasn't returned home. We were able to identify two of the pamphlets from his house as originating with the AMA, which would help us make our case with DGSI. But I don't think we'll need it. The big news is, I just got my hands on the intel dump from the DRM exchange. It looks like they already suspect Martin, or at least they've tied him to Lefebvre's money through a Swiss account owned by Salmah. Lauren, he is the executor of the account! Not Sharif, Martin! They think he's been using money from the account to buy properties using his family's company as a front."

Lauren began to respond but Thomas cut her off. "No wait, there's more. You remember the sticky note in Sharif's apartment desk?"

Lauren was one step ahead of him. "The Potsdam address. Is it one of the properties Martin bought?"

"Yes! It could be where our three Algerians are hiding out. Who knows."

"It could also be where Dolan is headed. He could already be there. I just returned from Anne Bernard's house, and she told me she'd let Dolan borrow her car to travel to Germany. Thomas, I think Dolan initiated the exchange, got the information before we did, and for whatever reason he decided to act on it alone."

There was a moment of silence while Thomas digested the idea and the potential ramifications. "Holy shit."

"Yeah, holy shit."

"Well, now we have a lead on where he might be. Are you going after him?"

"Yes. I'm going to fly to Berlin. But I'm at a real disadvantage. If Dolan went straight from his meeting with Anne to get her car, and from there to Potsdam, he'd be there already. Retask the satellite on Martin's home to the Potsdam address immediately. The techs are there, right?"

"Yes, we are all here."

"How long to get it done?"

"Well, the NRO is rather good about giving us priority, until they don't, like what happened in Marseille. Hopefully in two to three hours."

"Shit. OK. Ask Dittrich to weigh in and escalate. We need eyes now. I'm going to wake Mike Collier up and have him send a team over to the address. It'll take a couple of hours probably, longer if he has to use the BND. I'll reassess once I'm on the ground. When you call Dittrich, please bring him up to speed on everything. Then call Tony and do the same with him. Oh, and make sure both Sharif's and Martin's vehicle information and Sharif's suspected destination is included in the data dump for DGSI."

"I'm on it. Do you want me to connect with Berlin Station as well?"

"Not yet. No one there at this hour will have any idea who we are. It will raise too many questions. We must work through Mike, period. He's our only play."

"Got it."

"Thanks Thomas."

Lauren wanted badly to take a shower and eat a proper meal, but there was no time. She booked the first available direct flight on her phone, brushed her teeth, put on some deodorant and perfume and asked the attendant call her a taxi. Then she picked up the secure telephone again and called Collier.

"Mike, hello this is Lauren Rhodes. I'm so sorry for calling at this hour, but I have an important favor to ask."

He answered in a hushed voice. "Lauren? Oh wow, look at the time. Give me a second."

She could hear him getting out of bed, probably tiptoeing out of the bedroom. *Doesn't want to wake Mrs. Collier...*

"OK, what's up?"

"The three Algerians. I think I have an address where they might be hiding, or were hiding. I'm on my way there from Paris, but it will take me a while. Could you send a recon team out as soon as possible? I could get Dittrich to call you, but I'd lose time doing it. To watch and verify, and to kill or capture if it comes to that."

She heard him sigh. "Well, I can of course but could you give me a little more? Are you expecting them to move, or worse, is an attack imminent? Does this have anything to do with the cable cancelling public Fourth of July events across Europe?"

"Thanks Mike. Very grateful. Yes, this is what prompted us to send the cable, though we had less information at the time. They may have left already, we suspect for Paris, but it's just an educated guess. They are highly likely armed and could be transporting a chemical weapon. Again, an educated guess. Call it very educated. And there's more. One of our team went dark yesterday, and he could be in the vicinity or even in the house. His name is Michael Dolan, six feet tall, black hair. Probably wearing a black overcoat. He drove there in a dull red, nineteen ninety-eight model Peugeot sedan, French plate number…you have a pen?" She fished the note out of her purse. "Alpha Sierra One Four Three Juliet Charlie."

"Got it. *Christ* Lauren, this really sounds like something I should have known about already. Please tell me you just got all this information?"

"Mike, of course, *yes*." She was getting frustrated. "Can you send the team now? I'll be in Berlin in three and a half hours or so and will call you then."

"I'll send a team, but it will have to be the BND. They should let us send someone to tag along. Ever since the 2010 Wikileaks State Department cables fiasco we've had to be much more transparent. Lauren, I *really* like my job—I do not want to be sent home under a cloud. If they found out I left them out of the loop about a possible chemical attack orchestrated on their turf I'd immediately be Persona Non Grata, and every bit of trust we've regained would be undone. They'll need chem gear and suits. The BND already has profiles on these three, so they'll be ready if the shit hits the fan. It'll take two hours at least before they get there. What kind of gas are we dealing with, is your guy armed, and is he carrying a cell?"

"Fine. I'll take what I can get. Full MOPP gear won't be necessary, it's only dangerous when inhaled. Treat it like ammonia, or chlorine—gas masks will be ineffective. M40, M42, MCU2AP and STANAG filters won't protect against it. It's colorless and odorless. The first indication you've inhaled it is drowsiness and confusion, and by then it's probably too late. None of our current patches or sensors will detect it. Now pay attention, this is important. You will have to find a way to tell the BND as little about the gas as possible while giving them enough to protect themselves. Believe me when I say there is a very good reason we do not want them to wonder how we know so much about it.

"Now, Michael is likely carrying a Beretta APX that we need to recover, and he does have a cell phone, but as I mentioned he's had it turned off." She told him the number. "If they identify him, have them take him into protective custody, and to be careful about it OK? We can collect him later. He speaks some German, much better with French. Make sure they tell him that it's protective custody—I don't want him thinking he's being arrested. Also, he's a fourth degree blackbelt in taekwondo. And Mike…"

"What else?"

"My guy, he has no diplomatic status. Not in Germany, not in France, not anywhere. You'll have to call in a favor I think, to keep them from pressing him too hard for information."

"*Perfect*. OK. They owe us a few so that shouldn't be too difficult. Why do you want Dolan detained? Have you had trouble controlling him? Is he operating outside the scope of his mission?"

"Good question. He's a bridge agent. Actually, *agent* might be the wrong word. Let's just say that Dolan's unaware of recent developments and doesn't know that his mission has changed. The most effective thing I can do is to contain him for the time being. I'll call you on the ground."

"Just like old times, eh?"

Lauren was too spun up to play the reminiscence game but unfortunately, he was right. "Yeah, just like old times."

CHAPTER THIRTY-SIX

Dolan placed the two cylinders on the ground behind the large rock where he was hiding and covered them with leaves. Turning back to the house, he waited. After about fifteen minutes the garage door rumbled open again, and again three men walked out from behind the drop cloth. This time they were carrying smaller luggage. *Briefcases.* As they walked to the path a fourth man appeared from the garage, remaining just under the eve of the roof. Thin, shorter. Dark hair. *Martin.* He yelled something and waved to the men, who all turned and waved back, yelling something in return. The rain was really making it hard to hear. The fourth man then returned inside the house and the door closed. Dolan immediately left his vantage point and crept stealthily after his prey.

Again he followed at a safe distance, Beretta ready. At the tunnel Dolan had a sinking feeling as he realized the old railroad trail could very well connect to the road at the trailhead where he parked Anne's Peugeot. *If they get that far.* It could be a good thing. It will slow them down, give more time for the gas to work. He'd noticed no ill effects from his minimal exposure. *So far, anyway.*

He decided not to enter and laid down on the left trail bank, just able to peek over the edge. They could drive through at any moment—the car was parked facing the tunnel. Sure enough, a light appeared at the entrance, and he heard an engine as the Citroën entered at the far end. A moment passed and it sounded as if the car had slowed. A metal-grinding screech then echoed down the length of the tunnel, continuing for a few seconds and fading to a stop. *That's it then,* Dolan thought. He jumped up from the bank and jogged the fifty meters to the entrance. Then he slowed. *The gas is now contained, only two places for it to go.* He stopped about ten meters away and looked inside. The car had scraped up against the right wall of the tunnel, headlights on and engine running. The passenger door was open, and a figure was sitting against the far wall, clearly in distress. Dolan inhaled deeply and held his breath, then ran at full speed into the tunnel toward the man on the ground, weapon out and trained. Ten more meters. Just as he was about to pull the trigger the man noticed Dolan and lifted a handgun with his right hand and fired. Dolan fired at the same time, two shots to the body and one to the head. The man crumpled to the ground. Dolan dropped his Beretta and exhaled forcefully as a bullet entered his right forearm, tearing through and out the other side, lodging in his chest. He stumbled backwards and began to gasp for air. The sudden surge of adrenaline impaired his thinking for only a moment, and he held his breath again, turned and sprinted out of the tunnel and thirty meters beyond before collapsing in the mud. Still gasping for air, he unbuttoned his coat with his left hand and ripped open his shirt, buttons flying. Despite the pain he prodded the wound. The bullet had entered at the thickest area of his pectoral muscle, just left of the nipple. He could feel the bullet inside, lodged against his ribs. His forearm had saved his life, at least temporarily. Whatever the gas was, he had inhaled at least some of it and he was clearly feeling much worse than he should right now.

Dolan stood up and pulled up his right sleeve, gingerly. His shirt and jacket were soaked with blood and both the entry and exit wounds were bleeding heavily. As far as he could tell the bullet had travelled between the radius and ulna without breaking either. Another stroke of luck. He glanced back at the tunnel. Seeing nothing he took off his overcoat and ripped off the right sleeve of his dress shirt, wrapping and tying it tightly around his right arm. His chest wound wasn't bleeding too badly so he left it alone, donned the jacket and walked back to the tunnel. He held his breath again, this time walking inside. No change—dead bad guy on the ground, two lifeless forms inside the car. The dead bad guy looked more like a boy, now that he thought about it. Then he realized this was the first time he'd killed someone without being thousands of feet away. He had been close enough to see the whites of his eyes as he pulled the trigger. Unlike his combat experience piloting the Spectre gunship it wasn't so impersonal, clinical. Routine. The antithesis of that, actually. And without the right training, much more dangerous. He picked up the Beretta and walked back out. By the time he exited he was experiencing extreme vertigo. He bent over with his hands on his knees and after a few minutes of deep breathing he felt better. As quickly as the gas had worked on the Algerians, he surmised he'd only gotten a small dose. Each moment he was feeling better, aside from the tremendous pain in his forearm and the thudding ache in his chest.

Dolan forced himself to get back in his zone, to kill off the adrenaline. It was difficult but he was able to do it as he walked the path back to the house, now holding the APX in his left hand. Instead of going back to his hiding spot he turned left inside the tree line and circled the yard, watching for movement through the backlit curtains covering each window. As he was circling the back yard, he noticed motion in the far-right window, probably a bedroom. He continued around until reaching the far side of the property. There was a covered vehicle parked there at the edge of the yard. Dolan left the tree line and approached the vehicle, crouched. He knelt and removed the valve stem covers on the passenger side tires and deflated both.

There were no windows on the garage side of the house. Unable to low crawl because of the pain, Dolan hunkered down and moved steadily until he was up against the outside wall, then slid along toward the back. He quickly moved along, ducking under two windows, until he was at the back door. Locked. He'd never shot left-handed before. This worried him a bit. But he had the element of surprise, and it will be tight quarters inside. He should be able to get close.

With one swift, powerful move Dolan kicked in the door, splinters of the frame spraying in the doorway. Then he stopped, head down and listening. A rustling sound to the right. Dolan bolted down the hall to the door he was sure led to the room where he saw movement and kicked it in as well, immediately diving through the doorway with the Beretta elevated toward the middle of the room. The second he saw Martin standing to the left he fired off a volley of shots. Martin sprinted toward the door he'd just come through, firing as he ran. Dolan paused for a microsecond and decided he hadn't been hit. But how could he have missed Martin? As he got up off the floor bursts of plaster erupted from the wall as Martin let loose a barrage of bullets through from the other side. *They're all rookies*, thought Dolan. He immediately fell back to the floor, left arm with the Beretta trained on the doorway and waited. He heard clicks as Martin repeatedly pulled the trigger on his empty weapon, then retreating footsteps and a door slamming. *Out of bullets.* He popped up and grimaced as a bolt of pain coursed through his arm, then raced out and down the hall to a door at the end, *to the garage*. He noticed a few spots of blood on the floor. *His or mine?* He could hear the garage door opening, not sure how much longer he could continue. He was gasping, in pain and out of energy.

Gritting his teeth, Dolan flattened his back against the wall, turned the doorknob and pulled the door open. Nothing. He held out the Beretta and took one stride into the doorway only to see Martin in his peripheral vision on the right swinging a two-by-four over his head. There was a wet, deep red stain on his shirt. *Ah, got him in the shoulder.* Dolan made a move to get out of the way and squeezed off a round toward him just as Martin hit his gun hand. The bullet struck the floor and ricocheted through the wall as the Beretta was knocked free. Dolan immediately leaned to his right and landed a punishing roundhouse kick to Martin's kidney and he doubled over. He followed with an axe kick, his right heel dropping swiftly to impact the top of his head and Martin dropped to his knees.

Dolan turned to look for the APX. Seeing it about three meters away he noticed the panel truck, bright green with 'Baumservice Berlin' painted on the side. *Berlin Tree Service.* As he reached for the handgun, he became lightheaded, almost falling. He tried to grab the handle, but his fingers weren't working. His hand was swelling. *Broken metatarsals...* Martin then got up behind him, picked up the two-by-four and swung it like a baseball bat, hitting Dolan squarely on the side of the head and he crumpled to the floor on top of the gun.

Dolan lay face down and couldn't move. He wasn't in pain. A warm, surreal sensation engulfed him as blood ran across his cheek and onto the floor. He could smell it, sickly sweet. *So this is it then.* He heard Martin, saying something. Angry. Impassioned. He forced himself to listen.

"You cannot stop me!" he yelled. Then in a measured but elevated voice, "Allah wills it. Don't you understand? The United States attacked my people without provocation, as you have done time and time again. I am the Deathbringer, the hand of Allah, his instrument of justice and I will deliver our vengeance with great fury and wrath. Notre Dame was the harbinger, and what follows is apocalypse!"

Still face down, Dolan strained to see Martin. *The harbinger.* He had set the fire? Or perhaps Sharif? No, Sharif wouldn't have. He remembered back to his conversation in Sharif's apartment. He'd been genuinely upset. He'd said *"I didn't agree with it. I don't know why anyone would want to destroy such an historic monument to God."* Dolan had believed him then and still did. Martin had done it without Sharif's consent. Out of the corner of one eye he could see Martin winding up with the two-by-four to finish him off.

With effort Dolan turned his head enough to look up at Martin who waited to see if he would say something, two-by-four held high above his head. "You know Martin, those who believe they are invincible are quickest to demonstrate their mortality." With pain screaming up his arm he clawed for the Beretta with his right hand and rolled to his back, bringing the weapon to bear. Martin's eyes went wide and he immediately dropped the board, bolting around to the driver's side of the truck. Dolan shot twice and struggled to keep the Beretta trained on him but couldn't. He didn't have enough strength to pull the trigger a third time. Martin started the engine and drove off with tires screeching through the drop cloth and into the night.

Dolan chuckled to himself at the turn of events, then decided to clean himself up and finish the job. It was clear the van was involved in some aspect of the attack, a second attack that would take place not in Paris but in Germany, most likely on Independence Day. Everything had happened so fast he didn't get the license plate number. He wasn't sure he'd have been able to read it anyway, as his vision was now blurred. But the van stood out like a sore thumb. *Unless it was painted to look just like any number of other 'Baumservice Berlin' vehicles in the area…*

He laid there for a few minutes and by degrees gained enough strength to get up and stand. He looked around the garage and walked to the two work benches. On the floor to the left he noticed a brown paper bag. He reached down and picked it up gingerly, dumping the contents on the bench. Papers and cell phone pieces scattered across the work surface. He swept the phone parts onto the floor and arranged the papers. One sheet had hand-drawn schematics of various parts of a device, annotated in French. Another showed the completed device within the outline of a vehicle—the panel truck. The rest were spreadsheet printouts. Test data.

It only took about ten minutes of review to understand exactly what the device was built for. To launch gas canisters like the ones he grabbed from the Citroën, only larger. The test results were specific to range and accuracy. Average maximum distance was 320 meters, accuracy was exceptionally good, within 0.2 meters. A closer look revealed two specific requirements: a minimum range of 250 meters and minimum entry angle of 60 degrees. Dolan scanned the various tables and spotted the correct one, test data for range at a 60-degree entry. The average maximum distance was 262 meters.

Dolan took a roll of duct tape and a pair of needle nose pliers from the bench. He gathered up the papers, folded them and put them in his coat pocket. After another look around, he closed the garage door, turned off the light and went back into the house, quietly and methodically searching each room. There were three bedrooms, including the one where he'd surprised Martin. He found some personal items and clothes but not much else. He grabbed a pair of pants and a shirt that looked like they would fit, along with an additional tee-shirt and then went to the kitchen. He took a paring knife from one of the drawers and sterilized it along with the needle nose pliers on the gas stovetop. Then he went to the bathroom. He downed five acetaminophen tablets from a bottle in the medicine cabinet. Undressing slowly, he tossed his bloodied, muddy clothes in a pile and took a hot shower. Blood from his wounds ran like thin, dark rivers down the length of his chiseled body, pooling and swirling towards the drain. As he scrubbed, he ran through all the data in his mind and concluded that whatever the target was, the gas canister didn't just need to clear an obstacle—the maximum apogee was realistically much higher than would be needed for any barrier. A minimum entry angle meant that Martin needed to avoid two obstacles, one in front of, and one beyond the target. It could also mean that he wanted to prevent the canister from rolling or tumbling too far past the target.

The paint scheme on the van was for cover, of course, but it also meant that the launch site was probably in or near a wooded area. This would provide additional cover and while the van stood out, no one would question why it was there. So, his target was within 250 meters of a wooded area. Unfortunately, Berlin probably had more trees per square kilometer than any other city of comparable size in Europe. But the target? The target was Americans—Martin had made that clear. From his travels to Berlin when he was at the Sorbonne, he remembered that the U.S. Embassy sponsored a large, public Fourth of July event in the Grunewald, a huge park area in the Charlottenburg-Wilmersdorf borough. He'd never attended but knew it was a big deal, with a concert, lots of food and fireworks. But the test requirements didn't support that location—there just weren't any obstacles in the

Grunewald besides trees. And the effectiveness of a chemical gas would be mitigated greatly if dispersed outside in an open area.

He'd also had a tour of the U.S. Embassy itself, together with Claire, Sharif, and Anne. From their visit he knew it was five stories high with a large courtyard in the middle, open to the sky and closed in on all four sides. The courtyard would contain the gas, and a sixty-degree entry angle would clear the inner side of the leading part of the building without hitting the inside wall of the far part of the building. *He wants to make sure the canister doesn't go through a window, potentially sparing people in the courtyard.* This made more sense. It all meant that the attack would happen during the day, when some kind of event is going on. Perhaps a large, formal VIP event. A Fourth of July luncheon hosted by the Ambassador.

Dolan toweled off and picked up the paring knife from the sink. It was still difficult to use his right hand, but possible. He watched in the mirror as he made two short, deep cuts on either side of the bullet hole in his chest, then dropped the knife in the sink and applied a towel quickly to staunch the fresh flow of blood. He held it tightly for a moment, then used the pliers to probe inside the hole until he felt the bullet and pulled it out, letting it drop to the floor. He cleaned the wound, the gash on his head, and the two holes on his forearm with rubbing alcohol from the medicine cabinet. He cut the additional tee shirt into strips using the knife, dressing his arm and chest wound, using duct tape to secure it. Then he tightly rewrapped his left hand, which by now had swollen considerably.

After donning the pants and shirt he'd found he grabbed some water and snacks from the kitchen and quickly replenished himself. He was in rough shape, but more concerned about his head injury than anything else. He had some of the symptoms of concussion—the blurred vision, some dizziness, sluggishness. And as hard as Martin had hit him, his skull could be fractured. But he was still mobile, and still able to think. The acetaminophen had reduced the pain in his right arm, and he could now use it to a reduced degree. He cleaned the mud off his overcoat as best he could, then set about removing all evidence he had been there. He used bleach from under the kitchen sink to clean up the blood in the garage, the hallway, Martin's bedroom, and the bathroom. He wiped down all the surfaces and items he had touched and put his old clothes, the bullet and blood-soaked arm dressing in the paper bag from the garage. With the Beretta and the paring knife in his overcoat pocket Dolan exited out the back doorway.

He retrieved one of the gas canisters from his hiding spot and wiped down the other, re-hiding it. Cradling the canister and paper bag with his arms on the walk back to Anne's Peugeot, the effects of his probable concussion became more pronounced. With his injuries, lack of quality sleep and his recent foray into drinking and questionable substances he would need to get to a hospital soon. The sum of all of it was taking an unprecedented toll that would eventually overcome his conviction and resilience.

Once at the car he put the bag of clothes in the trunk and the canister in his backpack. Then he sat down gingerly in the driver's seat, closed the door and drank impulsively from the bottle of cognac until it was empty. *That should provide some relief.* Almost immediately he cursed himself—it was too much. His driving, already a challenge due to his injuries, could be comically bad. If he were pulled over by the Polizei he would fail to stop Martin. People would die. He picked up his iPhone from the passenger seat and stared at it, realizing he should tell the team what had happened. Let them know Paris was safe, the Algerians were dead. Give a description of the panel truck, his analysis of the test data and the probable target and launch site, and then let the cavalry do the rest. It almost didn't matter at this point if he trusted any of them, whether they had used him or were operating without any real plan. He had already taken out a big part of the cell and would give them the plan for Martin.

Dolan was feeling lightheaded once more as he typed in his password. He wasn't angry or even irritated that he had to give up, which seemed strange. It was against his code. He wasn't sure he'd been doing things to the best of his ability. But it no longer mattered, he was spent. As his mind drifted, he noticed gratefully that the pain had ebbed considerably. He was feeling at peace. Floating, deliquescent. He felt as if his very existence was at the precipice of evanescence. Curiously, at this moment slipping away seemed like the right thing to do. As he eased into the darkness, he became disembodied and saw himself, not sitting there in the car but standing, staring back. In his vision he wasn't hurt, in fact he seemed fine save the look on his face. Sardonic, twisted. Evil? The scene panned wider to reveal a crumpled form at the feet of his doppelganger lying in a pool of blood, the hilt of a knife protruding from his side. *From Dolan's side.* He went cold with horror. *The victim is me. The killer is me. They are both me.* The revelation of the true meaning of his recurring nightmare overcame and consumed him. And just as he fervently committed to endure, to fix everything, to fix himself, the vision faded, and he fell into nothingness.

CHAPTER THIRTY-SEVEN

Tony was pissed. Things hadn't gone according to plan. His position in SCALPEL was in jeopardy. And he'd been sent on a goose chase that would probably net nothing. The entire seven hours of his drive to Marseille he'd spent searching for a way to get out of his predicament with Lauren. He was quite sure he could get Dittrich on his side. After all, he had done just as much to enable their success in Algeria as Collier had. In fact, he'd done better than that—Collier was the one whose cover was blown.

Thomas called him and brought him up to speed a couple hours back. By the time he verified Sharif wasn't at Salmah's house and drove back, the attack could have already either happened or been prevented by the DGSI and police. He was irrelevant. But then he wondered if the attack might be postponed, that the cell might regroup since all public events were cancelled. If that were the case, he would still have a job to complete. Any issues between him and Lauren would have to wait, and he could work things out in the meantime. *And Dolan, holy shit.* Tony couldn't believe the balls on that guy. He'd been quite effective, good in fact. And he seemed to relish the role. But to go rogue like that? He probably has the Beretta with him. They didn't understand his motivations at the moment, but it was likely he would either end up in jail or dead, unfortunately. He hoped not. He liked him.

As he reached the Lefebvre estate Tony saw that it was grand—a sprawling property on the far east side of the city surrounded by an eight-foot wrought iron fence and a gate with a callbox at the driveway. He drove past without slowing, noting the security cameras on either side of the entry. He kept driving and the horizon flattened up ahead, the beautiful blue waters of the Mediterranean. Eventually the road ended at Chemin des Goudes, which followed the coastline. There were no real beaches to speak of this far east—instead, it was several kilometers of rocky shore and craggy cliffs, in some places quite high above the water. Stone made a left turn and drove a little further before pulling over into an overlook area. He got out of the car and walked to the cliff's edge, taking a moment to appreciate the beauty of the place. *God, how I love this country...* It was almost eight in the morning, and though the traffic was picking up he was alone in the small turnoff.

Stone walked back to the car, opened the trunk, pulled out a large backpack, and slung it over his shoulder. He was wearing black jeans, brown hiking boots and a pea green tee-shirt emblazoned with a black fleur-de-lis. He closed the trunk, locked the car and crossed the street. As he walked along, he looked for cameras or typical security devices along the fence. Once Stone was satisfied there was no electronic surveillance he stopped and waited for traffic to clear. While he waited, he pulled a rope from the bag. As soon as no vehicles were visible in either direction he broke for the fence, lobbing the noose end over the continuous row of spikes at the top.

In about ten seconds he was on the other side with the rope back in his pack, moving cautiously but quickly to a grove of trees nearby. Positioning himself where he was sure he couldn't be seen from the road, Stone took his handgun and a flat case from the backpack. He tucked the gun inside the backside of his pants and quickly assembled the sniper rifle, attached the high-power scope and loaded it. Then he sat down and opened the Google Earth app on his phone, noted his position and the location of Salma's residence and plotted his approach. Lauren expected him to locate Sharif and report in. If he got a good shot, Stone intended to take him out.

◆

Sharif sat with his mother on the veranda. He'd asked the nurse to make certain she spent at least an hour on the veranda each day so she could enjoy the fresh air and a little bit of nature. Especially when the weather was beautiful, as it was today. Nothing was said. There was nothing to say. She didn't remember him anymore. He knew it was irreversible and it had been difficult to come to terms with. She was all he had left, and now she was essentially gone. He wept quietly for a moment, then composed himself.

His life was about to change, and in no small measure. Martin had called him early that morning informing him of the incursion at the house in Potsdam. He'd been shot by an American, probably CIA, grazed across the shoulder really. He'd been able to escape in the panel truck with the gas. The plan was still on track in Berlin. As for Paris, the American Independence Day celebration was cancelled, and his Algerian recruits had now missed two check-ins with Martin. Everything pointed to a complete failure for Paris, and the Americans were after them. It was OK. *Berlin is all that really matters.*

They had breakfast early. Mother usually woke around five a.m. The temperature was beginning to rise but was still comfortable. He had packed already and would be leaving within the hour. This was likely the last time he would ever see her, the only woman who had ever truly loved him. *The only person who ever loved me.*

"Mother, would you like a Pastis?" He didn't wait for her to answer. "I'm going to make us some Pastis." She loved them, especially during the summer. Though he'd never particularly enjoyed the taste of anise in general, he'd grown up with the refreshing drink and it brought back fond memories.

He got up from the wicker chair and walked into the house towards the kitchen. As he was making their drinks, he heard an unfamiliar beeping from across the house. The beeping stopped, then started again. Sharif put the pitcher down and walked brusquely to the library. His father had bought the property and built the house. He'd made sure it was secure as well. There were four kilometers of fence surrounding the estate, with an extensive array of cameras and motion sensors. Most of the cameras were hidden or difficult to spot. In the library he looked at the twelve monitors, each alternating between feeds from four individual cameras. If a camera or sensor detected significant movement the monitor would automatically display the associated feed and display a red border. Two monitors currently had a red border.

His father had originally planned to move here to be with them. He'd taken every precaution—he knew he had enemies. There was even a footlocker with loaded guns in the room, right next to the monitors. No one had ever taken them out of the locker, never mind used them. In the end, his father's dedication to an ideology and his vast empire had proven more important than any dedication he might have had to his family. Salmah had kept the security system maintained and even upgraded it a few years back. Salmah never gave up on him though and would tell Sharif that *it is only a matter of time before he comes back to us.* His time was up long ago. Instead, Sharif would be going to him.

Sharif looked at one monitor and then the other. He didn't see anything abnormal. *It could have been the trees swaying in the wind,* he thought. As he turned to go back to the kitchen, he saw something out of the corner of his eye. A tiny flash. He looked closer and saw it— there was a man sitting in the shrubs with a rifle. The flash was a glint of sun off the front lens of the scope.

Sharif read the camera location penned on a piece of masking tape across the top of the monitor. South-middle. *Someone jumped the fence.* Sharif hurriedly opened the footlocker and selected a semiautomatic, scoped long rifle. It hadn't been shot in many years. Maybe not at all. *Hopefully, the scope is not out of alignment.* He checked the magazine, chambered a round and sprinted back to the veranda. Without saying anything he set the rifle on the patio and grabbed the handles of his mother's wheelchair, spinning her around and inside. He pushed her down the hall to her bedroom, yelling for the nurse.

"Chloé, I'm putting mother in her room. Can you please come here and stay with her for a while?"

After a moment she appeared, an open book in her hand. "Is everything OK? What's wrong Sharif?"

"I think someone is on the property. The security alarm has been tripped. I am going to check it out. In the meantime, I want the two of you to stay in here with the door closed."

"Should we call the police?"

"No—please just stay here while I check it out. It could be nothing."

Sharif returned to the veranda and picked up the rifle, then went back to the library. Still beeping, there was now a single monitor with a red border. Back yard. Sharif strained his eyes for a moment and then saw him. He was within fifty meters of the house, peering from behind a large umbrella pine, rifle trained on the residence. He appeared to be wearing a backpack and looked like your average Frenchman. *He is here for me.* He paused to see if the man would stay put, then bounded out of the room and up the ornate curved staircase to the second floor. Down the hall on the left he opened the door to his old bedroom. The window would overlook the intruder's position at a good angle.

Sharif moved quickly to the side of the window and looked out with one eye, being careful to keep his body from view. The man was still there. He carefully unlatched the window and opened it a few inches, just enough to let the rifle barrel through without blocking the scope. He located the intruder again visually and then through the scope, placing the crosshairs chest-high and just to the right of the side of the pine tree.

◆

Stone shifted left a few inches to get a better view of the area east of the house. All clear. Back at the house, he checked each of the second-floor windows and then the first without noting anything. The stone manor was majestic. It wasn't very old; however, the architect had stayed true to southern French provincial characteristics. High, arched second-story windows, balanced proportions, and a steep hipped roof. There was a modest veranda with a table and chairs off the back of the house on the right side. It broke the symmetry of the structure, but this was the back of the home—certainly not unheard of. The door to the veranda was open. *Someone was inside.* It was probably Salmah and her live-in nurse. Breakfast outside on a beautiful morning.

He was probably too close right now but needed to get around to the garage side of the house to determine if Sharif's car was there. Seeing no movement, he selected his next place for cover, a large fountain with a mermaid in the middle, water gracefully spouting upward from her mouth, about fifteen meters to his left. He took his first step and instantly fell backwards. He dropped the rifle as he hit the ground, confused by what had just happened. He must have stepped in a hole or…then he felt it. As if a concrete block had been dropped on his chest and was still there. He craned his neck forward and saw the blood. So much blood. At that moment he found it odd his final thought would be that the beautiful poem Dolan had penned for his dead French girlfriend, the one Dolan had left on the street where she perished, would be found in his wallet. Then Stone's head fell back as he died, the fleur-de-lis on his tee-shirt disappearing in a dilating circle of deep red.

CHAPTER THIRTY-EIGHT

Lauren was already on the phone as she stepped off the jetway. Thomas answered.

"Hi Lauren. We have eyes on the house in Potsdam. The BND team is already on site and have surrounded the property, though they are standing back pretty far. Looks like they're in full MOPP gear. There is one vehicle in the yard, near the trees and it's covered with a tarp or something. Lauren, we don't see anyone in the house. There's no one there."

"Shit." Lauren was walking rapidly through the airport. Collier had sent a car to pick her up. "OK, how wide is your view right now. How much of the property can you see?"

"We have infrared pretty tight, the house and the yard. Visual spectrum is a little wider. The sun is up now so we have a good view."

"Go wider. We should be checking a quarter mile radius at least. It's a rural area and there could be other buildings on the property. Then call me back."

"OK, will do Lau..." She hung up and dialed Collier.

"Hi Lauren. Welcome to Berlin. I have a team at the house. I told them they didn't need the gear, but without being able to tell them much they're going overboard with caution. Right now they've set up a perimeter and are watching and listening. They won't go any closer. No sign of the three suspects or your man Dolan. One of my top guys, Stan Bolden is with them, and I've brought him up to speed. If they encounter Dolan Stan will advise on the capture. They promised not to interrogate him. The team is GSG 9, BND's elite counter-terror unit."

Lauren's phone beeped and she looked at the screen, it was Thomas. She declined the call. "OK thanks Mike. I should arrive in about half an hour. Tell Stan I'm on my way and make sure the BND doesn't pull the local police into this. Will I see you there?"

"No, I have other things to attend to. I'll be escorting the BND President and his VP for Military Affairs today at a 'bruncheon.' Starts at ten. Potsdam is sure to come up, so if there's anything you haven't told me, tell me now."

Lauren thought quickly. "Mike, I need to collate this in my head a bit before telling you anything else. As I mentioned before, there are certain things we absolutely cannot inform the Germans about. Anyway, this event, it's not public, is it? Is it inside the embassy?"

Collier laughed. "Don't worry Lauren, it's inside the embassy. The Fourth of July celebration we usually have in the Grunewald was canceled, that's the public event. This one is VIP and by invitation only. There will be about twenty German dignitaries with their families, some from the Bundeswehr, Parliament, and some top executives from defense industry. The Ambassador is hosting. We do this every Fourth of July."

"Um, ok… Can I assume you have extra security measures in place, given current events?"

"Yes. Every Marine is on duty, we even pulled a few back who were on leave. And we've doubled our counterintelligence efforts in the vicinity. We'll be fine."

Thomas was trying her again. "Right. I must go. Talk again soon." She pressed end and accepted Thomas' call.

"Lauren, *major* updates. We widened the sat feed. There are no other buildings in the immediate vicinity, but there was a vehicle just down the road from the house. It was pulled into a trailhead and mostly obscured by trees, but I'm sure it was Bernard's Peugeot."

Lauren's hopes jumped as she got into the back seat of the black Mercedes. "Hold on Thomas." She put on her seatbelt and thanked the driver for picking her up. "Why are you sure it's Dolan? Is it still there?"

"Well, I couldn't tell for sure it was the same car, but it was the right color. There wasn't much of it visible. It left shortly after I widened the view. If you remember, there is about a five-minute delay in the feed from Dolan's phone. Just after the Peugeot was gone his phone went live. GPS coordinates showed him right there, in the car."

"Holy shit Thomas, that's good news. Are you tracking him?"

"Unfortunately, no. He turned his phone off minutes after he turned it on. Lauren, *he called Sharif,* and you must hear it. I'll let the translator tell you."

Lauren listened as the CIA French linguist read from the transcript. With each word her eyes grew wider with disbelief. When he was finished, she told Thomas to go as wide on the optical feed as he could for now, keep an eye out for the Peugeot, and put in another retask request with the NRO to center their view over the U.S. Embassy at Pariser Platz. If they could find Dolan, he might lead them to Martin. She also instructed him to update Dittrich and get approval for an immediate data dump with DGSI. With everything the team knew now, their focus should be to stop Martin at the border if he's headed back to France, and to put out an APB through French authorities and Interpol for him and Sharif.

Thomas wasn't done. "Lauren one final update. We now know that Rolf Haussmann is still alive and has assumed the identity of Albrecht Richter. He boarded a freighter at the Port of Split in Croatia a few weeks back. It stopped in four countries along the route, the final destination was Port of Iquique in Chile. I'll be following up and let you know if we locate him."

"Good work Thomas. Tell Dittrich immediately if you find Haussmann. He has a special plan drawn up for that."

Then she called Collier back. "Mike, I have more information."

"Hi Lauren, go ahead."

"Change in plans. I'm headed to the Embassy. We have confirmation that Dolan, the three Algerians and a fourth suspect were at the property earlier. The fourth's name is François Martin, a French citizen. He's five foot seven, slight build, black hair, brown eyes, short beard and middle eastern appearance. He is thirty-three years old. Martin could be suffering from a gunshot wound. Dolan was there, about a few hundred yards to the west from the Potsdam property driveway. He drove off in the Peugeot about ten minutes ago, not sure where. He might have driven right by your team. He terminated the three Algerians. If it was long enough ago your infrared may not be picking them up. And we have reason to believe the gas is no longer on the premises. We are confident Martin took it and is in the wind. He could be driving a large, late-model Mercedes sedan, black. Tell Stan to convince the team to go in and search the place—there could be critical evidence inside that will tell us where Martin and Dolan are headed. I'll have Thomas send you the Mercedes details from D.C."

"Thanks Lauren, good update, though if the gas is mobile now the Germans are likely to open this up to all law enforcement in the area. As for the Mercedes, there is a car that matches that description with a cover over it near the edge of the yard. There may have been another vehicle."

"Shit, OK. Well there's another reason to go in and search the house. We need to know what Martin's driving now. Will I see you at the embassy?"

"I'm on my way there as well. Our guests don't arrive for a couple hours still, so we'll have time to talk. You can meet me in my office."

"Thanks. See you there."

Lauren then called Stone to give him the latest information and most importantly, to let him know Sharif was likely there. He should verify and maintain surveillance until authorities react to the All-Points Bulletin. She also wanted to know if he noticed Dolan's phone had popped up on the grid and to monitor. But the call just rang and went to voicemail. She hung up and tried again. This time there was no ring, straight to voicemail. She left a message and told him to be careful. *I don't want him getting caught in any crossfire…*

CHAPTER THIRTY-NINE

Dolan's eyes hurt. His whole body hurt, and he was nauseous. He squinted but couldn't focus. At first, he didn't know where he was. Eventually he realized he was still in the car in Potsdam. The gravity of his vision, his nightmare, rushed to the fore. *Is this a second chance?* He saw the truth of the dream—that his carefully structured paradigm for managing life was deeply flawed. Ultimately, he would end in ruin. He needed to change things, and radically.

The sun was up now, and the rain had stopped. He checked his watch. Seven twenty. Every few seconds a vehicle drove by on the road. He took a moment to appreciate the fact he was still alive, and remembered he needed to contact the team. Then he would find a hospital.

The phone was in his lap. He was still a little inebriated from the cognac but would probably be safe to drive. As he keyed in the password, he realized he might get something useful out of Sharif if he decided to take the call. It made sense to do this one last thing before letting the team take over.

There were two messages, a voicemail from Anne and another from Lauren. He listened to both. He felt bad immediately for Anne.

Lauren had visited her, and she wanted to know if he was OK. He would give her a call after he was done with what he needed to do. The voicemail from Lauren was no surprise. No matter, he'd be in touch with her soon as well.

He tapped the cell number in Sharif's contact. The phone rang.

There were three seconds of silence after he answered, then "Hello? Michael?"

He sounded fragile. "Sharif, yes, it's me. How is Provence? How is your mom?"

Again, a short pause. Dolan thought he heard him weeping. "It's, well, it's beautiful down here, gorgeous weather. My mother is the same. She is healthy but doesn't know me anymore. It makes me sad."

He sounded truthful. He really was there in Marseille. "I'm sorry Sharif. It's a tough thing to go through. Listen, I don't have a lot of time. I've been through a lot myself today and there are two questions I need you to answer for me. It's important."

"Sure Michael, what is it?"

"First, I killed all three of your Algerian terrorist friends. I shot Martin, but he got away. The authorities will be after him soon. This whole terrorist plot of yours is falling apart. Tell me what Martin's target is. Second, why do it? Why Sharif? I know you, and this isn't you." Dolan expected him to hang up, but he didn't.

"You! You Michael? After everything, you are one of them? I can't believe it. Why? Why does it have to be you?" Sharif sounded simultaneously distraught and incredulous.

"Sharif, you're responding to my questions with questions. Not telling me the answers won't change how this is going to go down. At least you can prevent further loss of life."

"You bastard! You know I cannot. This is not what you think. I mean, it is for Martin but for me it's revenge! And yes, it's jihad too but your country killed my uncles, and almost killed my father. The Paris attack didn't even matter to me, that was Martin. Notre Dame was Martin. What's left is for me and for my father and it's going to happen, there is nothing you can do."

He's not going to tell me the target. Dolan realized he didn't have much time before Sharif cut it off. He was probably thinking Dolan was trying to trace the call. "OK Sharif, I get it. I'll never understand, how could I. But there's one last thing. Something that has bothered me for years and we've never properly discussed it. Whatever the answer is, it won't make any difference to what happens going forward, so please, tell me the truth. What really happened that night with Claire?"

Yet another pause. Then he truly was sobbing. Dolan could barely understand him. "We were talking about Mohammed Merah, in Toulouse. 2012. Remember, he shot a Rabbi, some schoolchildren, a few paratroopers. He was Algerian. She was making me angry, Michael. She was disparaging Muslims and Islam, saying they were ruining France, that immigrants were not properly acculturating, assimilating. That they were the problem. I tried to reason with her, but she kept on. We were drinking so much that night. Her death destroyed me, Michael. I agonized over it for weeks, just as you did."

Dolan almost couldn't believe what he was hearing. He'd asked Sharif the question to get more clarity, more details, more closure. Instead, this sounded like he was taking responsibility for her death. He was gripping the phone so tightly his forearm was numb from the pain.

Sharif continued. "I finally called my father, who I hadn't spoken to in years. He calmed me down. Gave me vision and purpose. Set me on a new path. I found Islam again. For the longest time I thought Claire's death was the catalyst of my own rebirth. Michael, *I killed her.* I shoved her and she fell. But I didn't mean for it to happen!

It was an accident! I wanted to turn myself in, but my father said I could make up for my misdeed by serving Allah. Except these past couple of months, I've been wondering if it was all worth it. Ever since Notre Dame. Martin kept saying that was *our harbinger*. I didn't want him to do it. It was wrong. So many things have gone wrong. *I am truly sorry Michael.* I can give you that, but I cannot give you everything you are asking for. It is a rite of passage to my father and whatever lies beyond. My life as I know it now is now gone, and so I am leaving it behind. In hindsight, to say that Claire's death was a catalyst for my own rebirth is not accurate at all. In truth, it was the beginning of the end of everything."

Before Dolan could respond the line went dead. He tried to call him back, but he'd shut off the phone. Dolan then began to feel something inside he'd never felt before. Something he'd always carefully controlled and boxed up before it could take effect. He'd gotten so good at it, by now it was automatic. But this, this could not be contained. Pure, unadulterated rage rose up inside him and took over. He let it out, encouraged it, fed it even. He screamed at the top of his lungs inside the Peugeot, gripping the phone so tightly the screen cracked.

When he was done, he was breathing heavily. *This changes things,* he thought. He might not be able to take revenge on Sharif, not right now anyways, but he could deprive Sharif of his. A new plan began to form in his head. It was much like the original plan but with a few modifications. He would go after Martin himself. If Martin wasn't staging where Dolan believed he would be, he'd call everything in to Stone and let them take it from there.

Dolan grabbed his backpack and felt inside until he found the jar of pills. He opened it up. There were five pills left. He quickly swallowed three of them, then waited two minutes. He was beginning to feel better, but better wasn't enough. He needed to be as sharp as possible. He put the two remaining pills in his mouth, chewed them and swallowed. A minute later his mind was clear, his eyesight sharp, and the nausea was gone. Despite his injuries, he felt…invincible. Which gave him a chuckle. He wiped the jar with his shirt to remove any fingerprints. Then remembering the cognac bottle, he did the same with it. *Shouldn't give anyone a reason to pull me over.* Grabbing each with the sleeve of his overcoat he opened the car door and threw them out onto the ground. Dolan picked up the phone again and opened the maps app. His fingertip catching a bit on the crack from top to bottom, he noted his location and the route to the Embassy, memorizing it. Then he put it back in airplane mode, pulled out of the trailhead and onto the street. *An rien peut arrêter moi konin la…*

CHAPTER FORTY

It would have been a forty-minute drive had traffic been light, but it wasn't. Several road construction areas along the way made things worse, but Dolan wasn't overly worried about getting there in time. If the target was in fact some lunchtime event in the embassy courtyard, he would probably have to wait for Martin to arrive, but he couldn't be sure about the timing. After fifty-five minutes he was pulling into the west entrance of the Tiergarten. The Tiergarten was opened in 1527 as a stocked hunting area for rich politicians. Now it was the third-largest urban park in Germany. With over 200 wooded hectares of trails, ponds, monuments and picnic areas it was a popular daytime destination for families and tourists, joggers, and downtown professionals on their lunch breaks. And the eastern border is approximately 50 meters from the west wall of the U.S. Embassy.

Martin wouldn't be able to stage that close. He would have to stand off a bit from busy Eberstrasse, which ran between the Embassy and the park. He would need to find a place with good cover and enough of a clearing overhead so the canister wouldn't strike any tree branches. But he'd be within about a 250-meter radius of the center of the embassy, as the test data for a 60-degree entry angle showed. All of which should make finding Martin easy. It wasn't a large area. He'd find a good hiding spot near the most likely place and wait. If he didn't show up, then something had gone wrong with Martin's plan or Dolan was wrong about the target.

The majestic Berlin Victory Column near the middle of the Tiergarten ascended in front of him as he drove along Strasse des 17. Juni. At the top of the column stood Victoria, an 8.3-meter golden statue of the winged goddess of victory Berliners had nicknamed *Goldelse*, or 'Golden Lizzy.' Dolan hoped she looked down on him favorably as he navigated the traffic circle around her. As he approached the eastern side, he searched for a parking spot. One that would be near enough for him to make a quick getaway if needed. He saw one and pulled in, not too far from the Brandenburg Gate. With the Beretta and knife still in his overcoat pocket, he reached into the back seat, grabbed his backpack and exited the vehicle. He then made his way along a path southward into the park. He searched for the green panel truck as he walked and noted there didn't appear to be any service roads. He passed a couple walking hand-in-hand in the opposite direction, both regarding him strangely. *I probably don't look too presentable right now...* If Martin was to launch within the required radius, he'd have to get there by driving along one of the many paved footpaths that meandered through the park. *It is probable that is what service vehicles do here as a matter of course,* he thought.

The path he was on cut straight through this part of the park and as he neared the southern edge, he realized he was probably outside the radius—he needed to move farther east. Dolan backtracked a bit, then cut in on a connecting path in the general direction of the embassy. Before he'd walked too far, he came across a line of red and white tape stretched across the walkway emblazoned with the word POLIZEIABSPERRUNG at regular intervals, tied to trees on either side. *Police barrier.* He hadn't seen any police or much activity at all, in fact. The park was sparsely occupied this morning. It was Martin. In the United States a tactic like this might be a bad idea, as passers-by would stop and try to see what they could see, and in the absence of any enforcement venture beyond to get a better look. In German culture this would be far less likely to happen. *Ordnung muss sein.* He decided to step off the walkway and moved stealthily while maintaining cover, keeping the path in sight.

There you are. The truck was parked next to a sculpture in the middle of a treed area with a small window of sky above. It was the Löwengruppe, a magnificent brass monument atop a pedestal depicting a lion standing guard over his dead lioness, with two cubs still nursing against her inert form. Crass graffiti desecrated the sandstone base. Dolan surveyed the area and saw no one, then looked back to the truck. He could launch at any moment. Now that he was sure of the target, he needed to warn the embassy. Sitting on the ground with his back to a large rock he took his iPhone off airplane mode and plugged the encryption dongle in, then dialed Stone. Something was wrong—it didn't ring. The was a buzzing sound and the line went dead. *I don't have time for this...* He pulled out the dongle and called him again in the clear. It went straight to voicemail. He left a quick message telling him the attack was imminent in Berlin and to contact the Embassy so they could clear the courtyard. Then he called Lauren in the clear. His feelings of invincibility were beginning to wane as her phone also went to voicemail. He left the same message for her, then decided to call the command post directly.

Just as he found the number online, he heard two pops in quick succession and instinctively scrambled to his left around the large boulder, away from the reports. With a terrible sense of failure and loss he thought, *I'm too late—Martin just launched the gas.* Dolan dropped the phone, fished the Beretta from his pocket and checked the breech. As he peered over the top of the rock, he saw blood spattered on the surface. And seeping down the front of his shirt as well. He felt faint and his knees were trembling; he was just able to remain standing. His heart was beating hard and fast. What he'd heard was Martin shooting at him. He must have seen or heard him. *I've lost my edge.* Then he caught sight of Martin entering through the rear of the panel truck and slamming the door. There was no time left. He was going to launch *now.*

◆

"The BND and Berlin police are searching for both Martin and Dolan. Public announcements are being made about a possible terrorist threat and all German government buildings are in lockdown. As soon as I told them the gas was mobile, they took off, full steam ahead."

He looks so smug, Lauren thought. "Listen, it's probably the right call. We just transferred a lot of information on this cell to the DGSI and they're acting on it there. They're likely to do something similar in Paris. In the meantime, all U.S. facilities across Europe are essentially in lockdown as well."

Collier's desk phone rang, and he picked it up. "Collier. Yes, she's right here." He handed the receiver to Lauren.

"Hello? OK, thank you." She handed it back. "Message from Thomas back in Clarendon. I need to call him back."

"You want to use my phone?"

"No thanks, I need to be monitoring my cell in any case. I'll take it outside."

"Right. Well I need to head down to the entrance and meet my guests. Everyone is assembling in the courtyard."

"OK. Will you be keeping your cell on during the event, in case I need you?"

Collier nodded seriously. "I'll have it on vibrate."

They both got up and walked out of the modern and modestly appointed suite of offices, out the cypher-locked door and into the hall where they retrieved their cell phones from lockboxes on the wall.

Lauren stayed there, impatiently waiting for her phone to boot up as Collier got in the elevator for the first floor. Despite all the recent activity and a real threat in the area they had yet to contain or fully understand, he felt good about himself and the job he'd been doing as Berlin Station Chief. Ironically, he had no idea it was his penchant for pushing the envelope that had led to this day, resulting in an imminent attack where he and his colleagues were the primary target. And as he introduced his VIP guests to his wife and two young children there in the Embassy courtyard, the possibility of such a thing couldn't have been further from his mind.

Lauren had five voicemails. She dialed Thomas.

"Lauren, thank God. I tried you three times. *Tony is dead.* The French police found him at Salmah Lefebvre's property, behind the house. Shot in the chest. Paris Station is sending a team immediately to contain the situation, but it's bad. There was a rifle with him, and he had his sidearm as well. No sign of Sharif, but his mother and the nurse are in the house and they confirmed he'd been there. Dittrich is all over it. You should call him."

Lauren thought she would cry. Tears welled in her eyes, but she held them back. She and Tony had never been overly friendly. In fact, there had always been a modest level of tension between them. They had different styles, different methods. He was a risk taker. But he was one of hers and he was a good officer, overall. To think she would have to walk past Memorial Wall at Langley time and time again knowing she was responsible for one of those stars…

She pulled herself together. "OK Thomas. I'll call Dittrich. I…"

"Hold on!" yelled Thomas. "Dolan just popped up on my screen, his phone is live! Holy shit, he's only about a block from you, to the east of the Embassy. It looks like he's in a park. And he's made two phone calls recently—one to Stone, and one to you…"

Lauren stopped listening and accessed her missed calls. Three from Thomas, one from Dittrich. *The fifth from Dolan.* She frantically tapped the message and went pale as she listened. Before it played back fully, she was dialing the command post. Three seconds later a startlingly loud siren accompanied by red flashing lights filled the hallway.

◆

Dolan stumbled around the rock and moved as fast as he could toward the panel truck. He approached it broadside and held up the Beretta. Aiming halfway down from the roof, he began shooting, left to right and every half meter from the driver's door to the back, then again right to left. He could hear the chugging of the compressor inside. The Beretta clicked on empty and he dropped it, now limping slowly while reaching around to pull off his Tumi knapsack and grab the canister of gas inside. He held it between his left elbow and his body while preparing to open the valve. If Martin's technical drawings were accurate, he could lob it into the truck through the moonroof opening.

In a split second he changed his mind and released his hand from the valve. The gas wouldn't kill him instantly. He could still get the launch off. And there were people in the area who could be affected. As he reached the side of the truck he went down hard on his knees, the canister falling from his grip. He reached into his overcoat pocket, took the paring knife and stabbed the rear tire twice. The truck settled back. *That should slow him down. He'll have to reset his firing solution.* Dolan then put the knife on the ground and grabbed the canister at the valve end with his right hand. With a herculean effort he stood up and walked to the front of the vehicle, testing the locked driver's door as he went.

As he crawled onto the hood, he was able to see Martin through the windshield. He was lying on his back covered in blood. An open laptop on his stomach, his right hand on the keyboard. Then Martin moved his head, hearing Dolan and straining to look in his direction. *He sees me.* Dolan used every ounce of fortitude and energy he had left to make it to the top. As he knelt at the edge of the moonroof opening he saw Martin raise his hand, staring up at Dolan with an evil smile. He hit the keyboard, mouthing the words *fuck you* with what little defiance he could muster in his last breath. At the same time, Dolan swung the canister with his right hand as hard as he could at the top of the metal tube. As he struck a loud discharge and whoosh of air made him lean back intuitively, the ejected tank whizzing by perilously close to his head. He caught himself from falling backwards, then leaned forward to look in again. Martin had taken at least two bullets and appeared to be dead. With nothing left to accomplish, Dolan fell slowly forward as he lost consciousness, landing face down across the moonroof on top of the panel truck.

CHAPTER FORTY-ONE

"Thirsty." A glass of water was pressed against his lips, and he drank it dry. His surroundings came into view slowly, beeping in the background. A plasma bag hung above him to the left next to two screens graphing his vitals. Lauren's face moved into view.

"Hey there, welcome back." She was genuinely happy to see him. "You had us worried. How do you feel?"

"Kind of numb. Not bad. What did you give me?"

"Morphine. And a few other things. You were shot in the chest. The bullet was lodged near your lung. The doctor was able to remove it and patch you up. It looked like you'd been shot through in your arm and again in the chest. You have a cracked skull and likely a concussion. We almost lost you a couple of times, it was touch and go. But you pulled through." She smiled at him.

"How long have I been out?" Suddenly the final events in the Tiergarten came rushing back to him. He didn't want to hear the answer. The results of his failure. "What happened at the embassy?"

"*You did it Michael.* Martin missed. No one there was hurt. The gas tank fell into the middle of the Jewish Memorial behind the Embassy. When it landed there were a few tourists within, two of them ended up in the hospital but they are going to make it. Luckily, it's a large, open-air area and no one died. You may not know this, but he was prepared to launch *two* tanks. And there was a third inside the truck, but it wasn't large enough to be launched by the device. You've been out for six days."

"Thank God." Dolan had never felt so completely relieved and grateful as he did now, hearing he'd been successful and that no one had been seriously hurt. He also felt good from the morphine, but he didn't want to. He wanted his head clear. There was a slight throb in his chest and another in his forearm. And he couldn't feel his head at all. "No more morphine, OK? That smaller tank was mine. I mean, I took it from the Algerians. There were three of those, at least. I used one to kill them, hid one behind a rock near the driveway in Potsdam, and kept the third to use on Martin. Turns out I didn't need to."

"We found the Algerians in the tunnel. There was a fourth smaller canister in the garage. I'll send someone to collect the one you hid." She turned and motioned to someone else in the room, then looked back to him.

"Where am I? This doesn't look like a hospital."

"You're at our safe house. Still in Berlin. Once you're stable, we'll fly you to a hospital back in the States."

Just then a young woman in a white lab coat walked into view. "We should let him rest. He still has a long way to go, and we can't risk a relapse."

"No, no," Dolan muttered. "Not yet. Rest can wait a few more minutes. Was that it? Are there any more? Terrorists, I mean? Did you get Sharif?"

"There are no more that we know of, Michael. Martin had a laptop in the truck to run the launch device. Their entire plan, all the details were on the hard drive. There is also a lot of evidence that

Hakeem Lefebvre was deeply involved and guiding Sharif on every decision, and that Martin was responsible for the fire at Notre Dame. You got everyone Michael, everyone except Sharif. He escaped, to Algeria we think. Records in his mother's house show she owns a large boat and kept it docked at a pier within walking distance of the property. The boat is gone. And in case you were wondering, we put Anne's Peugeot on a flatbed and sent it back to her, after we cleaned it up. There was a lot of blood inside."

"So that's it then, we're done with the mission." It felt good to say it. As if he had built something grand and beautiful, or composed a wonderful song. He could lay back and enjoy it now. "Where's Tony?"

Lauren looked suddenly crestfallen and he knew, immediately. "Michael, Tony didn't make it. He located Sharif at the house in Marseille, but Sharif shot him before he could call it in. I flew with him back to the States last week and informed his family. There was a nice service for him at Langley. Then I came back here to check on you. I just got back yesterday."

Dolan's sense of success and closure was instantly and significantly mitigated. At no point up until the moment the gas canister flew by his head did he think he couldn't handle everything by himself. Given the canister had missed its target and no one had died, those feelings had been revalidated. Sharif had seemed so fragile, so disassociated from his own plan that he never really considered him a threat. With Martin and the Algerians taken out, it was just a matter of collecting the poor, broken murderer Sharif. Except it wasn't.

"I'm so sorry Lauren. I wish there were something I could have done." As soon as he said it, he wished he hadn't. *Of course he could have done something.* He went rogue. He locked them out of their own mission and tried to do it all himself. It was possible Stone would still be alive if he hadn't been so selfish. If he'd put aside his worry and paranoia, just sucked it up…

"Listen, we can talk about all that later, once you've recovered. Before we transfer you to the States there is going to be a long debrief. You'll be asked a lot of questions by people you've never met. You don't have to worry about it though, it's a standard process. Yes, there were things you could have done better. Going dark and going it alone was a real bad idea—you made everything much more difficult than it needed to be, particularly on yourself. But in the end, you surprised everyone. No one had the slightest idea you would be so effective. What you did was nothing short of incredibly dangerous and stupid, lucky, amazing and heroic, all wrapped up into one."

He didn't feel heroic. He'd done things he can never take back, dark and troubling things forever seared in his memory. Right and wrong blended together over the past few months to the point he hadn't been able to tell them apart. It was easy to justify anything, anything at all in this line of work. If he had *really* done things the right way and to the best of his ability, they might have caught all the terrorists alive. Been able to question them. Get answers about the AMA, Hakeem Lefebvre and his whereabouts. Been able to prevent Sharif from escaping. *Prevented Stone's death.*

The lady in the white coat was at his side with a needle, ready to inject something into his IV. "No, no more. I must have my head clear, please…"

"Sorry Michael, you don't have a choice. We need you well." She injected the cocktail of morphine and other drugs into the line.

As it filtered into and up his arm a warm calmness fell over him. Again, he felt gratitude for being alive. So many things had gone wrong since his return to Paris, and due in no small part to the mental baggage he'd carried with him for so long. He remembered his vision of the dream, and what it meant. *One cannot be a victim if the damage is self-inflicted.* And the damage was deep. He remembered Père Aubertin and their discussion of the continuum of time. Nothing done can be undone—the only thing that matters is now. He had so much he needed to do *now.* He never called Amy to apologize. Heck, he hadn't called his parents since he first arrived in Paris. They tried to contact him, but for some reason he never responded. At the time it didn't seem to matter, but it mattered now. A lot.

And Anne. *She was the key,* he thought. His feelings for her, their feelings for each other in this instant became the catalyst of a wondrous epiphany. One that told him what he had to do. The key to opening a new, positive chapter in his life in which he is released from the need to compartmentalize, to hide from everything he disagreed with. Everything he thought might hurt him.

Dolan reached back into his mind and visualized them—all the semitransparent, cryptic boxes stacked too high to see, too deep to push through. He then gave each of them permission to set their contents free, all at once. And with that a great tidal wave of conflicting emotions rushed through him. An incredibly powerful and complex amalgam of things he hadn't experienced in years, some he couldn't remember experiencing *ever,* overpowered the morphine and prevented him for one last moment from falling into a deep sleep.

The moment lingered and the surge ebbed, leaving behind a vast area replete with self-realization and empathy…and love. It was curious and wonderful and fulfilling, and he knew he finally understood what love was. He knew that he loved his parents, and that he loved Anne. He loved her *deeply.* Aubertin told him the essence of love was to *desire the ultimate good for another person, unconditionally.* This is what he wanted for his parents, for Anne. *Love trumps everything.*

Before letting himself go he traveled to the far reaches of his mind, to a dark corner where one solitary box remained, pulsating. Flashing ghostly images of Claire falling from the balcony. He hadn't visited this one since he left her poem on the street in Paris and it was different now, as it showed a shadowy figure leaning against the balcony watching her fall. He would keep this one, at least until he was able to reconcile it somehow. *Someday.* And with that he floated off, content with the belief that from the time he awoke and onward, each stroke he painted on the broken canvas of his life would add as much to an unknown future masterpiece as his mind, imagination, and conduct could fashion.

TO BE CONTINUED IN *EVOLUTION*

Two years have passed since the dramatic conclusion of OPERATION EXCISE. Dolan has moved home to Boston to mend when once again, the Agency comes knocking. Terrorists have launched a bioweapon in the Middle East, thousands are dying of a horrifying virus with no cure, and Dolan is the key to preventing more attacks. Only this time, everything will be done on his terms…

ABOUT THE AUTHOR

JOHN CASEY is a novelist and Pushcart Prize-nominated poet from New Hampshire. *Devolution* is book one of *The Devolution Trilogy*. His first sequel, *Evolution*, was released in 2021 and *Revelation* rounds out the psychological spy thriller series. He is the author of *Raw Thoughts* and *Meridian: A Raw Thoughts Book* as well, both compelling and mindful fusions of poetic and photographic art. A Veteran combat and test pilot with a Master of Arts from Florida State University, Casey also served as a diplomat and international affairs strategist at U.S. embassies in Germany and Ethiopia, the Pentagon, and elsewhere. He is passionate about fitness, nature, and the human spirit and inspired by the incredible spectrum of people, places, and cultures he has experienced in life.